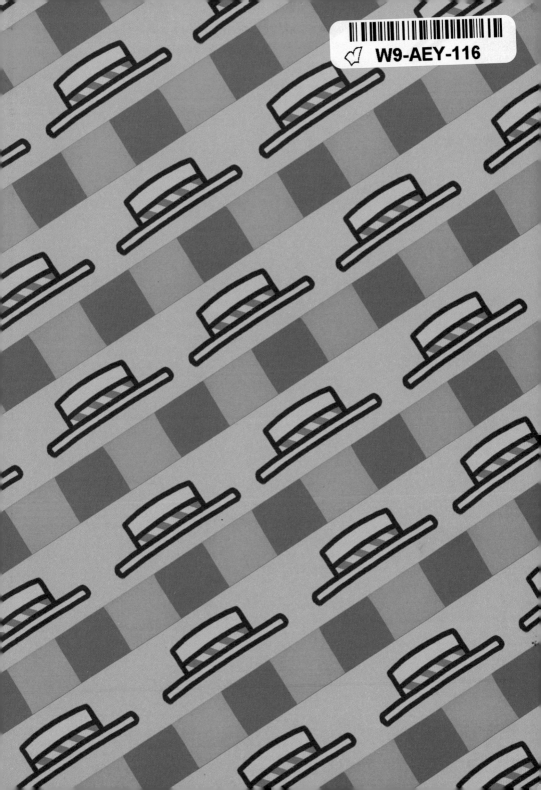

W9-AEY-116

P

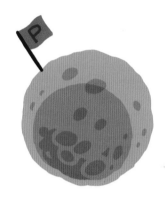

FOR ELENI, EVAN AND ROSA,
WHO, IN ALL THE VASTNESS OF
THE SOLAR SYSTEM, I WAS
LUCKY ENOUGH TO FIND IN
MY OWN NEIGHBORHOOD.

COPYRIGHT © 2023 BY PAUL GILLIGAN

TUNDRA BOOKS, AN IMPRINT OF TUNDRA BOOK GROUP,
A DIVISION OF PENGUIN RANDOM HOUSE OF CANADA LIMITED

ALL RIGHTS RESERVED. THE USE OF ANY PART OF THIS PUBLICATION REPRODUCED, TRANSMITTED IN ANY
FORM OR BY ANY MEANS, ELECTRONIC, MECHANICAL, PHOTOCOPYING, RECORDING, OR OTHERWISE, OR
STORED IN A RETRIEVAL SYSTEM, WITHOUT THE PRIOR WRITTEN CONSENT OF THE PUBLISHER — OR, IN
CASE OF PHOTOCOPYING OR OTHER REPROGRAPHIC COPYING, A LICENCE FROM THE CANADIAN COPYRIGHT
LICENSING AGENCY — IS AN INFRINGEMENT OF THE COPYRIGHT LAW.

LIBRARY AND ARCHIVES CANADA CATALOGUING IN PUBLICATION

TITLE: NEW IN TOWN / PAUL GILLIGAN.
NAMES: GILLIGAN, PAUL, AUTHOR, ARTIST.
DESCRIPTION: SERIES STATEMENT: PLUTO ROCKET ; 1
IDENTIFIERS: CANADIANA (PRINT) 2021033598X | CANADIANA (EBOOK) 20210336005 |
ISBN 9780735271906 (HARDCOVER) | ISBN 9780735271920 (SOFTCOVER) | ISBN 9780735271913 (EPUB)
SUBJECTS: LCGFT: GRAPHIC NOVELS.
CLASSIFICATION: LCC PN6733.G55 N49 2023 | DDC J741.5/971—DC23

PUBLISHED SIMULTANEOUSLY IN THE UNITED STATES OF AMERICA BY TUNDRA BOOKS OF NORTHERN NEW
YORK, AN IMPRINT OF TUNDRA BOOK GROUP, A DIVISION OF PENGUIN RANDOM HOUSE OF CANADA LIMITED

LIBRARY OF CONGRESS CONTROL NUMBER: 2021948305

EDITED BY PETER PHILLIPS
DESIGNED BY JOHN MARTZ
THE ARTWORK IN THIS BOOK WAS DRAWN DIGITALLY.
THE TEXT WAS SET IN SPINNER RACK BB.

PRINTED IN CHINA

WWW.PENGUINRANDOMHOUSE.CA

1   2   3   4   5   27   26   25   24   23

Penguin
Random House
tundra | TUNDRA BOOKS

NEW IN TOWN

PAUL GILLIGAN

tundra

CHAPTER ONE:

MIND BLOWN!

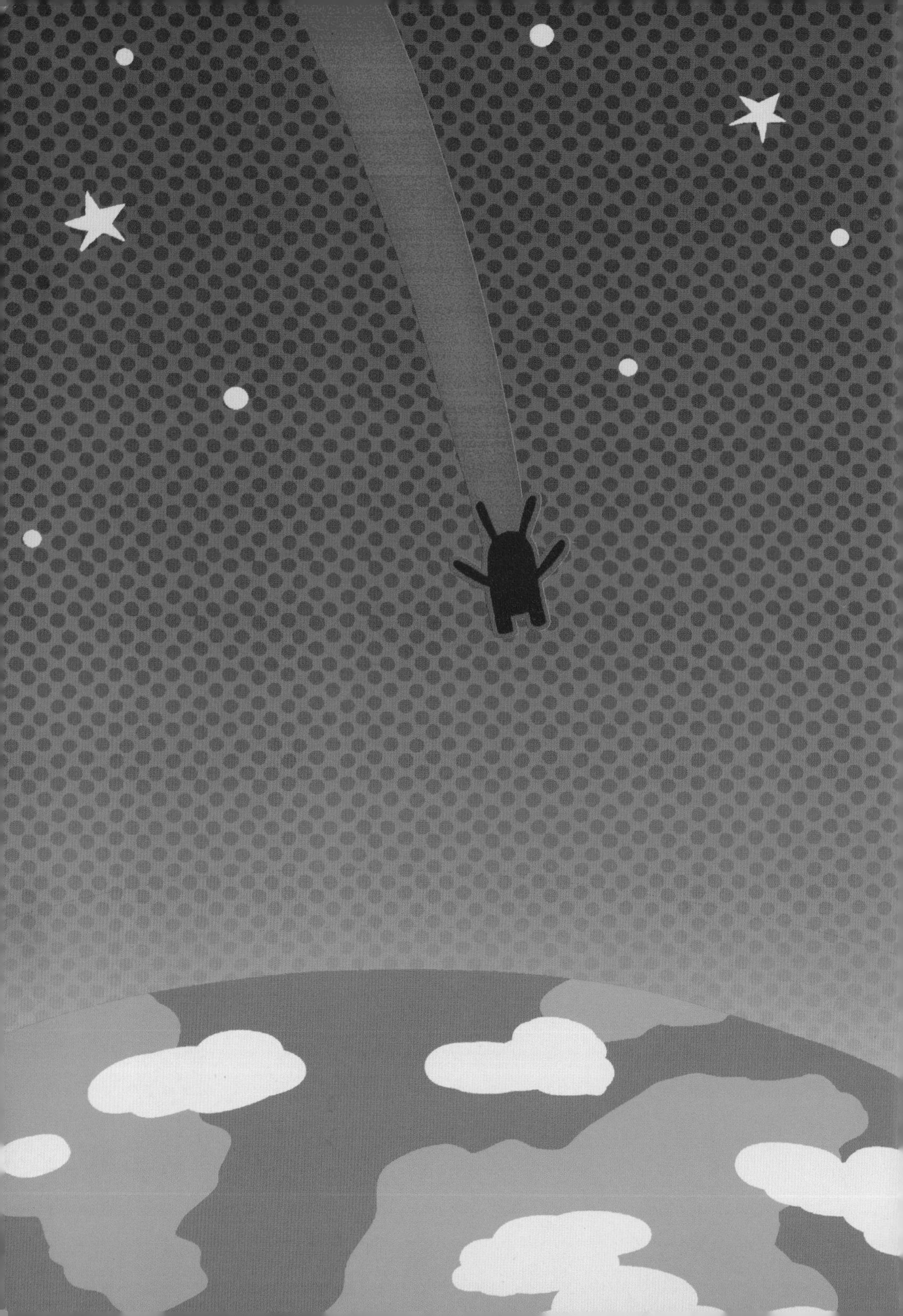

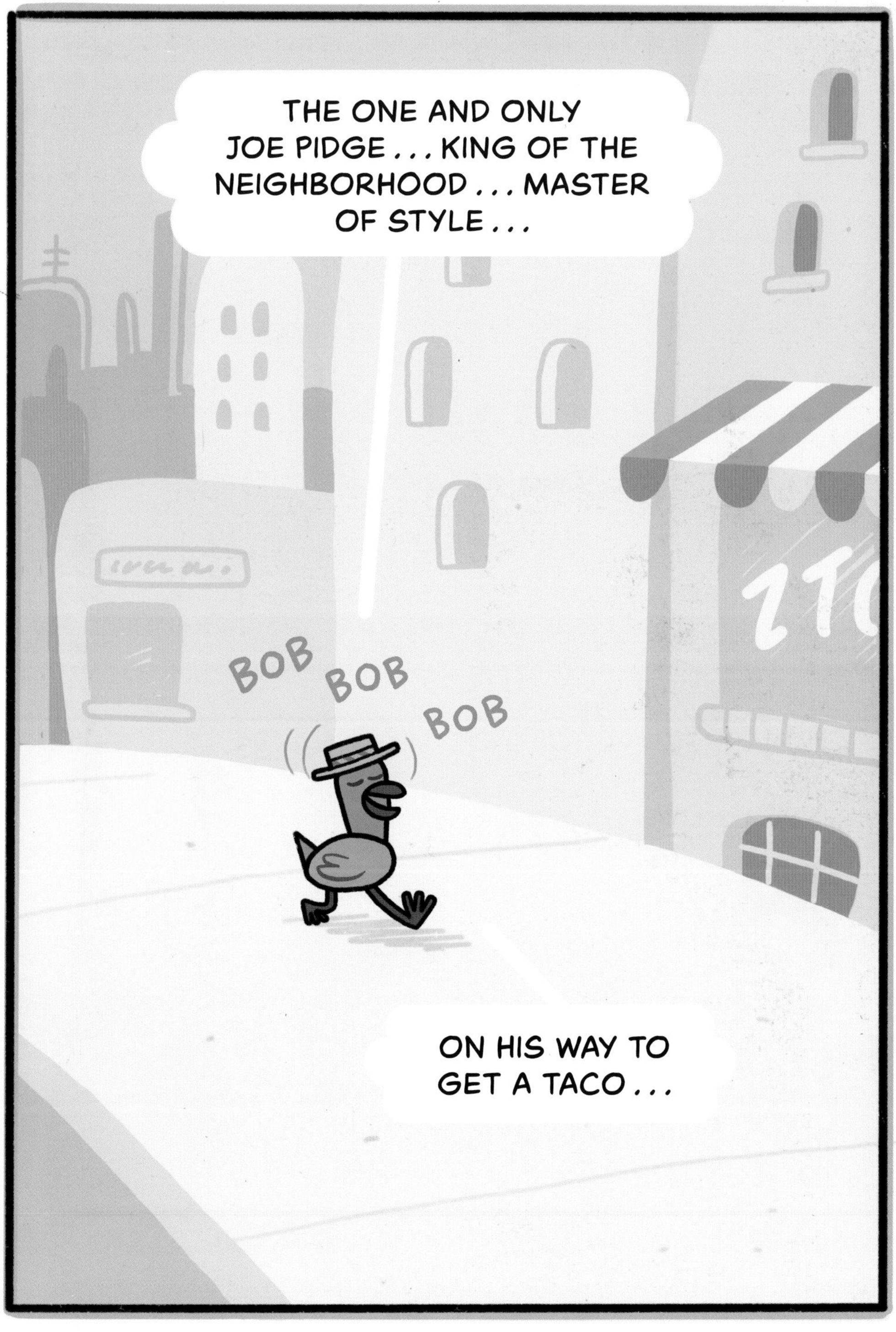
THE ONE AND ONLY JOE PIDGE . . . KING OF THE NEIGHBORHOOD . . . MASTER OF STYLE . . .
BOB
BOB
BOB
ON HIS WAY TO GET A TACO . . .

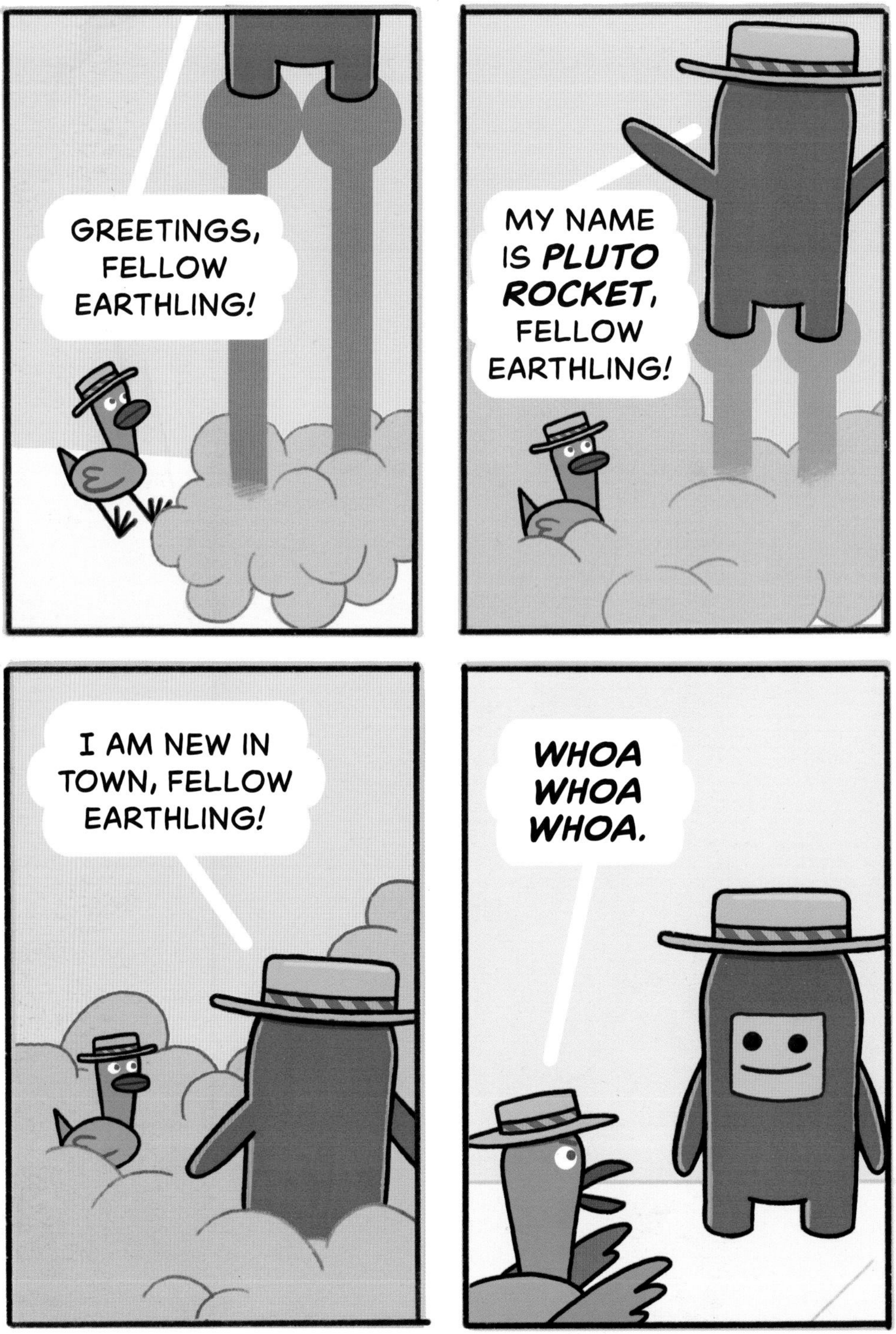
GREETINGS, FELLOW EARTHLING!
MY NAME IS PLUTO ROCKET, FELLOW EARTHLING!
I AM NEW IN TOWN, FELLOW EARTHLING!
WHOA WHOA WHOA.

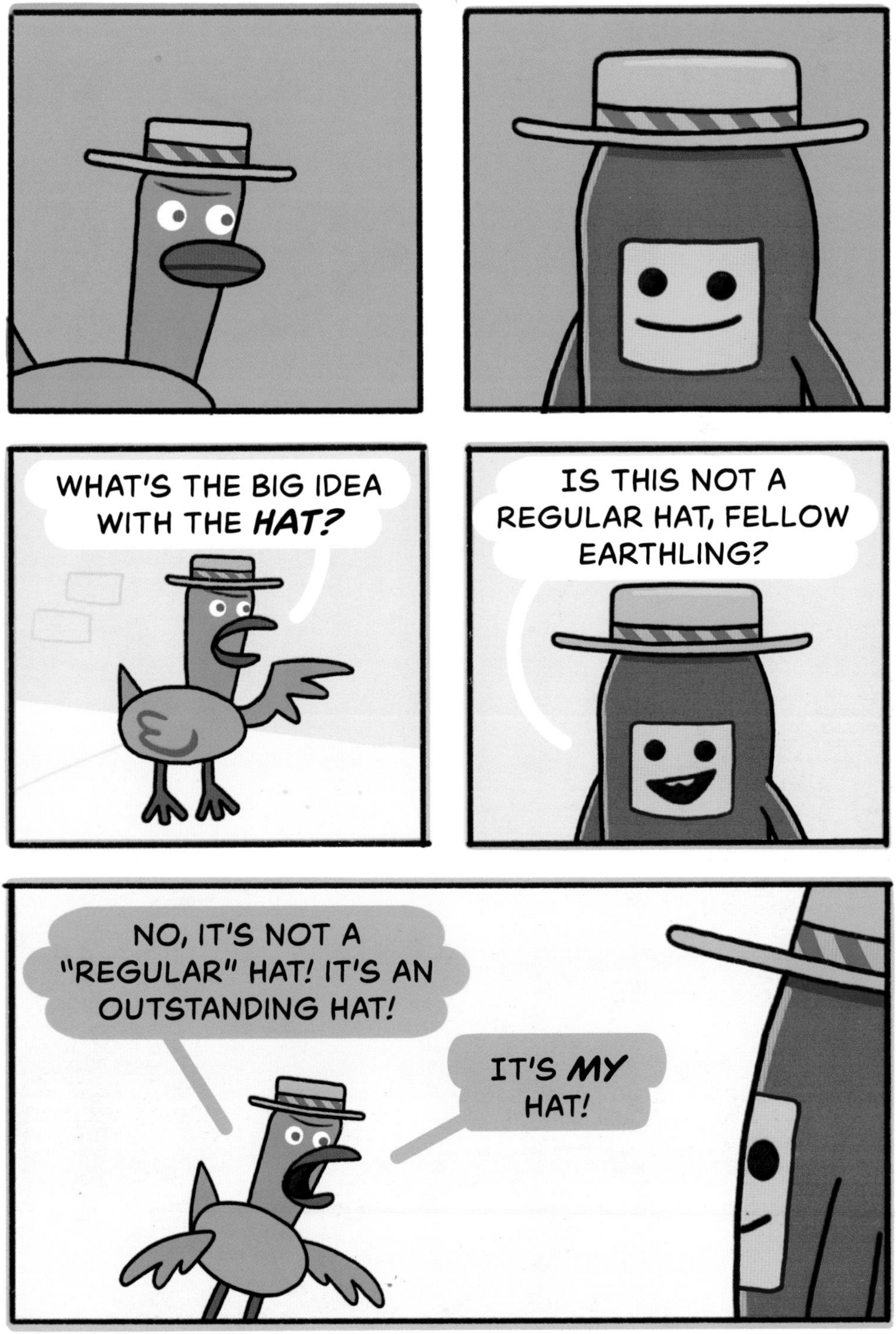
WHAT'S THE BIG IDEA WITH THE ***HAT?***
IS THIS NOT A REGULAR HAT, FELLOW EARTHLING?
NO, IT'S NOT A "REGULAR" HAT! IT'S AN OUTSTANDING HAT!
IT'S ***MY*** HAT!

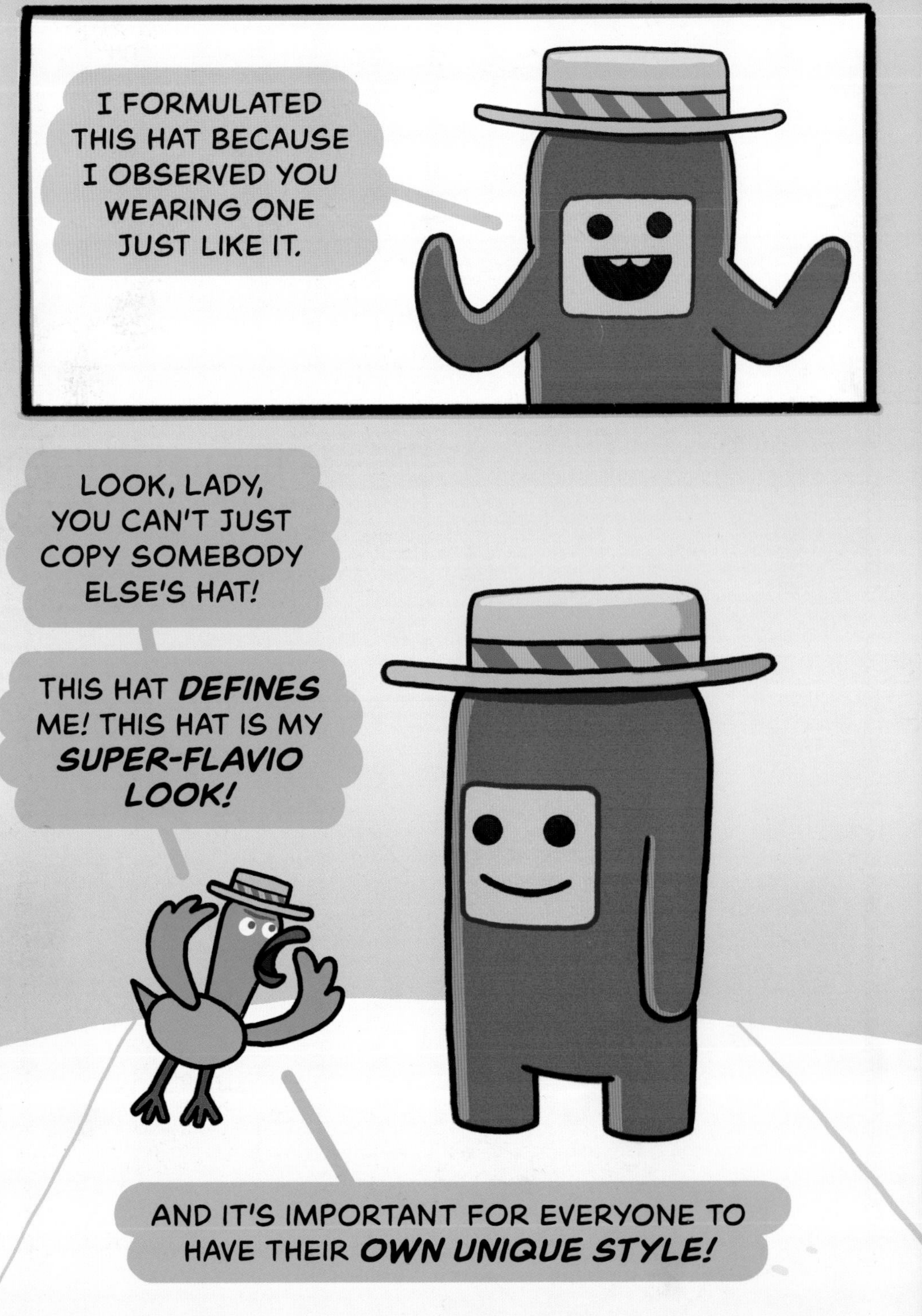
I FORMULATED THIS HAT BECAUSE I OBSERVED YOU WEARING ONE JUST LIKE IT.
LOOK, LADY, YOU CAN'T JUST COPY SOMEBODY ELSE'S HAT!
THIS HAT *DEFINES* ME! THIS HAT IS MY *SUPER-FLAVIO LOOK!*
AND IT'S IMPORTANT FOR EVERYONE TO HAVE THEIR *OWN UNIQUE STYLE!*

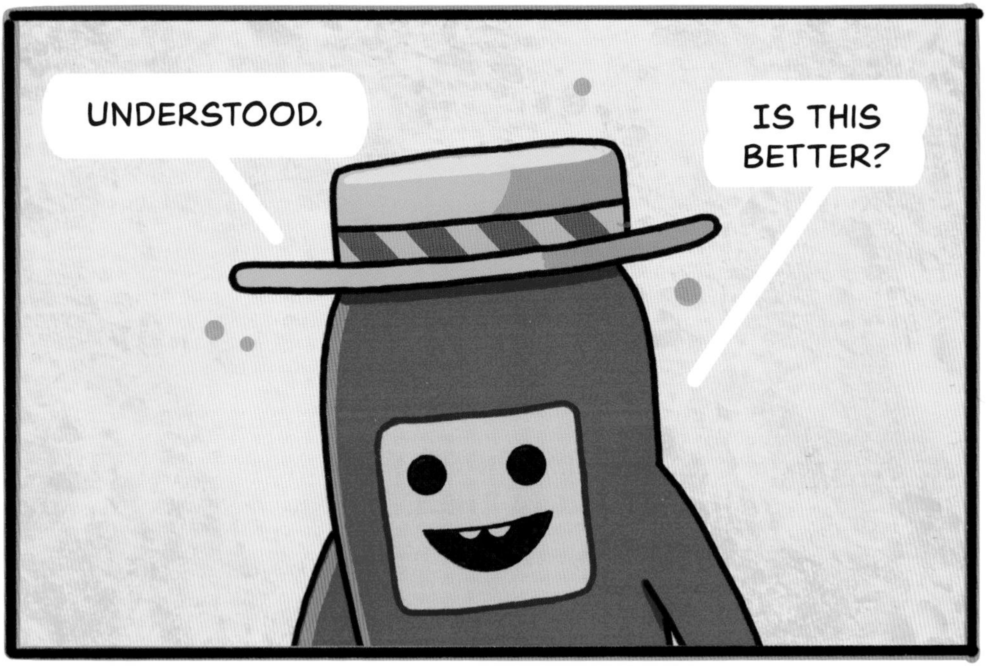
UNDERSTOOD.
IS THIS BETTER?

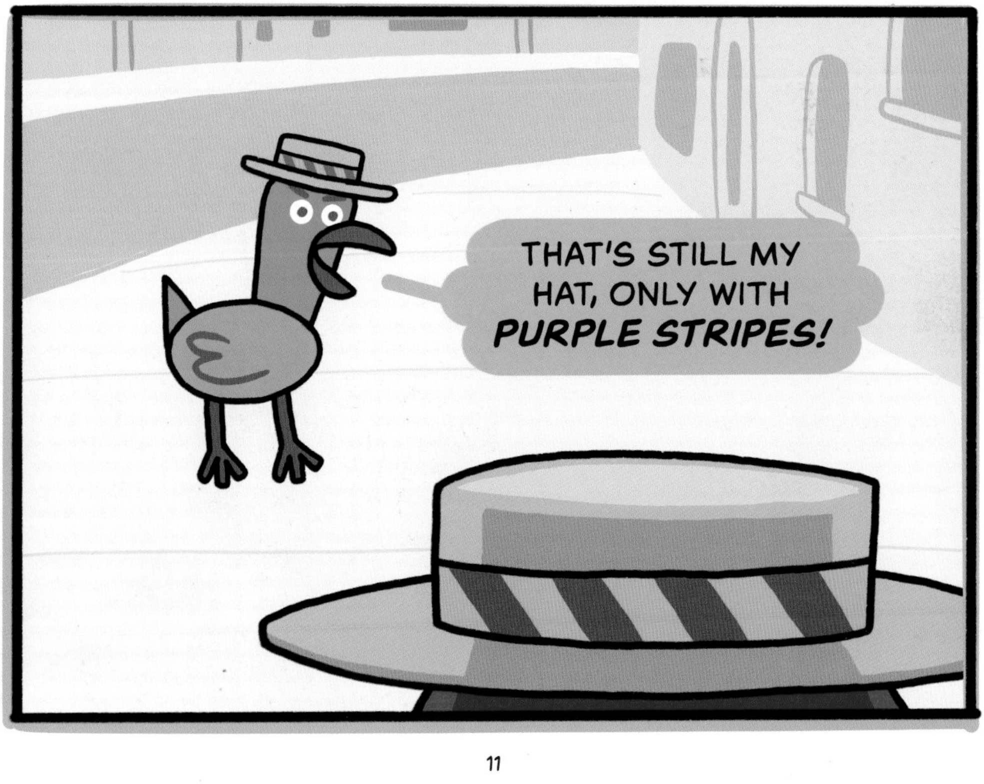
THAT'S STILL MY HAT, ONLY WITH *PURPLE STRIPES!*

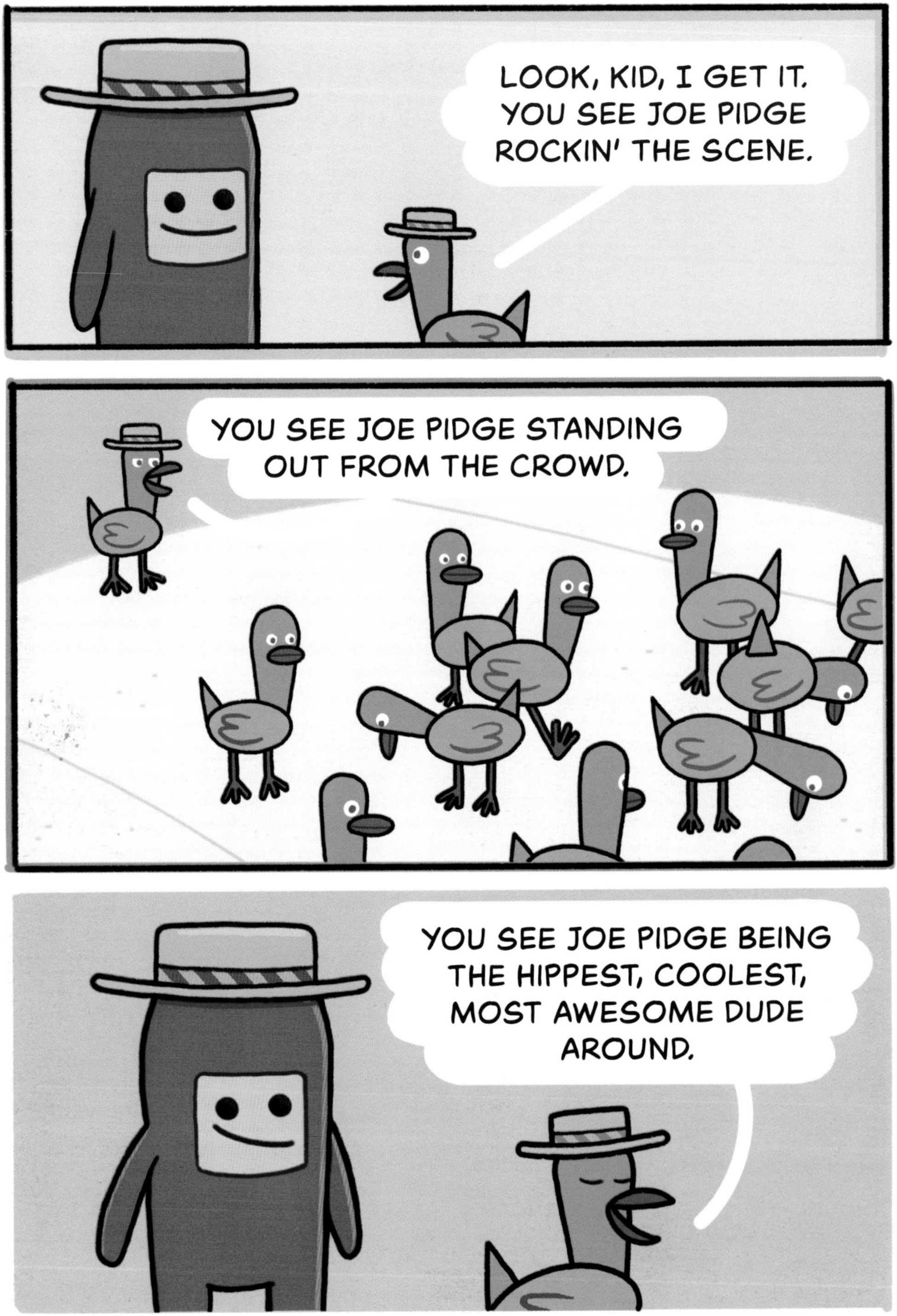
LOOK, KID, I GET IT. YOU SEE JOE PIDGE ROCKIN' THE SCENE.
YOU SEE JOE PIDGE STANDING OUT FROM THE CROWD.
YOU SEE JOE PIDGE BEING THE HIPPEST, COOLEST, MOST AWESOME DUDE AROUND.

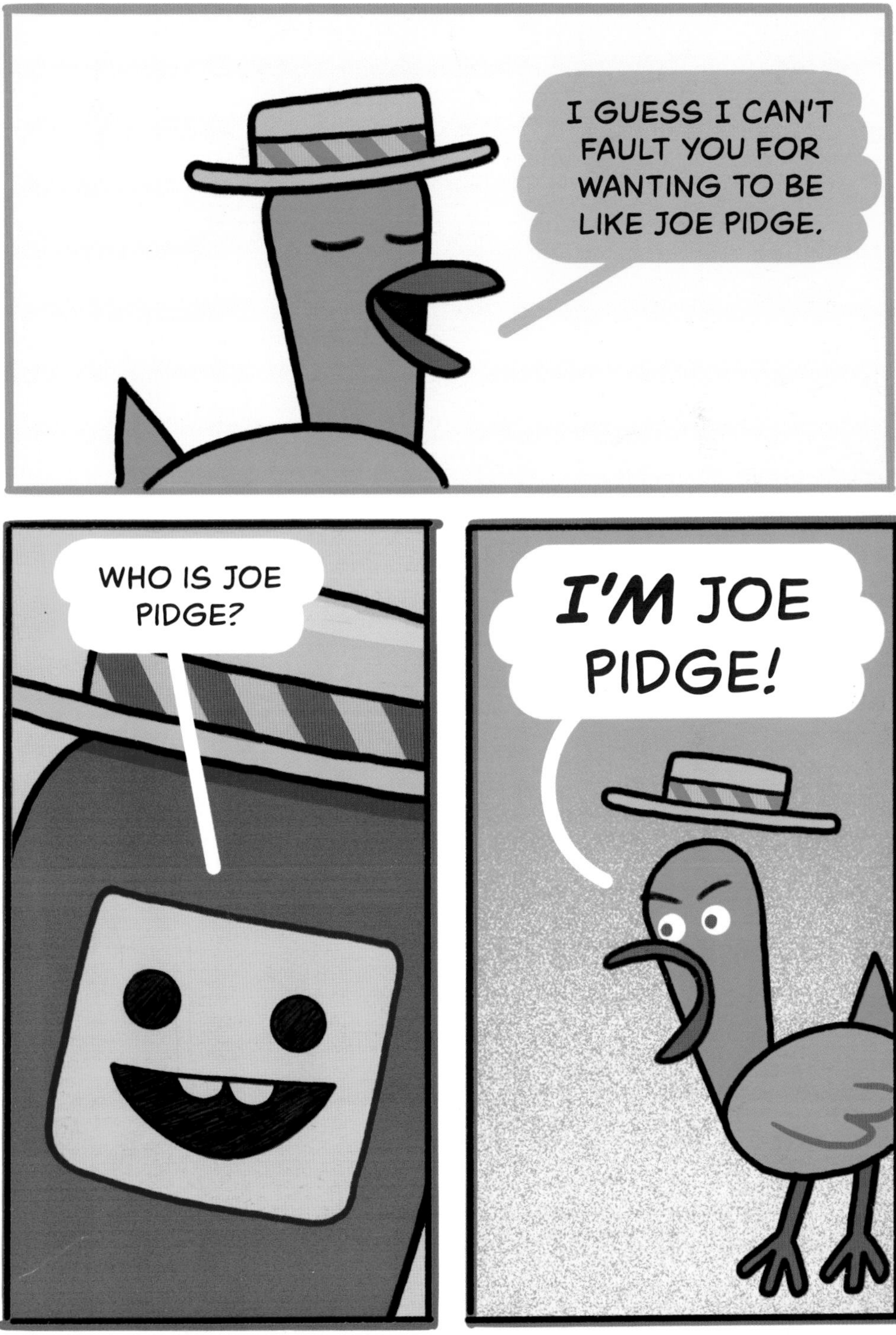
I GUESS I CAN'T FAULT YOU FOR WANTING TO BE LIKE JOE PIDGE.
WHO IS JOE PIDGE?
I'M JOE PIDGE!

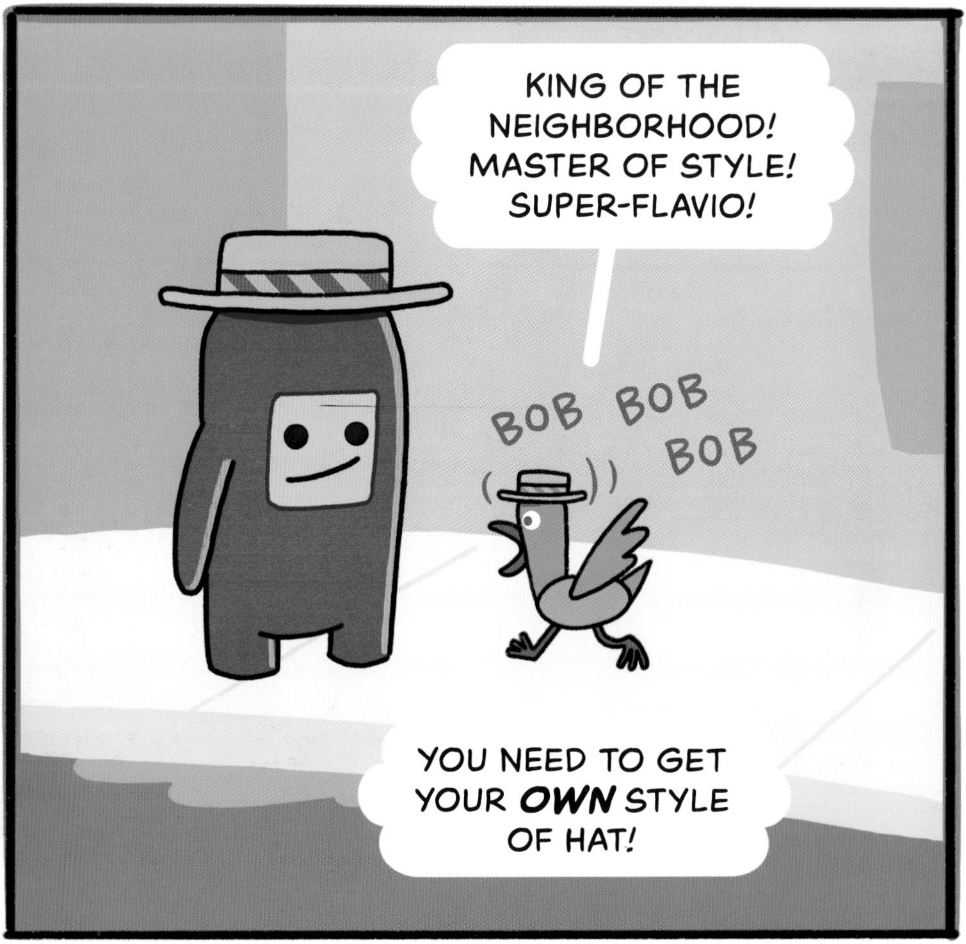
KING OF THE NEIGHBORHOOD! MASTER OF STYLE! SUPER-FLAVIO!
BOB BOB BOB
YOU NEED TO GET YOUR **OWN** STYLE OF HAT!

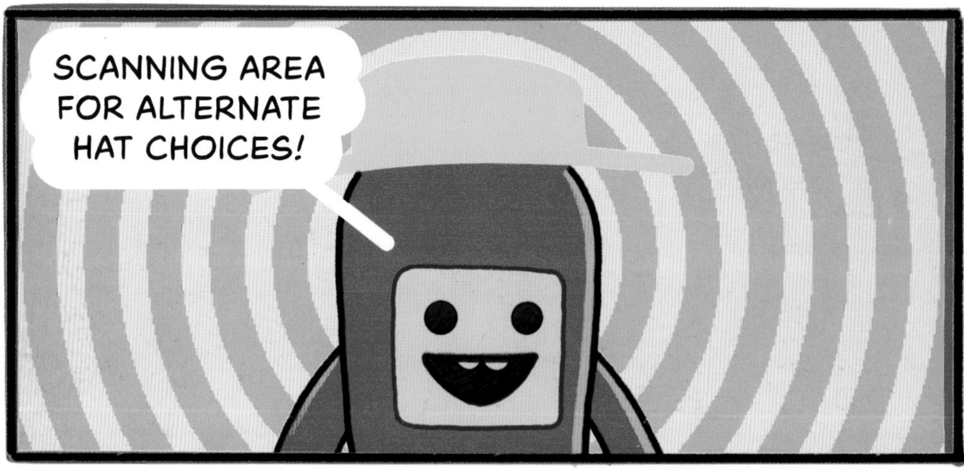
SCANNING AREA FOR ALTERNATE HAT CHOICES!

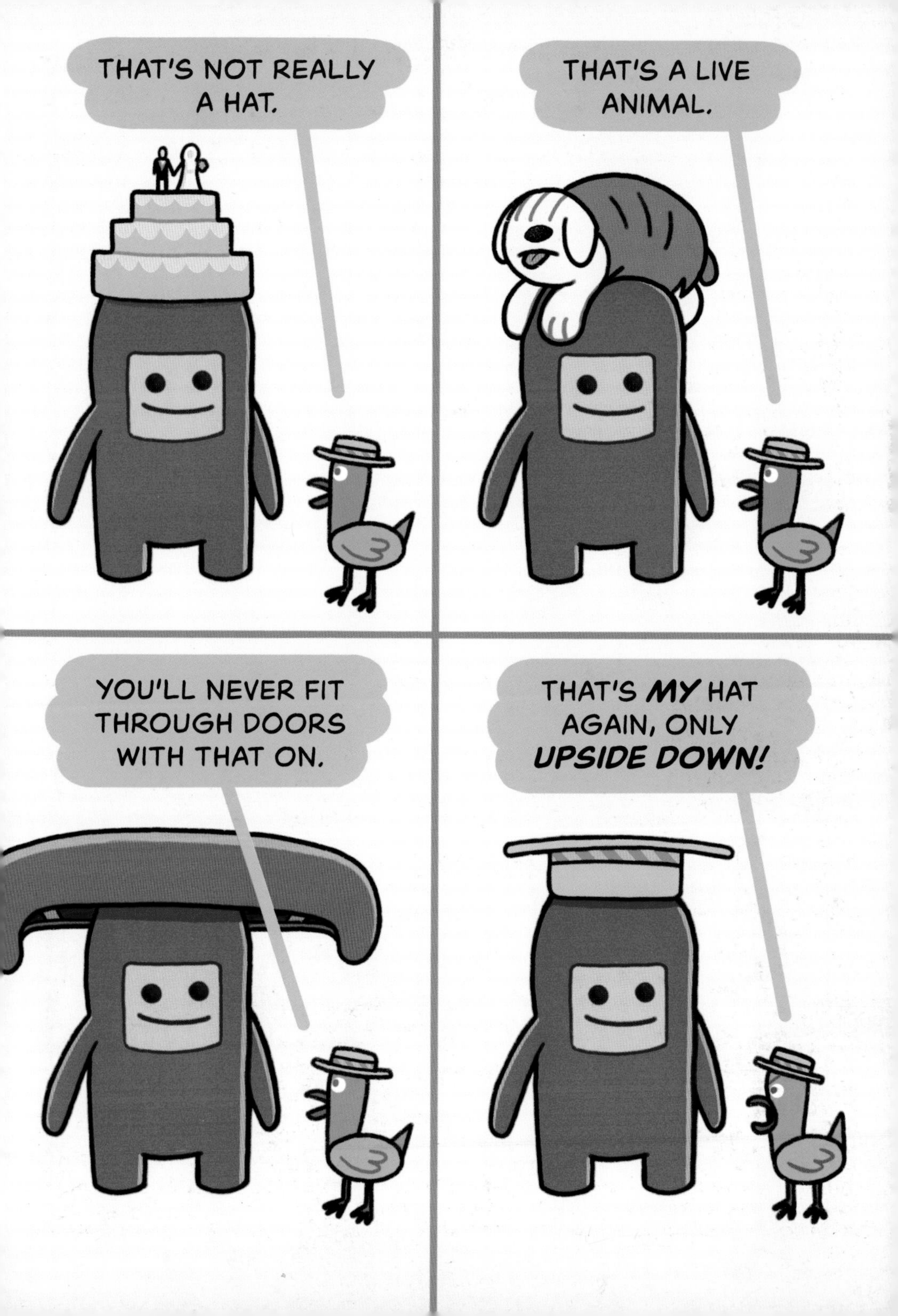
THAT'S NOT REALLY A HAT.
THAT'S A LIVE ANIMAL.
YOU'LL NEVER FIT THROUGH DOORS WITH THAT ON.
THAT'S **MY** HAT AGAIN, ONLY ***UPSIDE DOWN!***

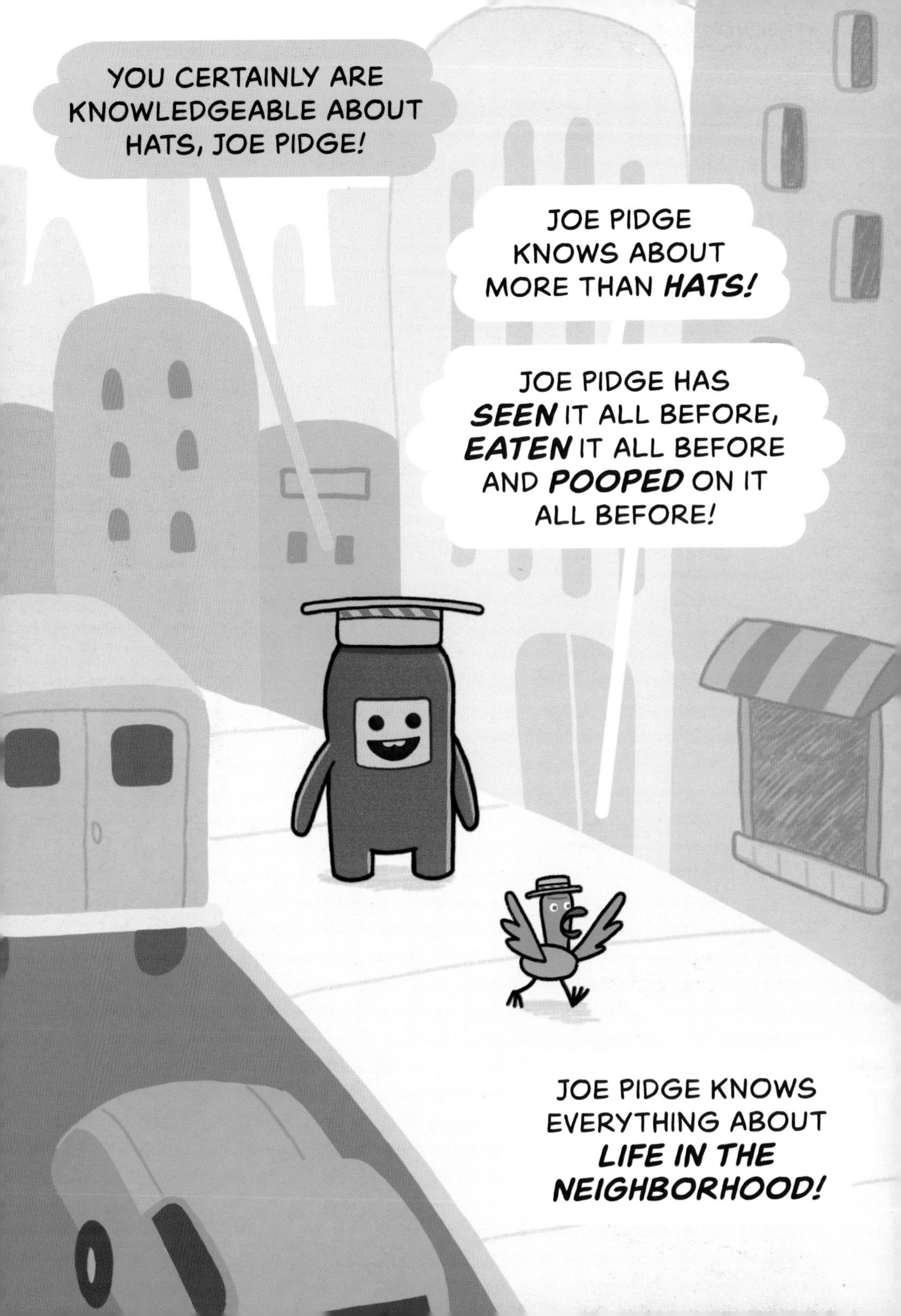
YOU CERTAINLY ARE KNOWLEDGEABLE ABOUT HATS, JOE PIDGE!
JOE PIDGE KNOWS ABOUT MORE THAN ***HATS!***
JOE PIDGE HAS ***SEEN*** IT ALL BEFORE, ***EATEN*** IT ALL BEFORE AND ***POOPED*** ON IT ALL BEFORE!
JOE PIDGE KNOWS EVERYTHING ABOUT ***LIFE IN THE NEIGHBORHOOD!***

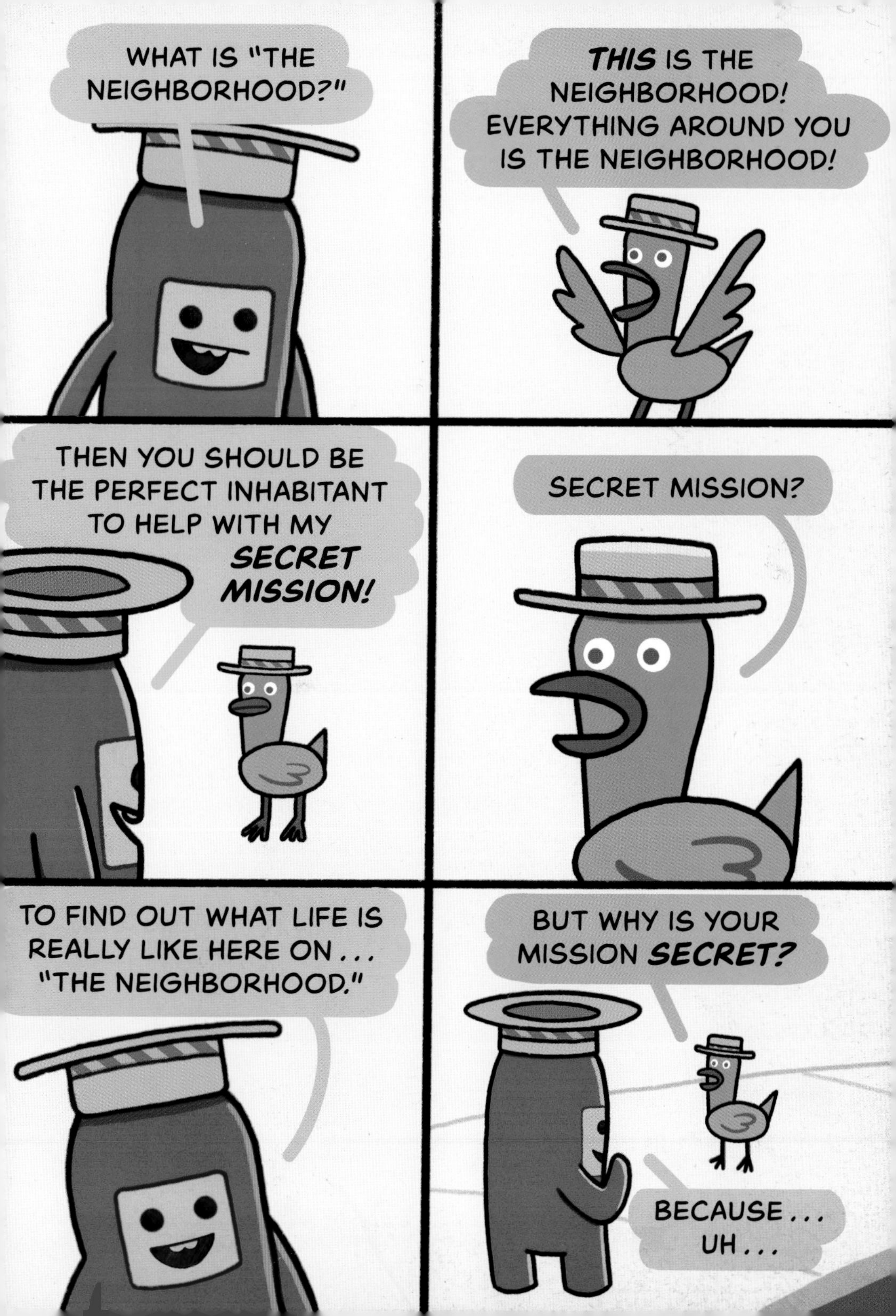
WHAT IS "THE NEIGHBORHOOD?"
THIS IS THE NEIGHBORHOOD! EVERYTHING AROUND YOU IS THE NEIGHBORHOOD!
THEN YOU SHOULD BE THE PERFECT INHABITANT TO HELP WITH MY SECRET MISSION!
SECRET MISSION?
TO FIND OUT WHAT LIFE IS REALLY LIKE HERE ON . . . "THE NEIGHBORHOOD."
BUT WHY IS YOUR MISSION SECRET?
BECAUSE . . . UH . . .

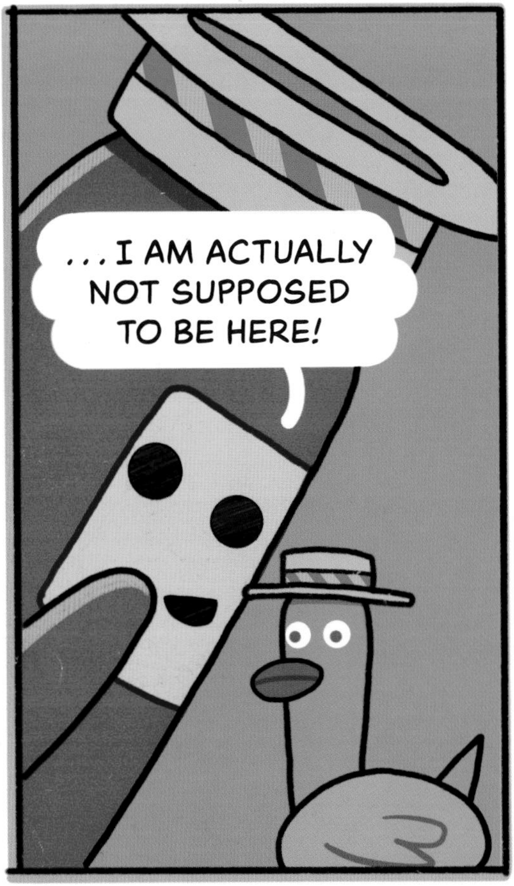
...I AM ACTUALLY NOT SUPPOSED TO BE HERE!

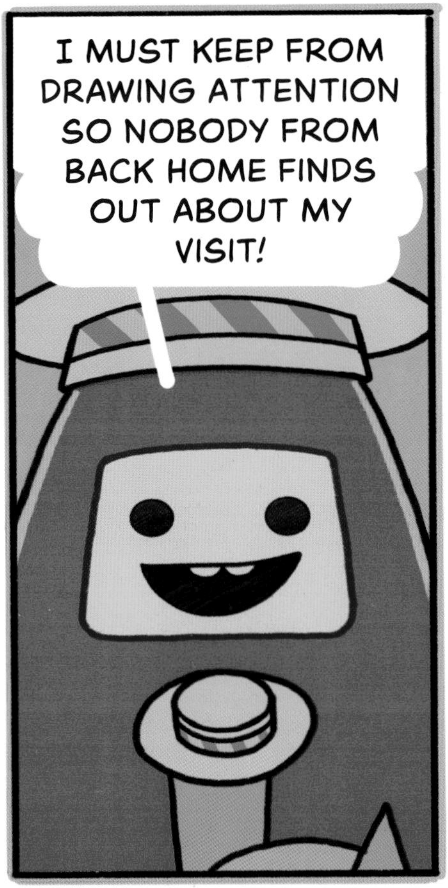
I MUST KEEP FROM DRAWING ATTENTION SO NOBODY FROM BACK HOME FINDS OUT ABOUT MY VISIT!

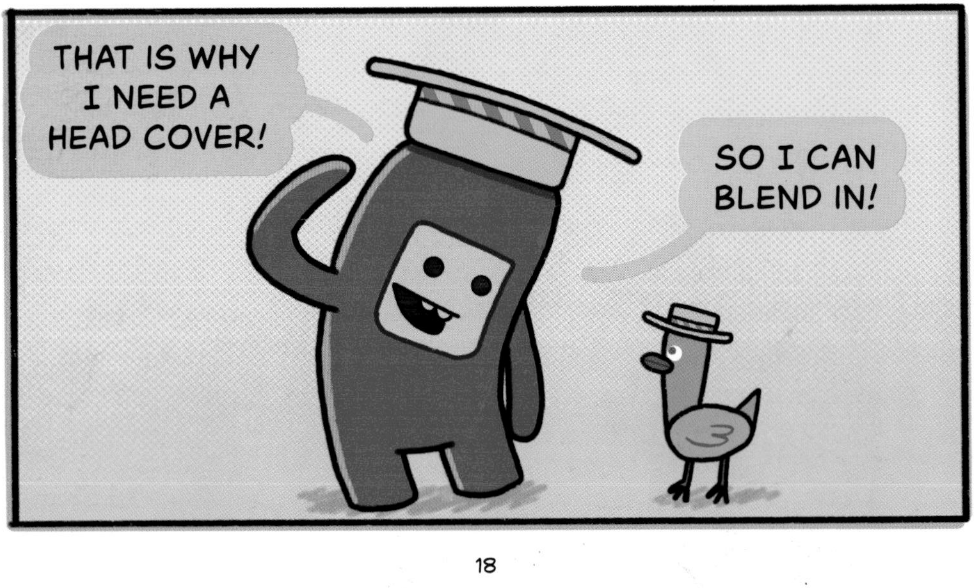
THAT IS WHY I NEED A HEAD COVER!
SO I CAN BLEND IN!

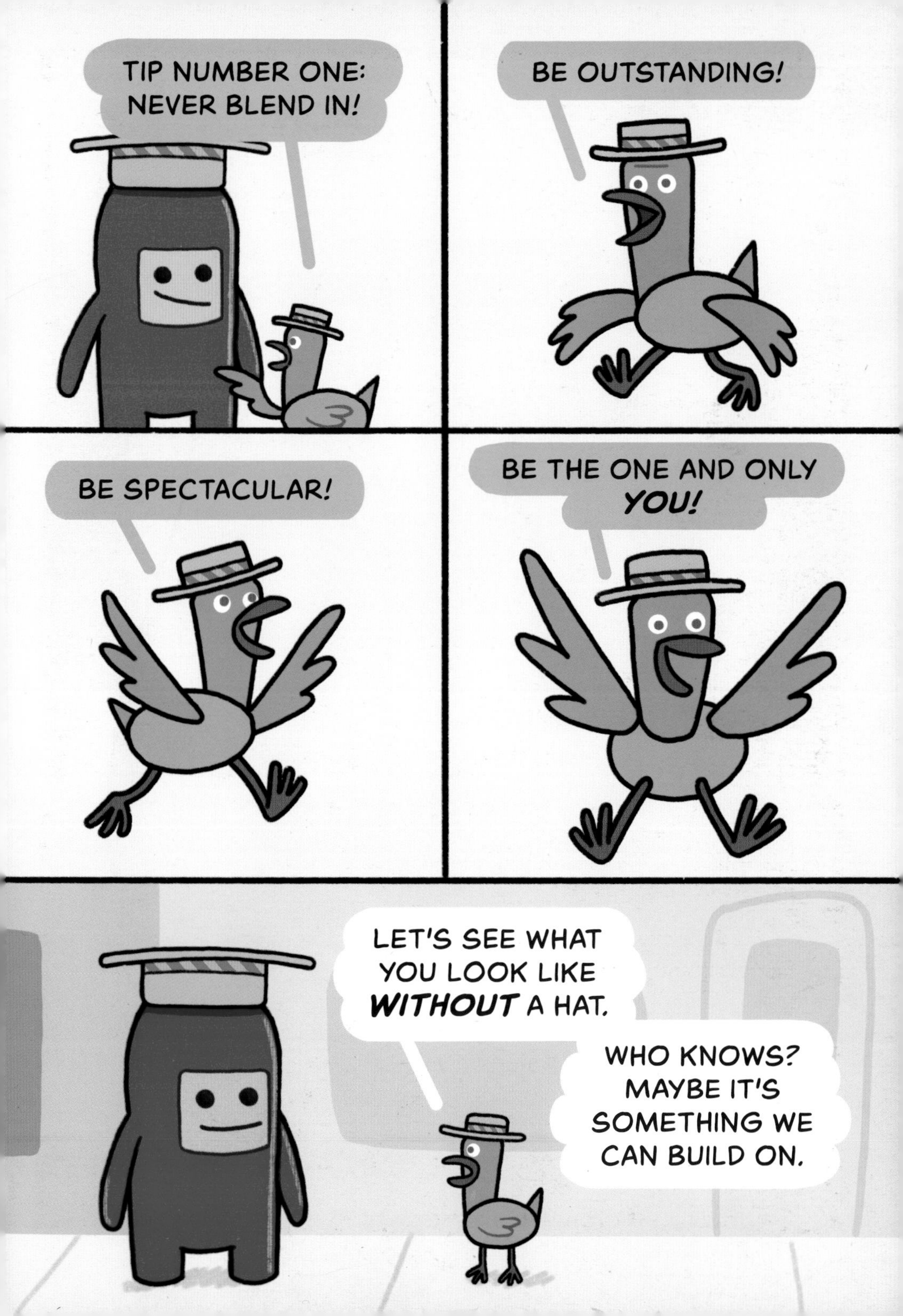
TIP NUMBER ONE: NEVER BLEND IN!
BE OUTSTANDING!
BE SPECTACULAR!
BE THE ONE AND ONLY *YOU!*
LET'S SEE WHAT YOU LOOK LIKE ***WITHOUT*** A HAT.
WHO KNOWS? MAYBE IT'S SOMETHING WE CAN BUILD ON.

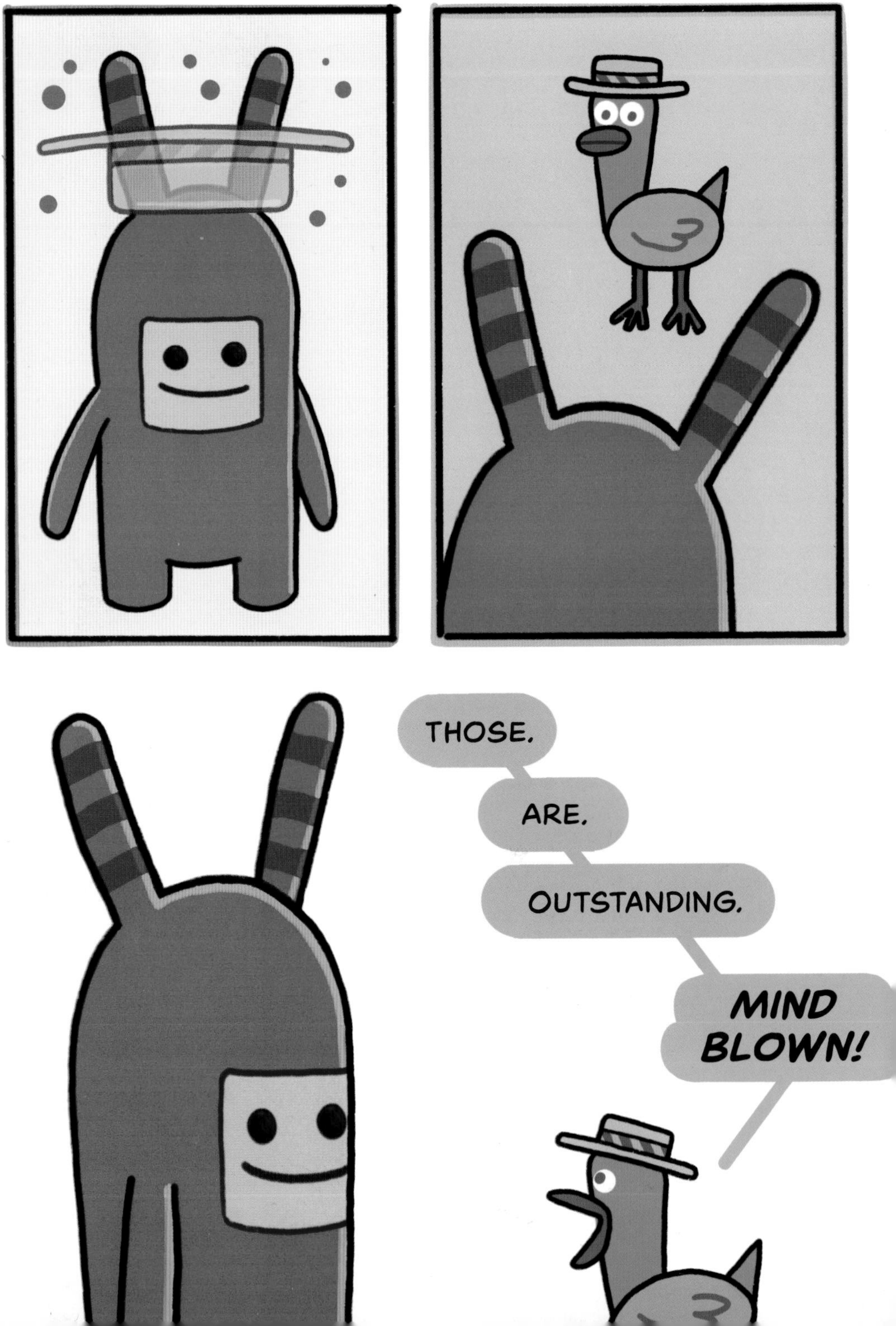
THOSE.
ARE.
OUTSTANDING.
MIND BLOWN!

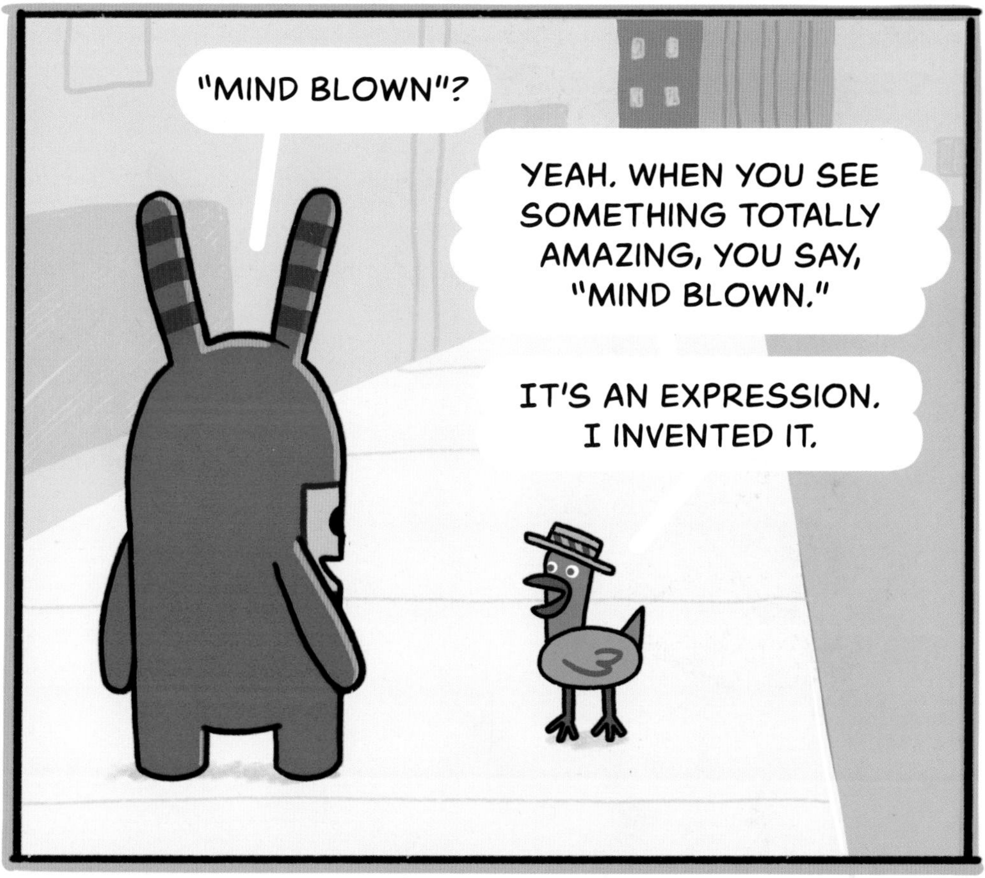
"MIND BLOWN"?
YEAH. WHEN YOU SEE SOMETHING TOTALLY AMAZING, YOU SAY, "MIND BLOWN."
IT'S AN EXPRESSION. I INVENTED IT.

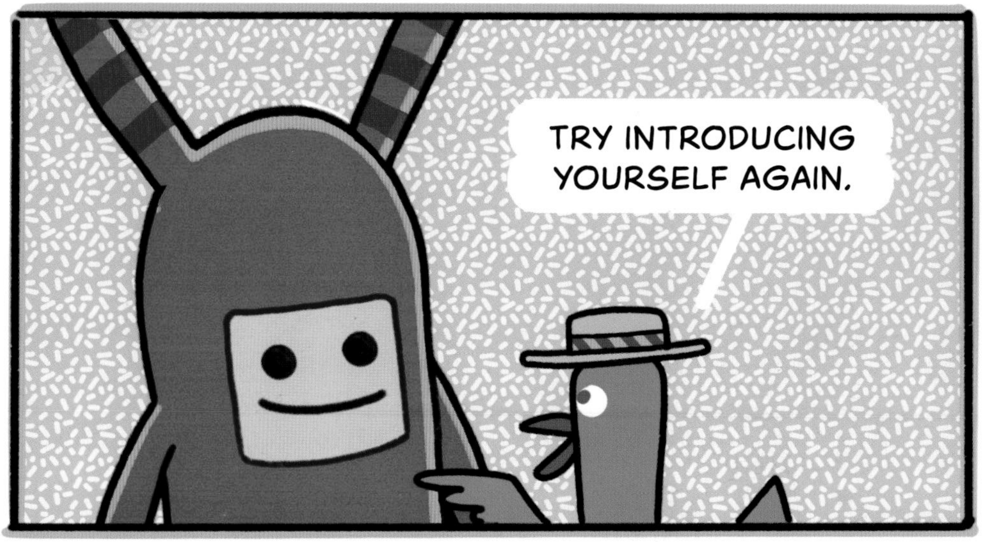
TRY INTRODUCING YOURSELF AGAIN.

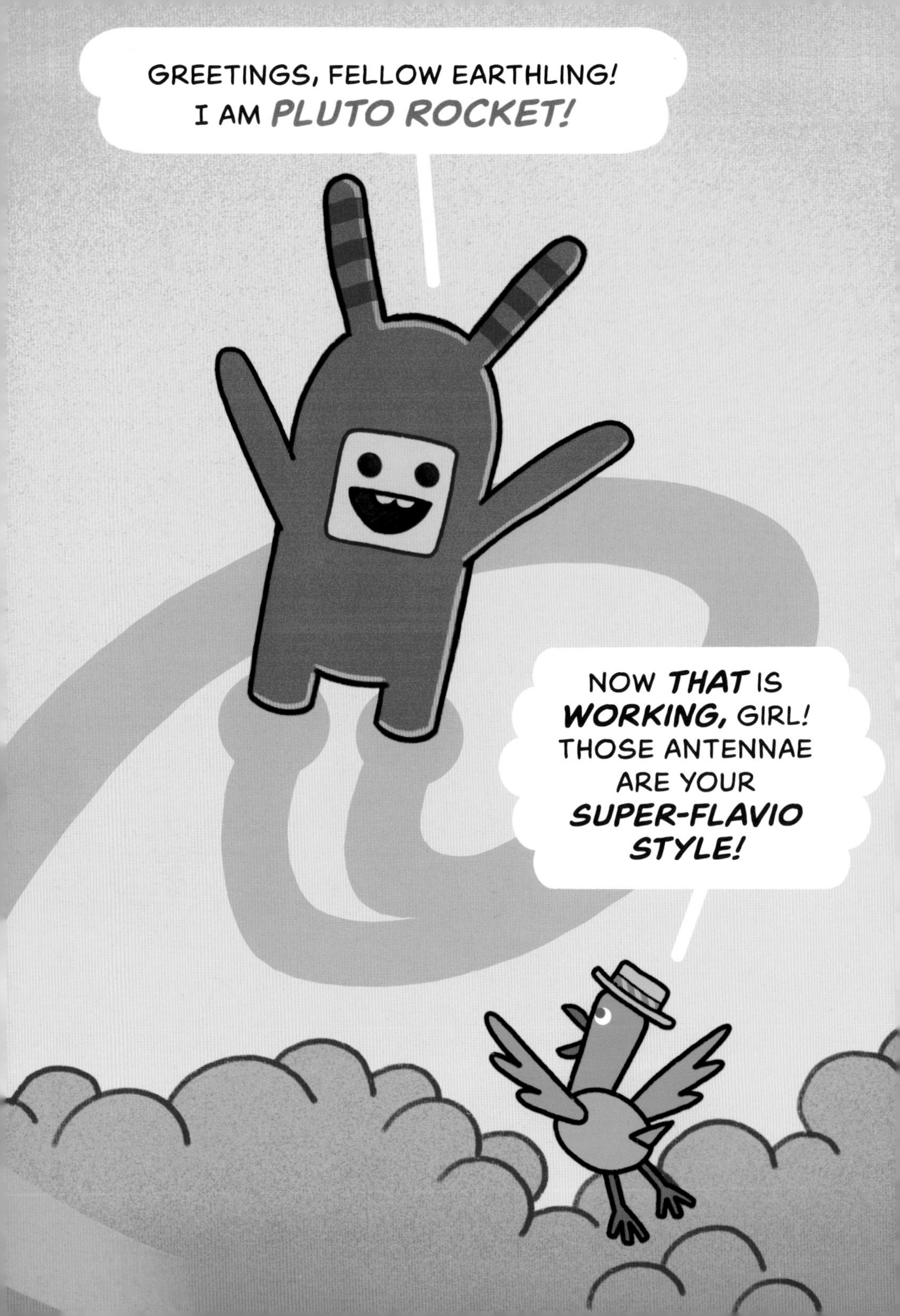
GREETINGS, FELLOW EARTHLING! I AM PLUTO ROCKET!
NOW THAT IS WORKING, GIRL! THOSE ANTENNAE ARE YOUR SUPER-FLAVIO STYLE!

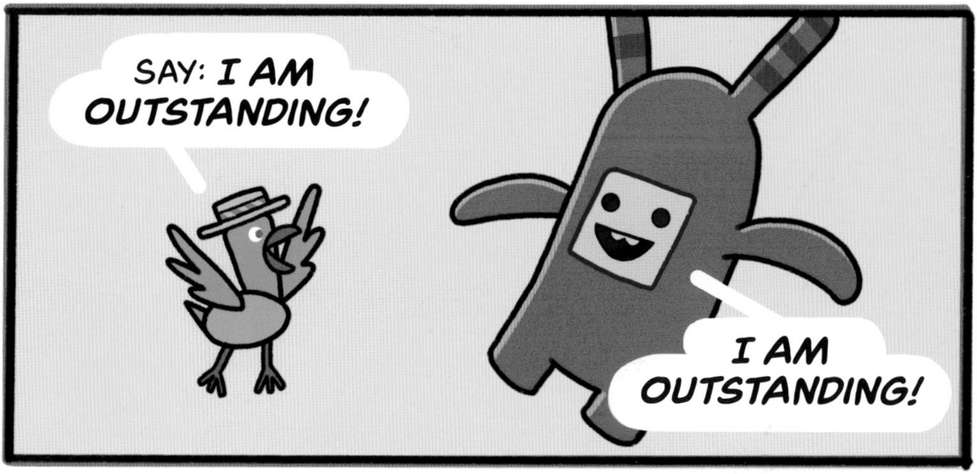
SAY: I AM OUTSTANDING!
I AM OUTSTANDING!

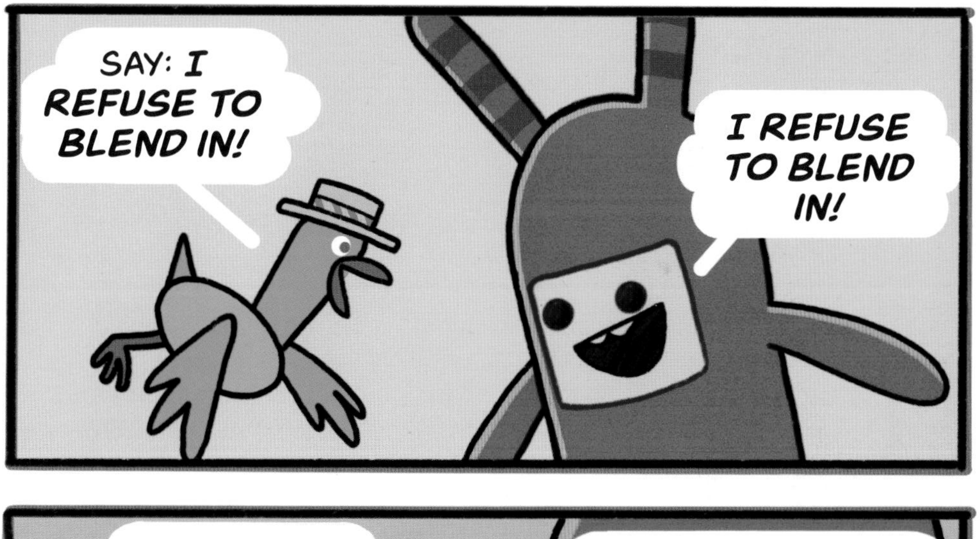
SAY: I REFUSE TO BLEND IN!
I REFUSE TO BLEND IN!

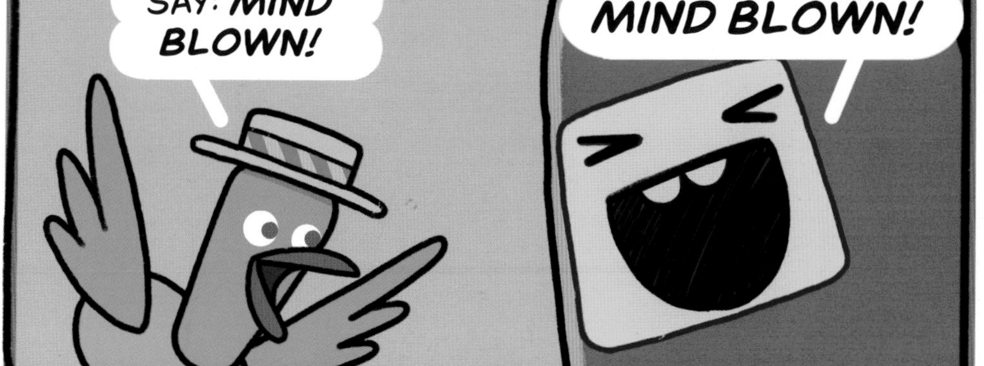
SAY: MIND BLOWN!
MIND BLOWN!

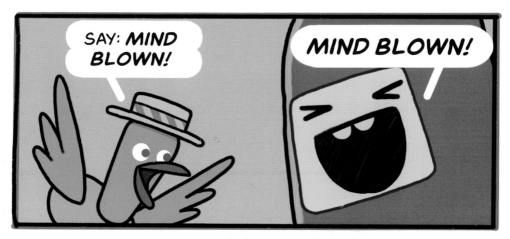

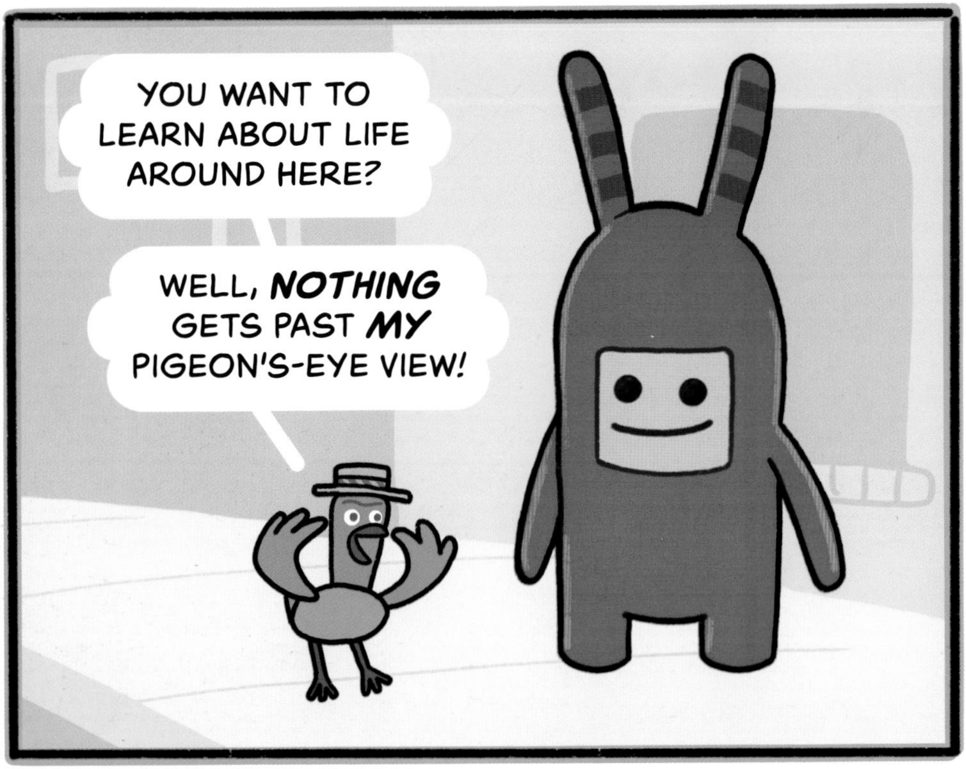
YOU WANT TO LEARN ABOUT LIFE AROUND HERE?
WELL, **NOTHING** GETS PAST **MY** PIGEON'S-EYE VIEW!

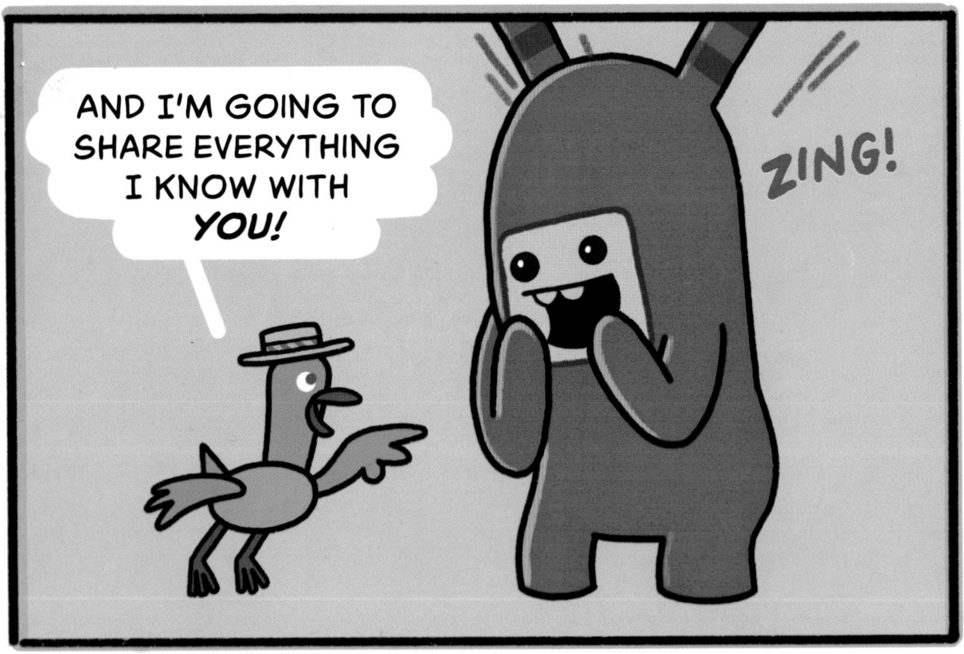
AND I'M GOING TO SHARE EVERYTHING I KNOW WITH ***YOU!***
ZING!

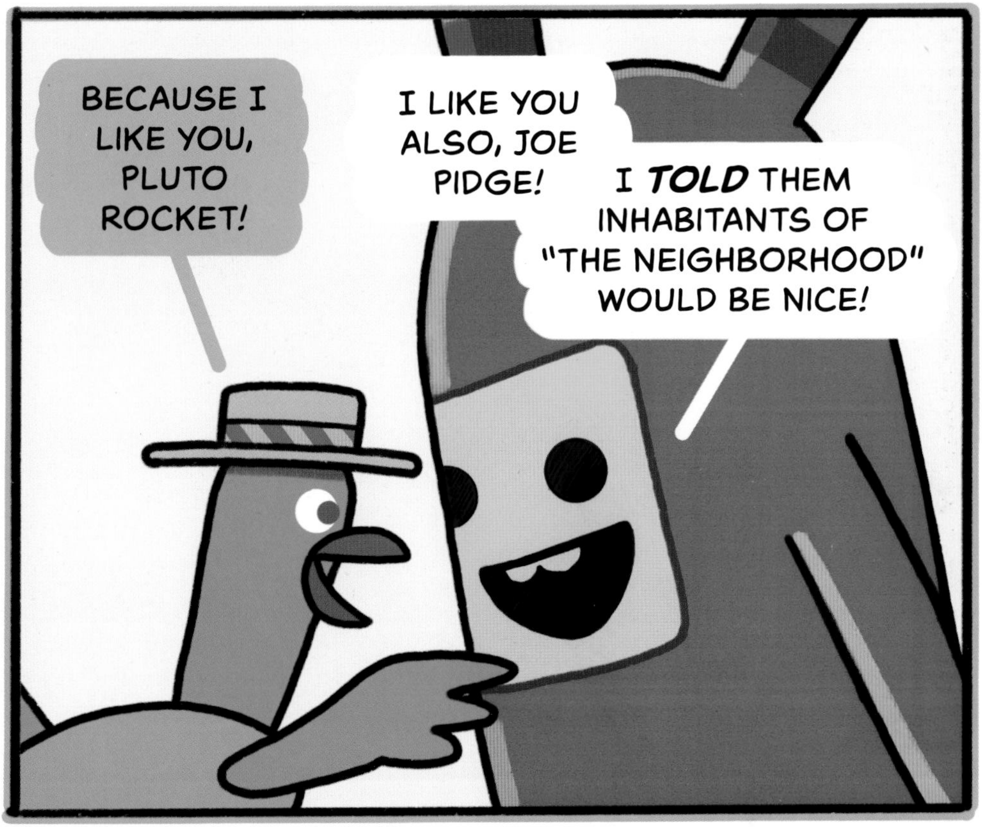
BECAUSE I LIKE YOU, PLUTO ROCKET!
I LIKE YOU ALSO, JOE PIDGE!
I ***TOLD*** THEM INHABITANTS OF "THE NEIGHBORHOOD" WOULD BE NICE!

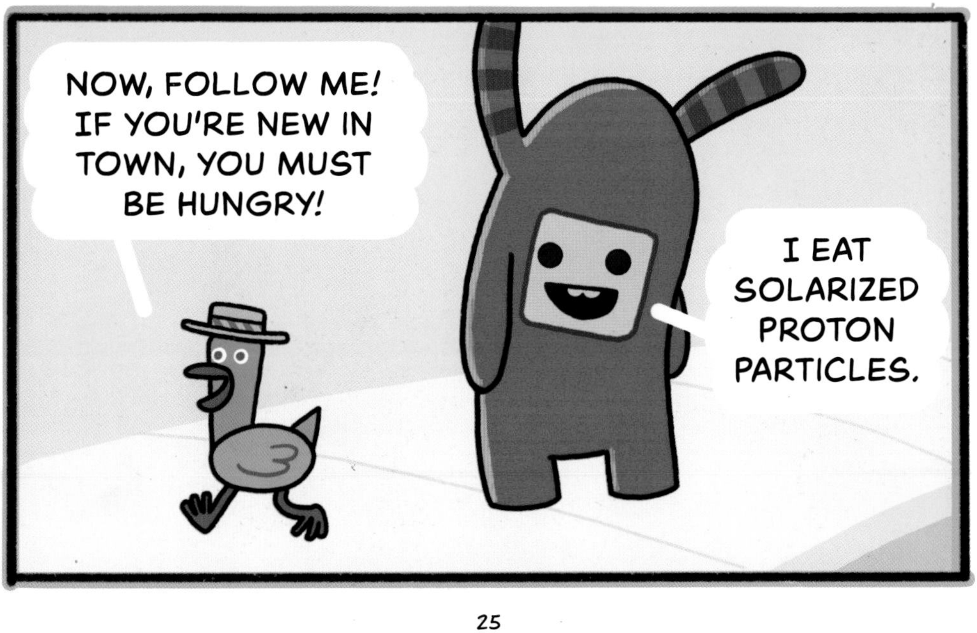
NOW, FOLLOW ME! IF YOU'RE NEW IN TOWN, YOU MUST BE HUNGRY!
I EAT SOLARIZED PROTON PARTICLES.

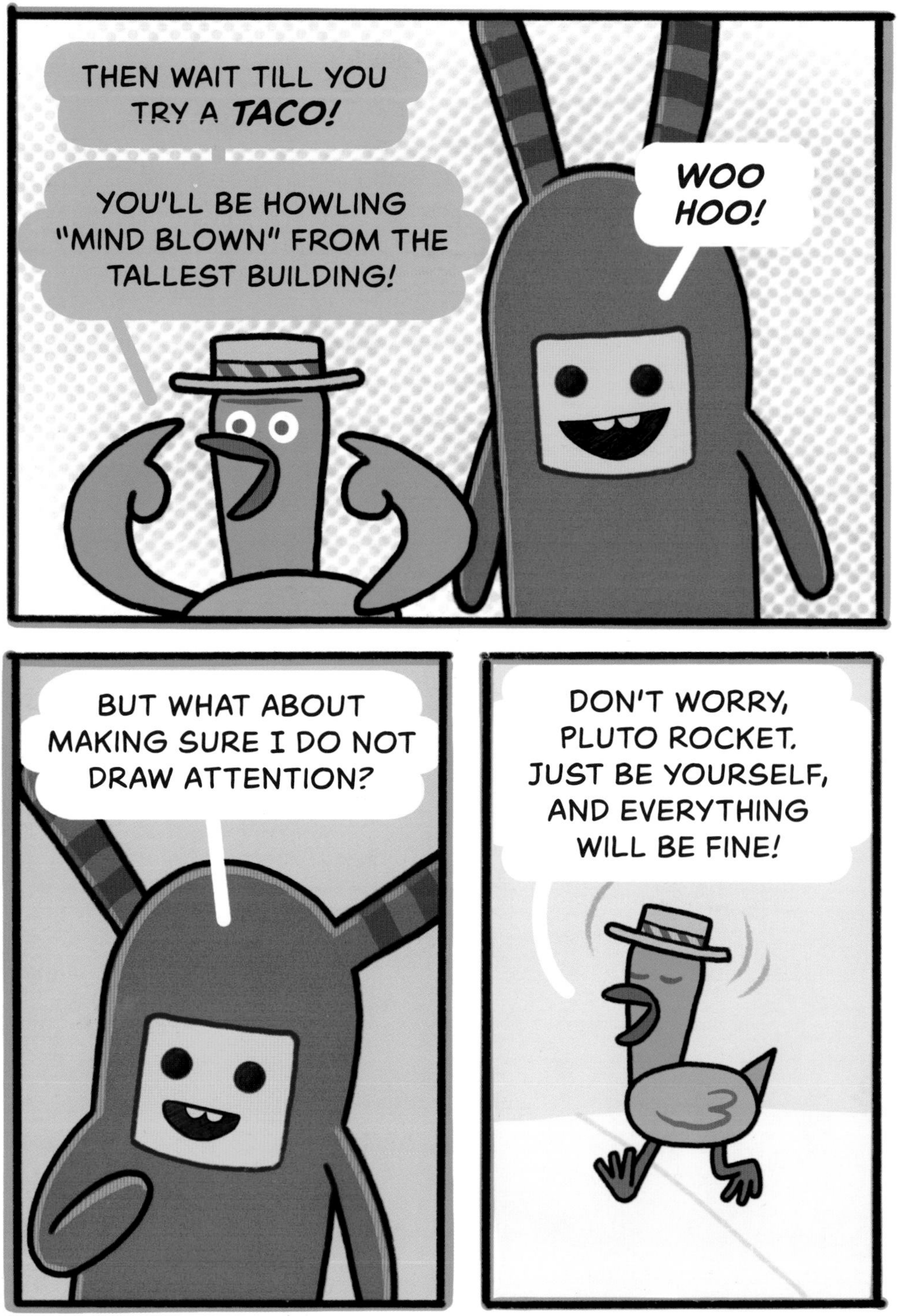
THEN WAIT TILL YOU TRY A *TACO!*
YOU'LL BE HOWLING "MIND BLOWN" FROM THE TALLEST BUILDING!
WOO HOO!
BUT WHAT ABOUT MAKING SURE I DO NOT DRAW ATTENTION?
DON'T WORRY, PLUTO ROCKET. JUST BE YOURSELF, AND EVERYTHING WILL BE FINE!

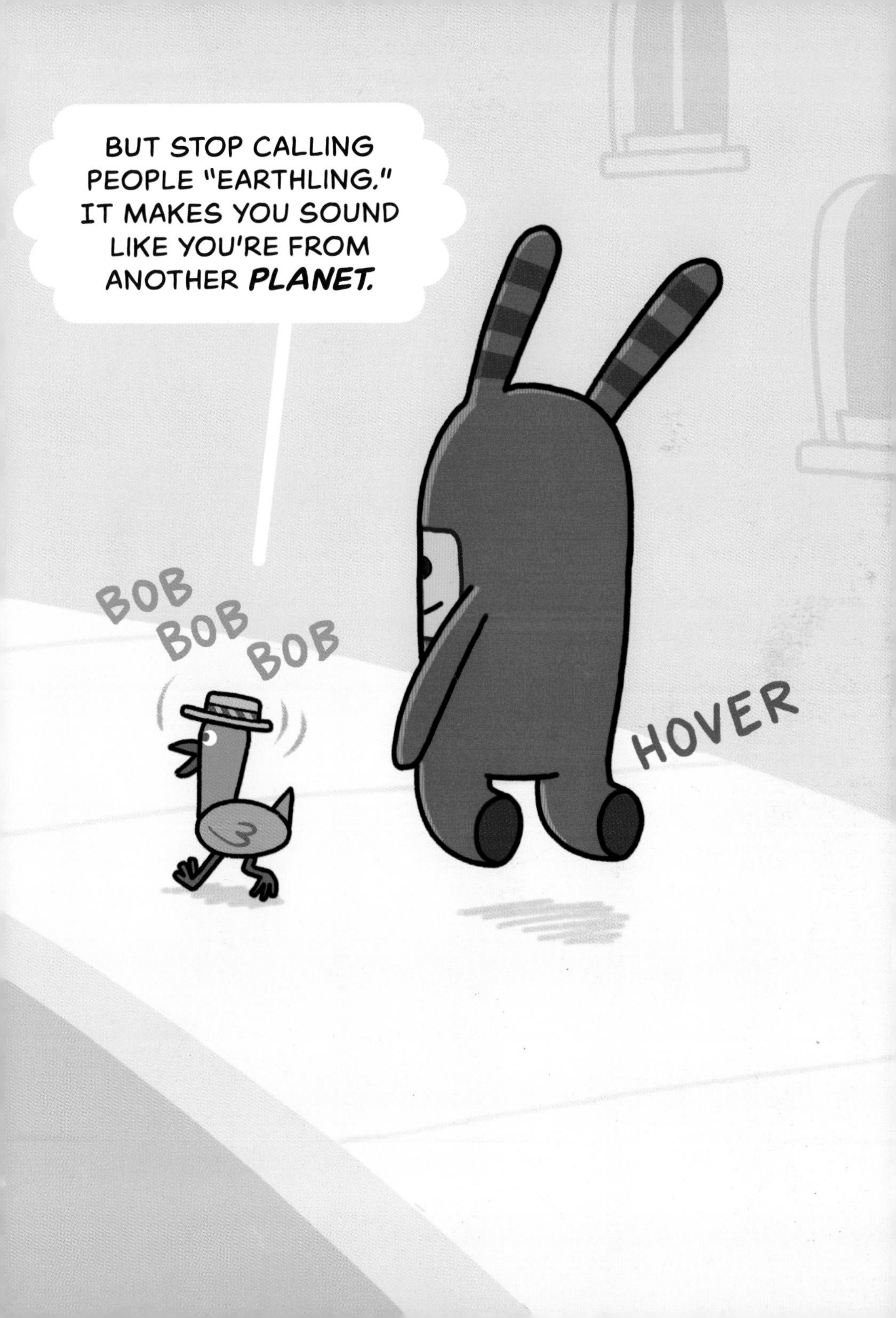
BUT STOP CALLING PEOPLE "EARTHLING." IT MAKES YOU SOUND LIKE YOU'RE FROM ANOTHER ***PLANET.***
BOB BOB BOB
HOVER

CHAPTER TWO:
LET'S GET A TACO!

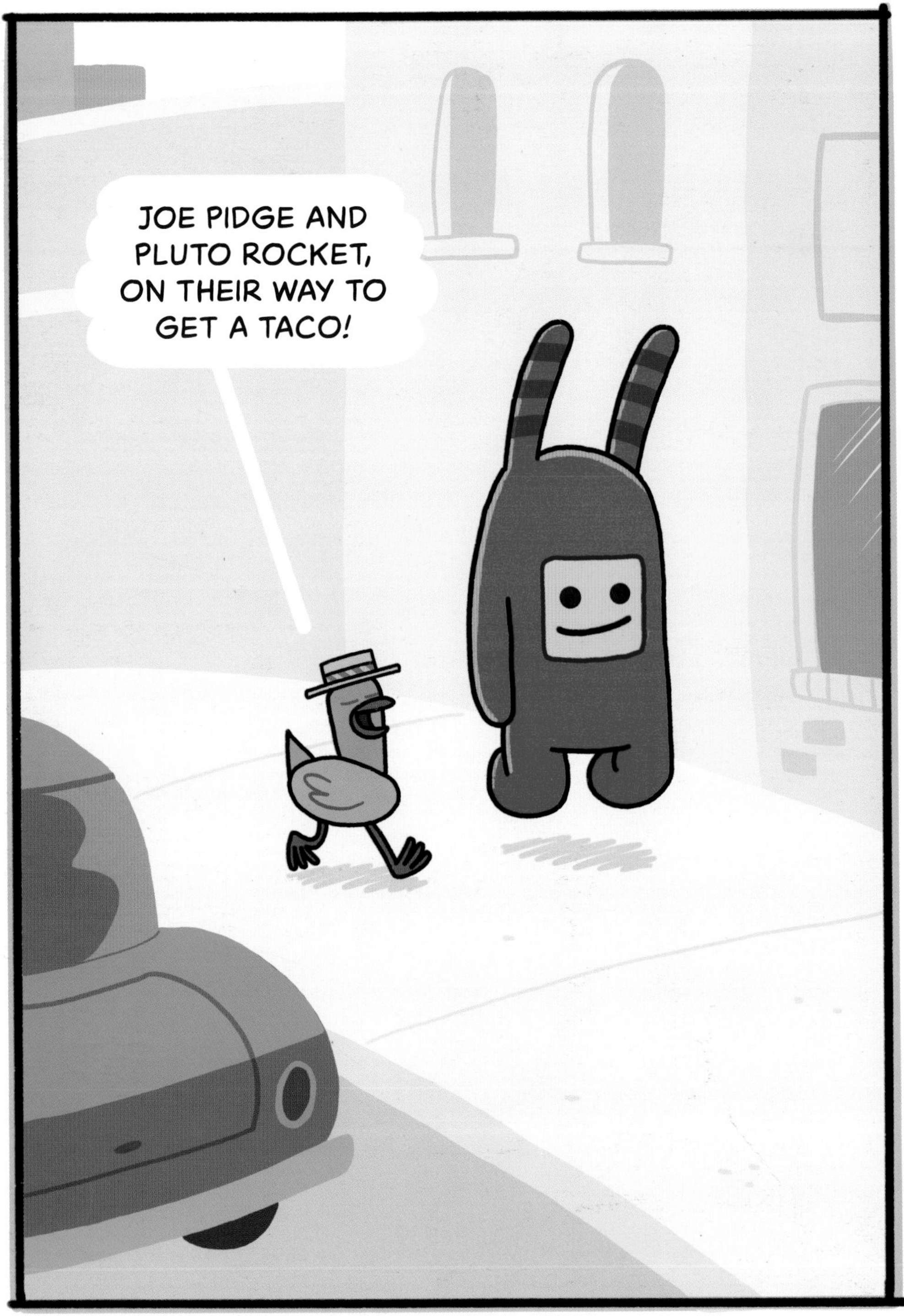
JOE PIDGE AND PLUTO ROCKET, ON THEIR WAY TO GET A TACO!

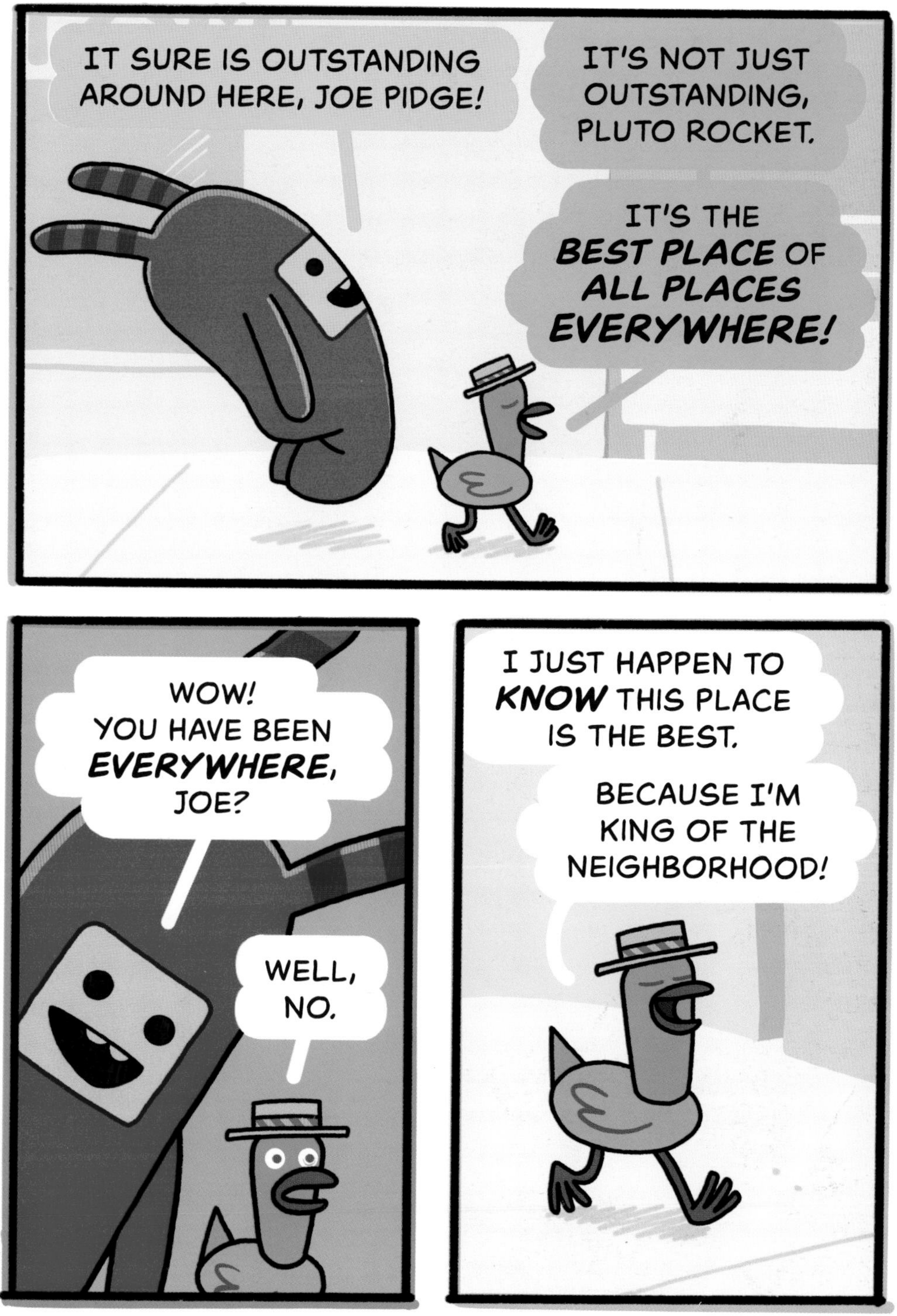
IT SURE IS OUTSTANDING AROUND HERE, JOE PIDGE!
IT'S NOT JUST OUTSTANDING, PLUTO ROCKET.
IT'S THE BEST PLACE OF ALL PLACES EVERYWHERE!
WOW! YOU HAVE BEEN EVERYWHERE, JOE?
WELL, NO.
I JUST HAPPEN TO KNOW THIS PLACE IS THE BEST.
BECAUSE I'M KING OF THE NEIGHBORHOOD!

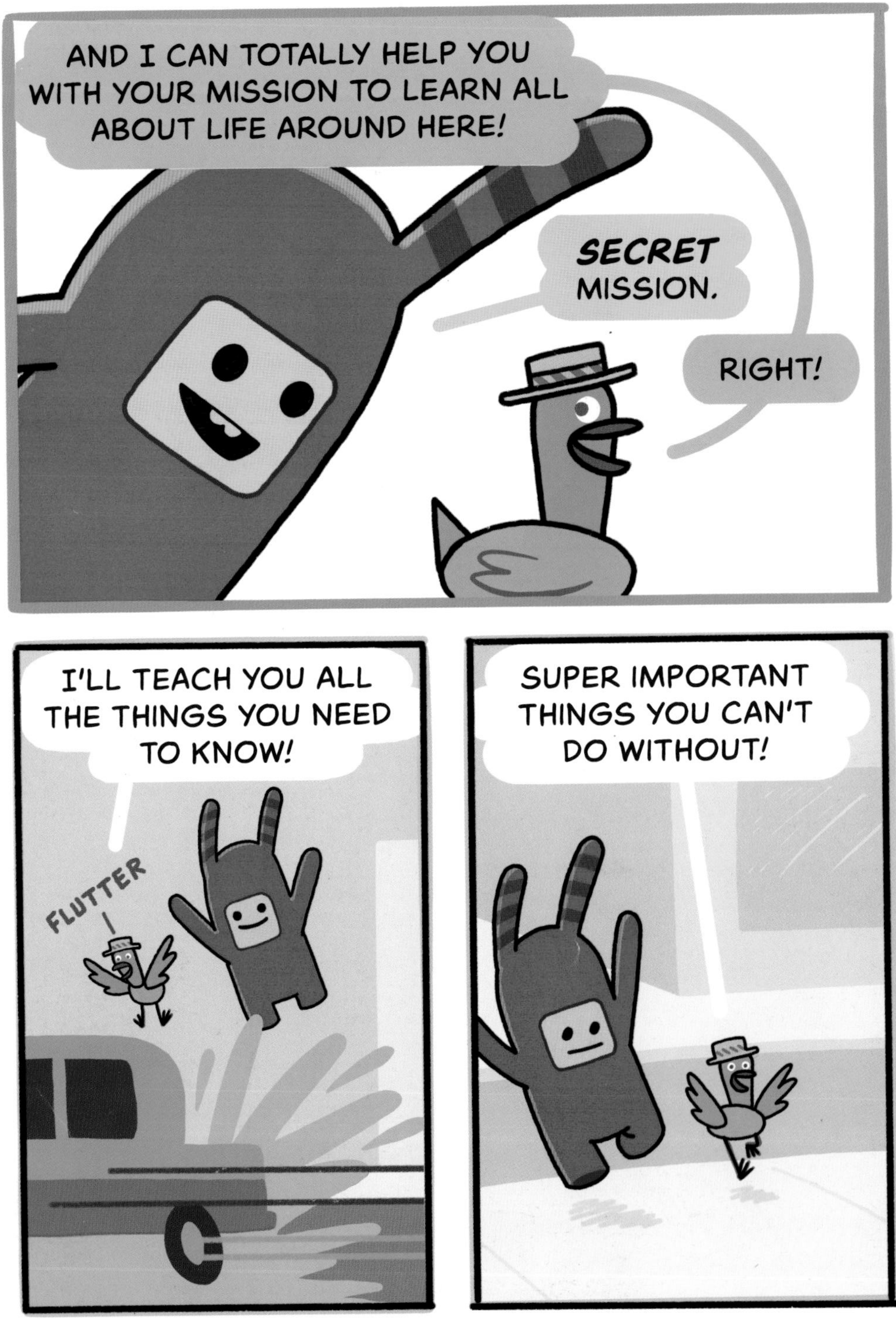
AND I CAN TOTALLY HELP YOU WITH YOUR MISSION TO LEARN ALL ABOUT LIFE AROUND HERE!
SECRET MISSION.
RIGHT!
I'LL TEACH YOU ALL THE THINGS YOU NEED TO KNOW!
FLUTTER
SUPER IMPORTANT THINGS YOU CAN'T DO WITHOUT!

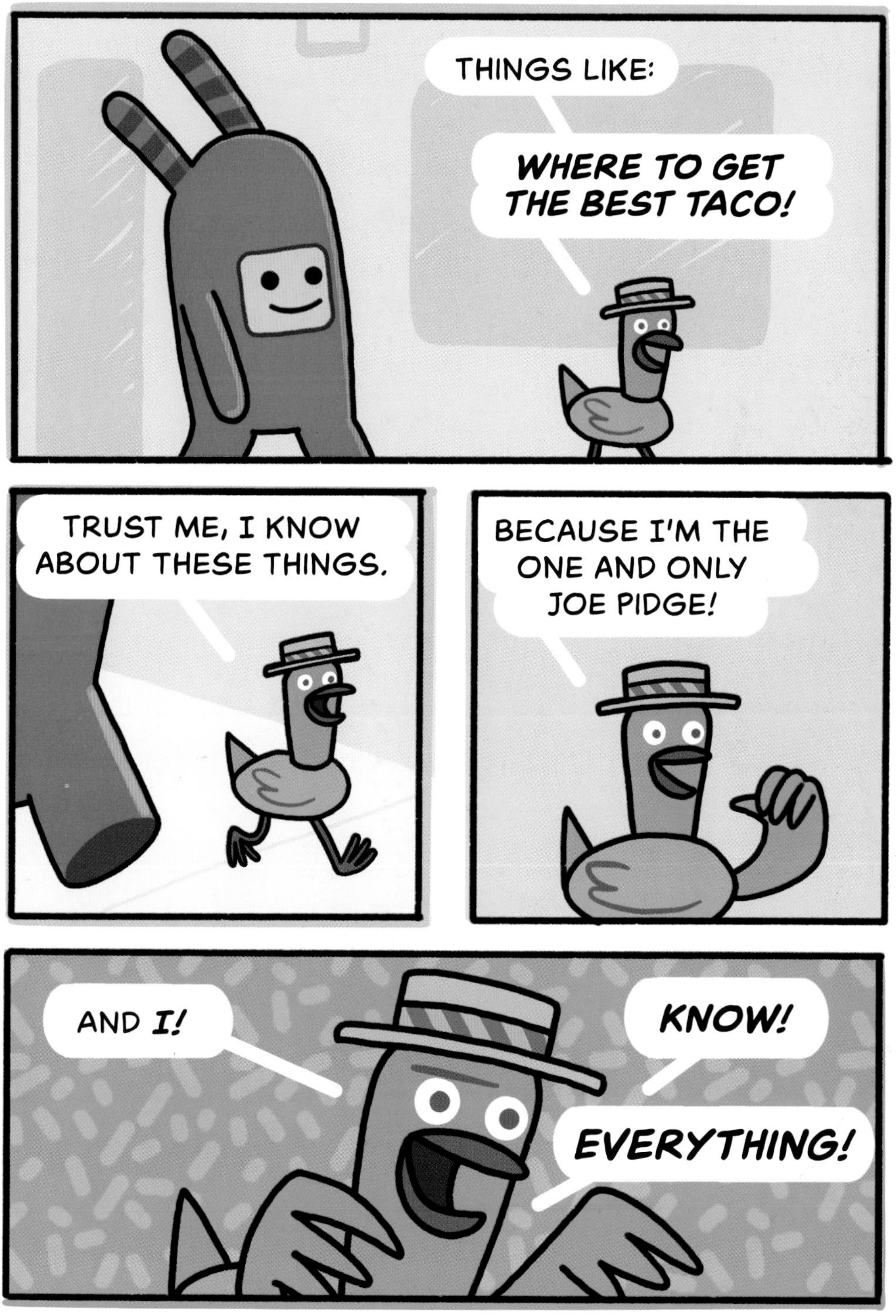
THINGS LIKE:
WHERE TO GET THE BEST TACO!
TRUST ME, I KNOW ABOUT THESE THINGS.
BECAUSE I'M THE ONE AND ONLY JOE PIDGE!
AND I!
KNOW!
EVERYTHING!

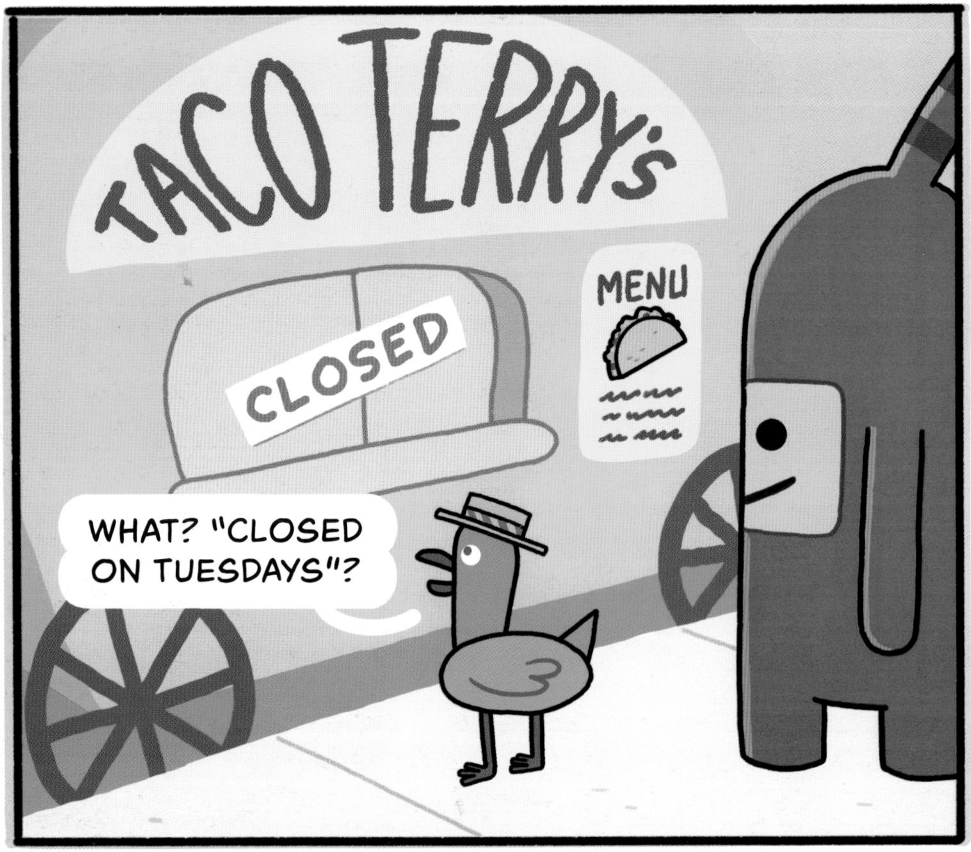
TACO TERRY'S
CLOSED
MENU
WHAT? "CLOSED ON TUESDAYS"?

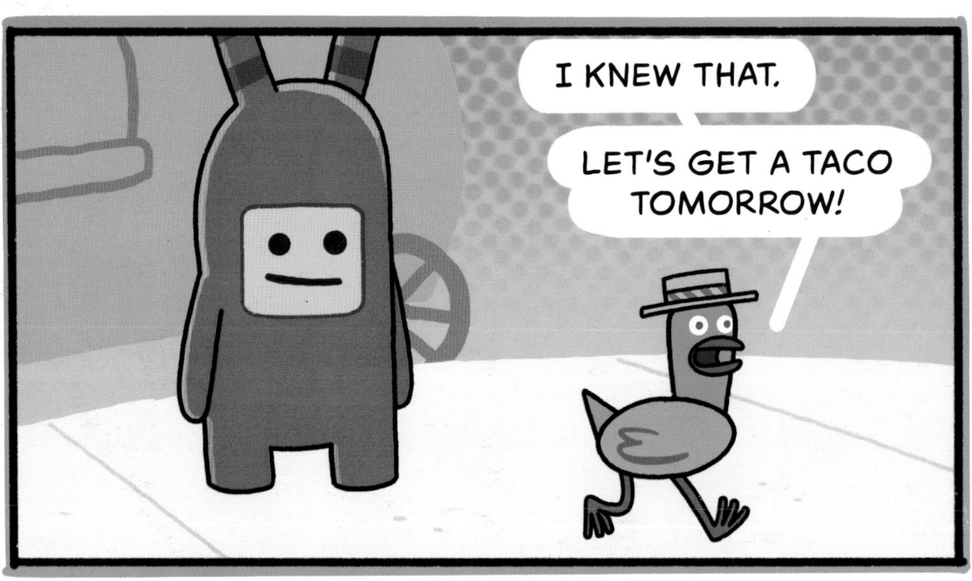
I KNEW THAT.
LET'S GET A TACO TOMORROW!

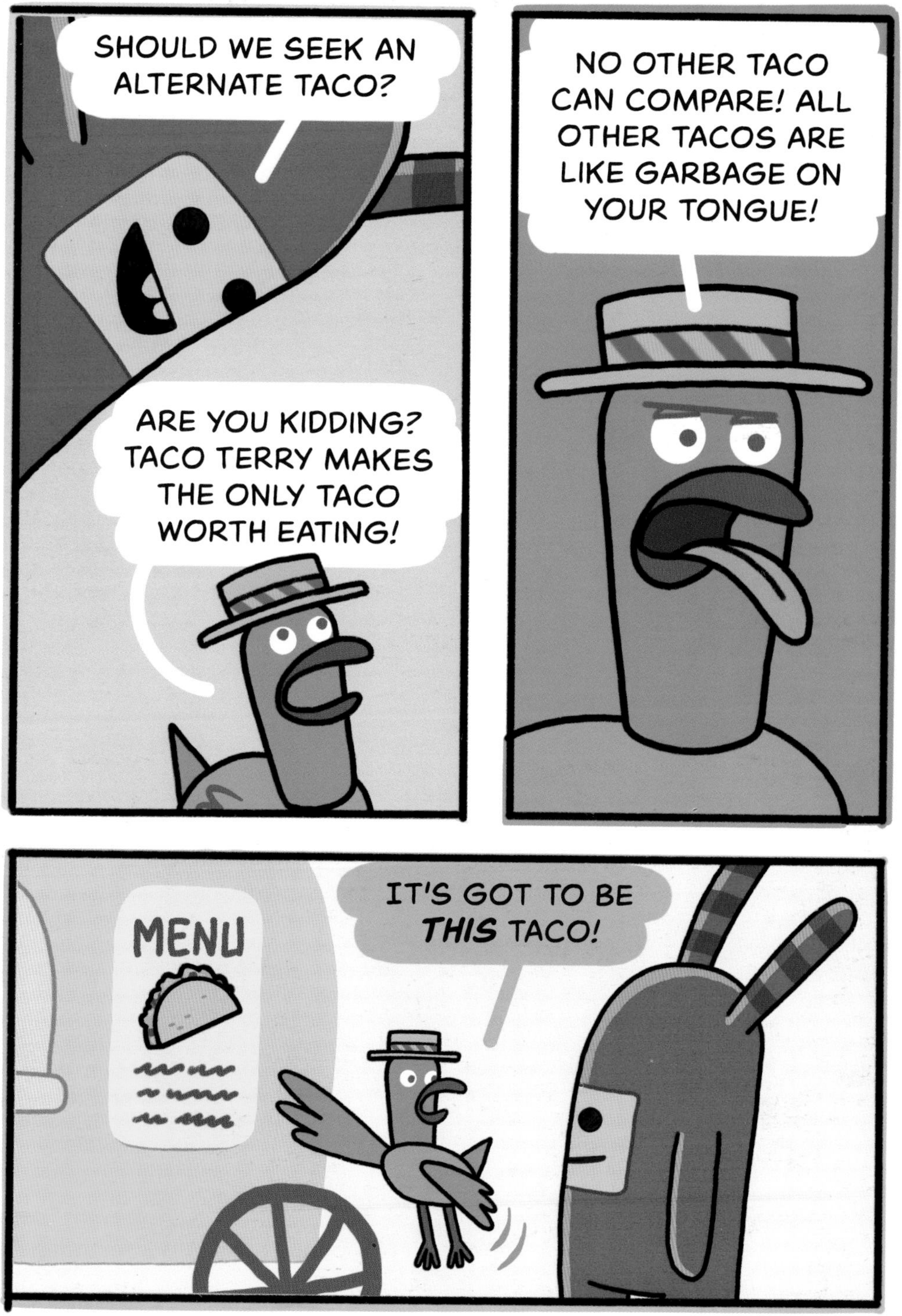
SHOULD WE SEEK AN ALTERNATE TACO?
NO OTHER TACO CAN COMPARE! ALL OTHER TACOS ARE LIKE GARBAGE ON YOUR TONGUE!
ARE YOU KIDDING? TACO TERRY MAKES THE ONLY TACO WORTH EATING!
MENU
IT'S GOT TO BE *THIS* TACO!

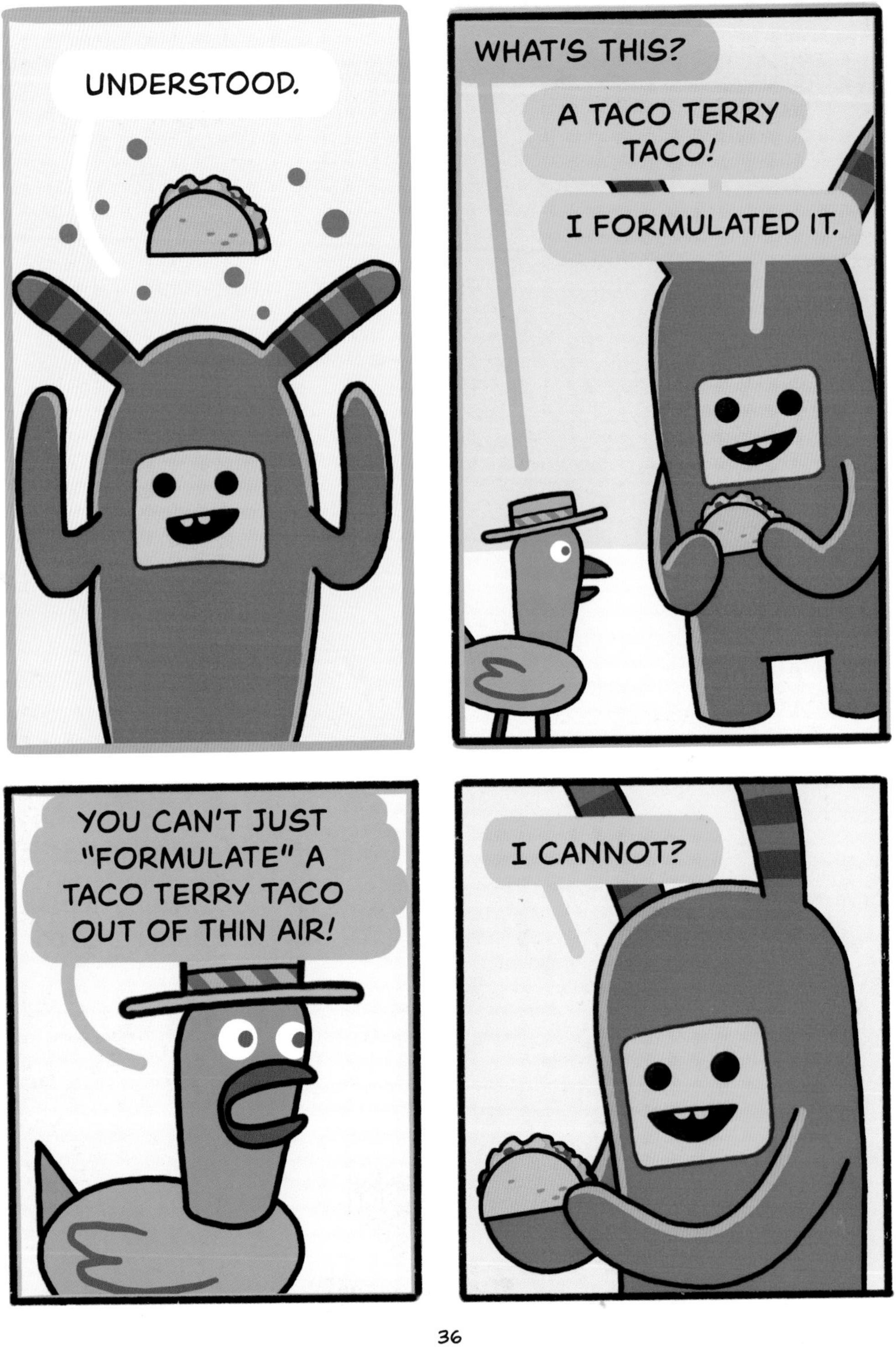
UNDERSTOOD.
WHAT'S THIS?
A TACO TERRY TACO!
I FORMULATED IT.
YOU CAN'T JUST "FORMULATE" A TACO TERRY TACO OUT OF THIN AIR!
I CANNOT?

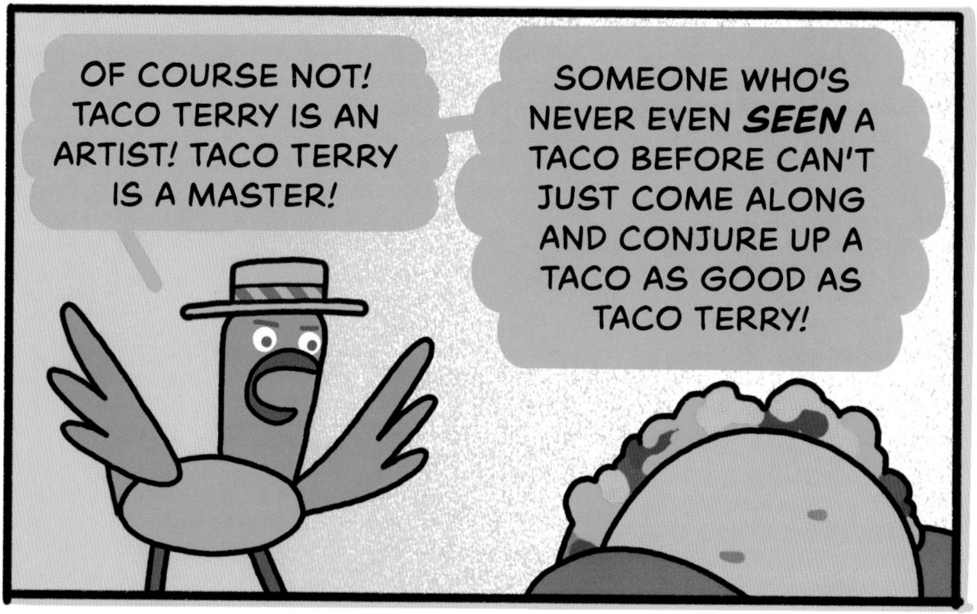
OF COURSE NOT! TACO TERRY IS AN ARTIST! TACO TERRY IS A MASTER!
SOMEONE WHO'S NEVER EVEN ***SEEN*** A TACO BEFORE CAN'T JUST COME ALONG AND CONJURE UP A TACO AS GOOD AS TACO TERRY!

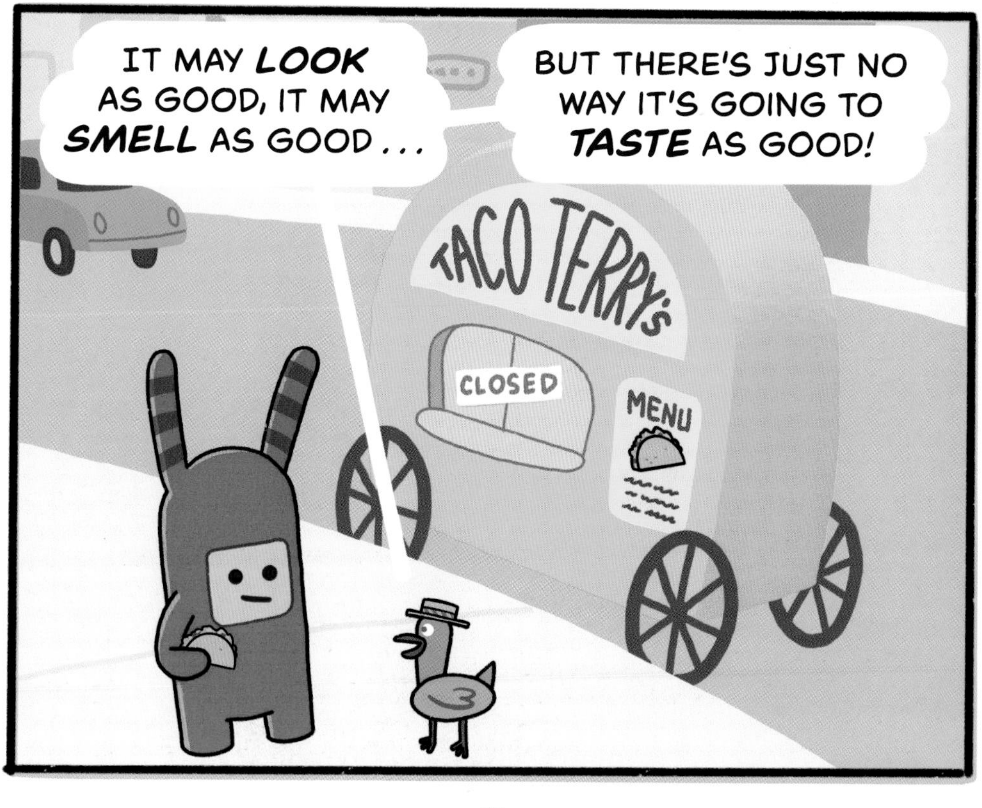
IT MAY ***LOOK*** AS GOOD, IT MAY ***SMELL*** AS GOOD . . .
BUT THERE'S JUST NO WAY IT'S GOING TO ***TASTE*** AS GOOD!
TACO TERRY'S
CLOSED
MENU

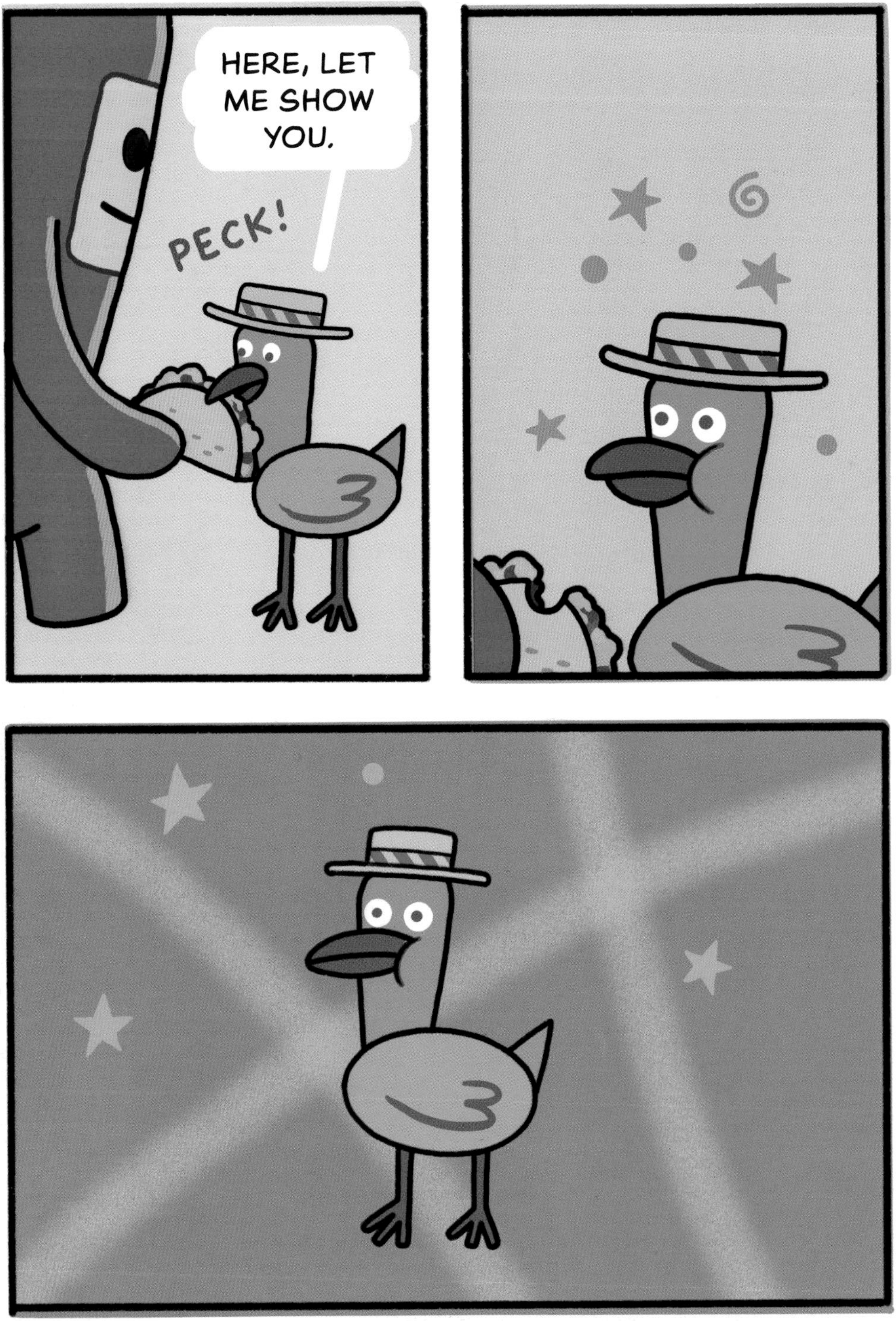
HERE, LET ME SHOW YOU.
PECK!

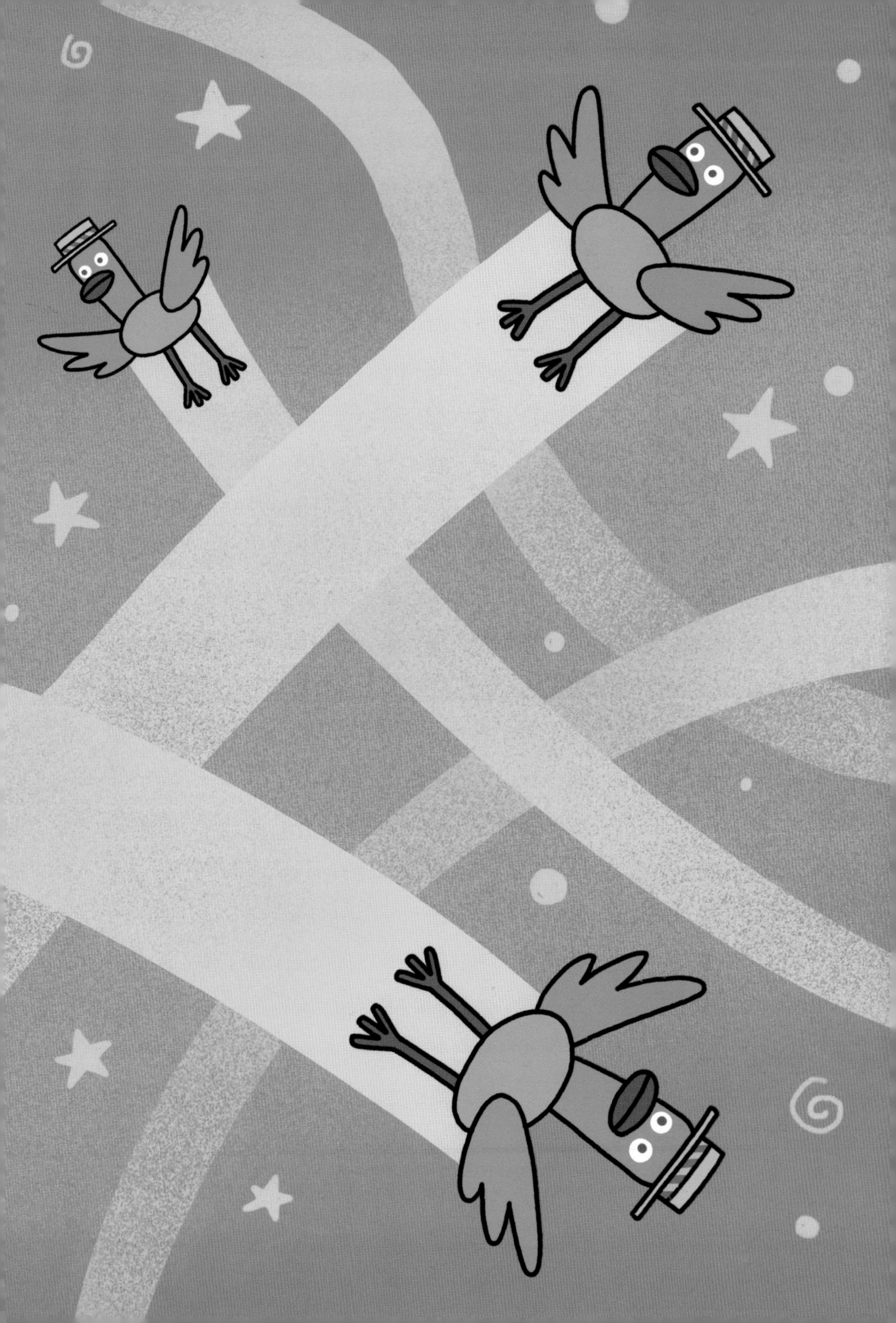

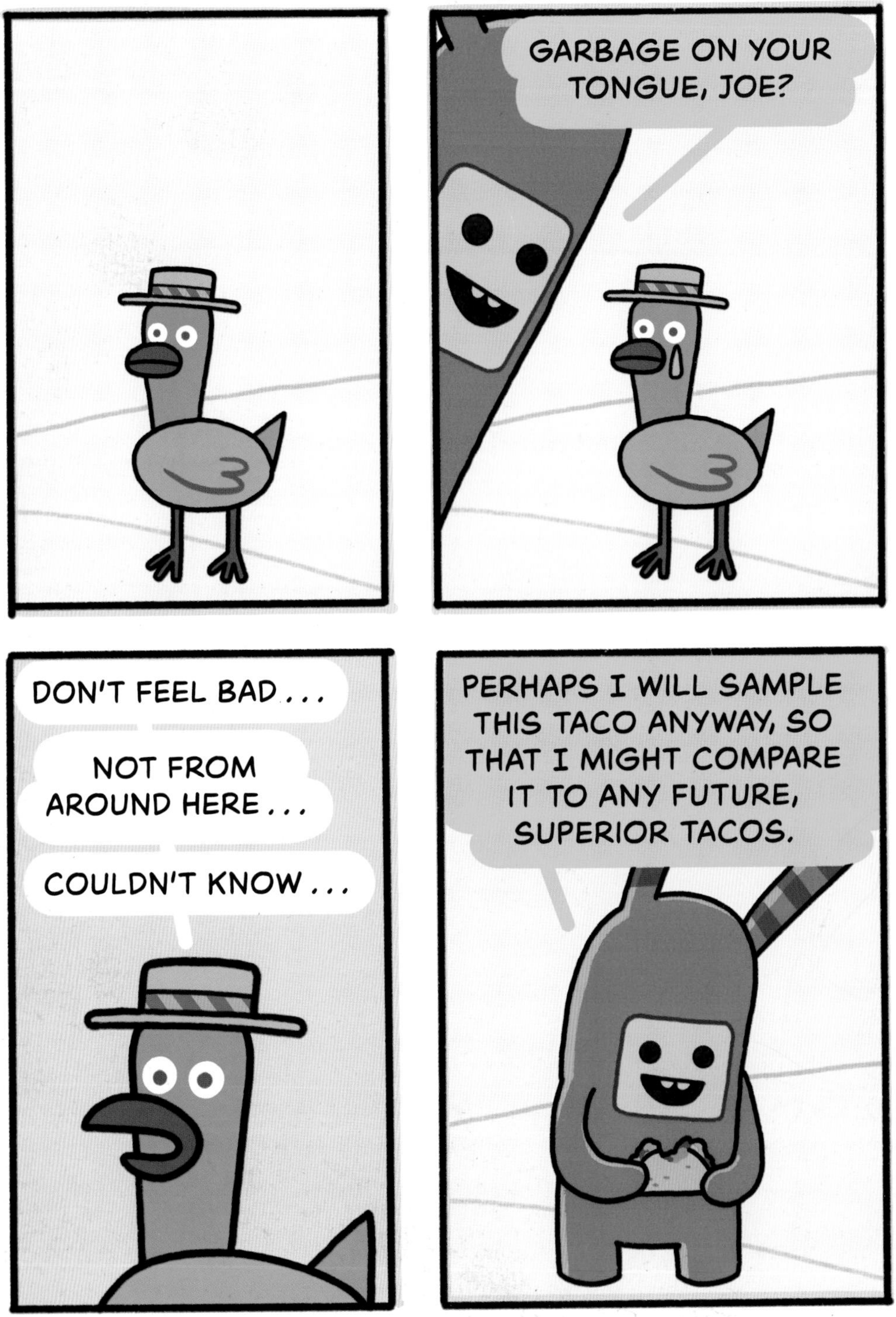
GARBAGE ON YOUR TONGUE, JOE?
DON'T FEEL BAD...
NOT FROM AROUND HERE...
COULDN'T KNOW...
PERHAPS I WILL SAMPLE THIS TACO ANYWAY, SO THAT I MIGHT COMPARE IT TO ANY FUTURE, SUPERIOR TACOS.

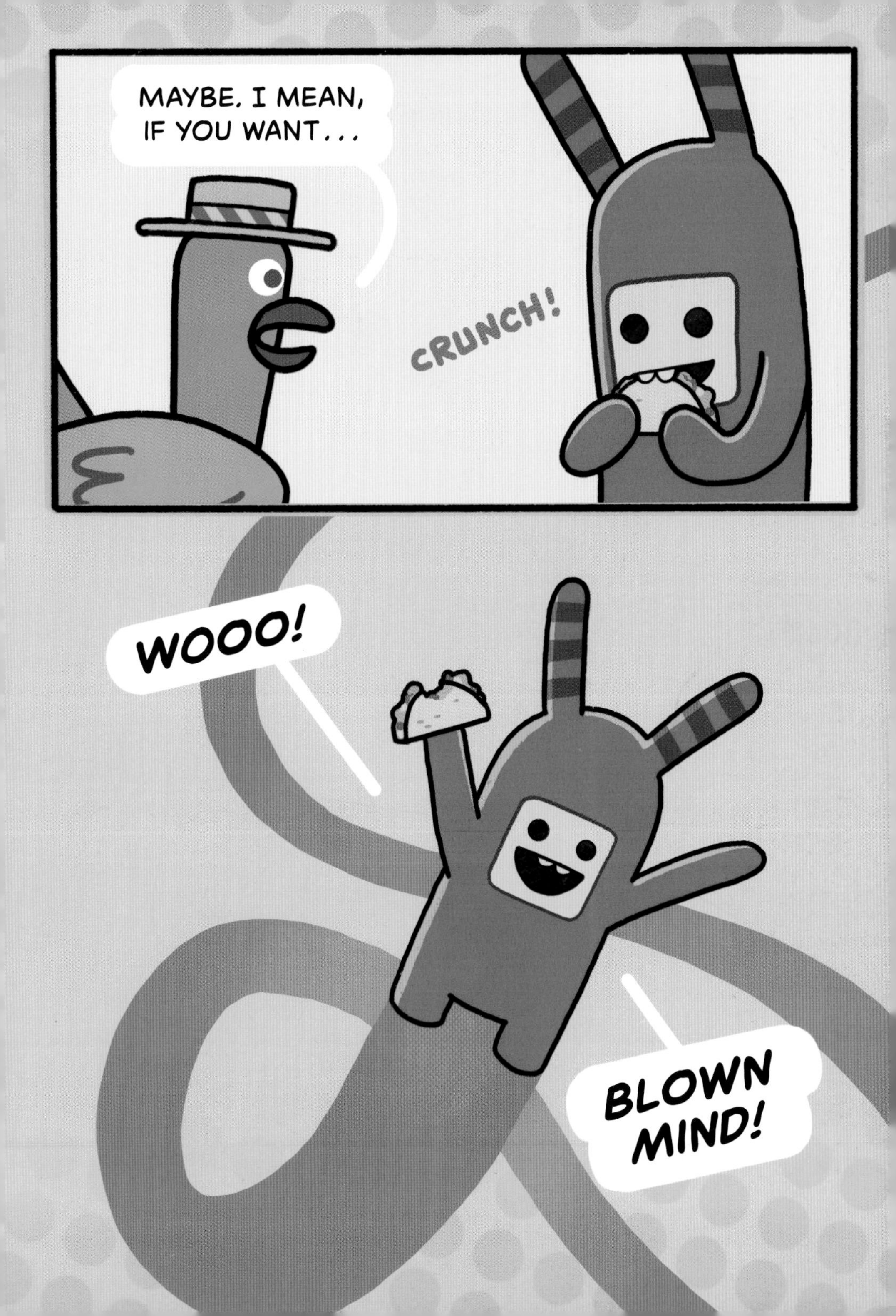
MAYBE. I MEAN, IF YOU WANT...
CRUNCH!
WOOO!
BLOWN MIND!

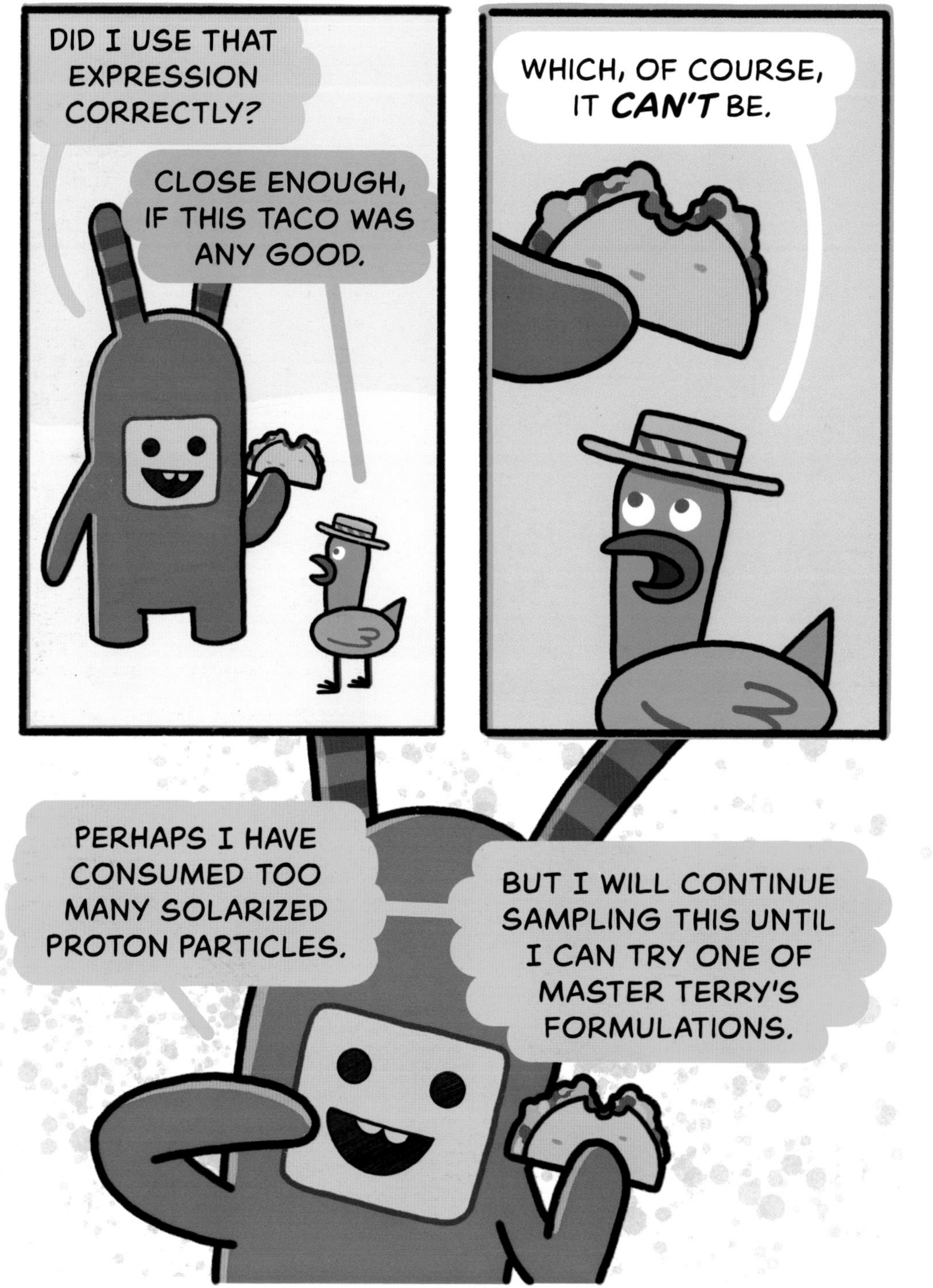
DID I USE THAT EXPRESSION CORRECTLY?
CLOSE ENOUGH, IF THIS TACO WAS ANY GOOD.
WHICH, OF COURSE, IT **CAN'T** BE.
PERHAPS I HAVE CONSUMED TOO MANY SOLARIZED PROTON PARTICLES.
BUT I WILL CONTINUE SAMPLING THIS UNTIL I CAN TRY ONE OF MASTER TERRY'S FORMULATIONS.

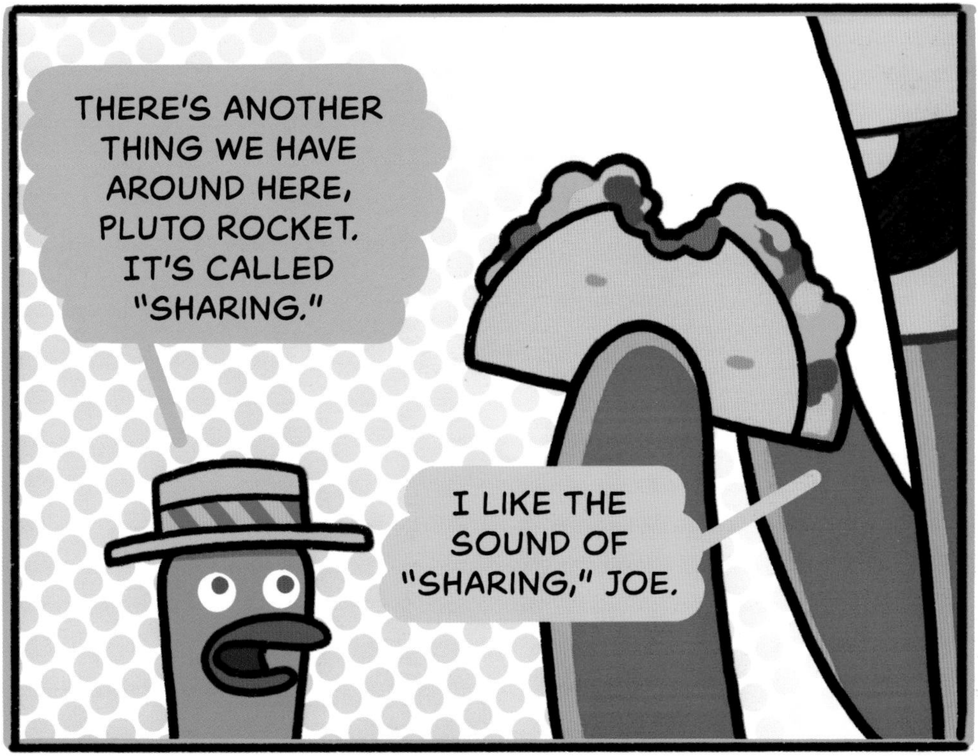
THERE'S ANOTHER THING WE HAVE AROUND HERE, PLUTO ROCKET. IT'S CALLED "SHARING."
I LIKE THE SOUND OF "SHARING," JOE.

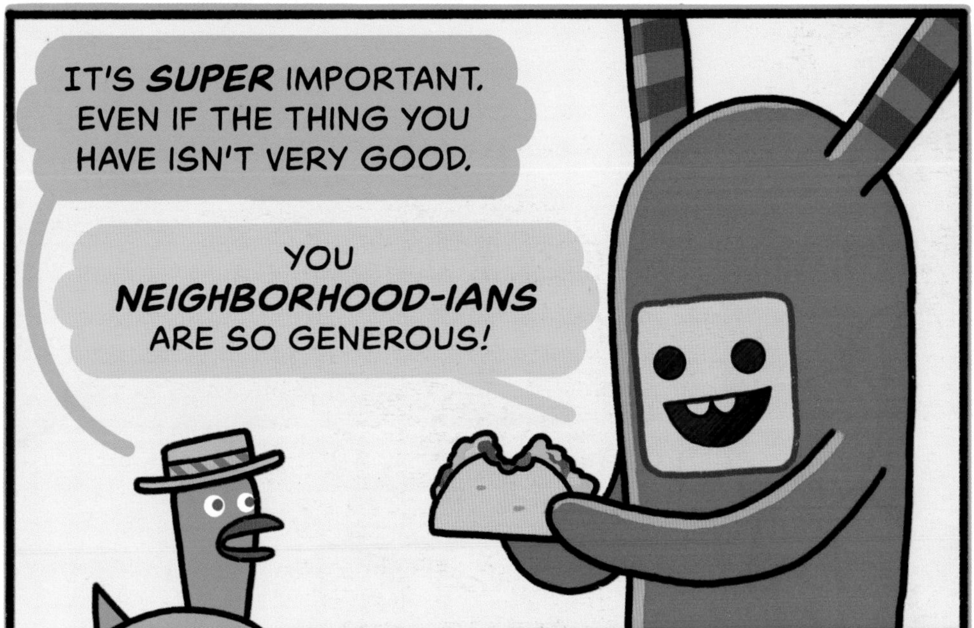
IT'S *SUPER* IMPORTANT. EVEN IF THE THING YOU HAVE ISN'T VERY GOOD.
YOU ***NEIGHBORHOOD-IANS*** ARE SO GENEROUS!

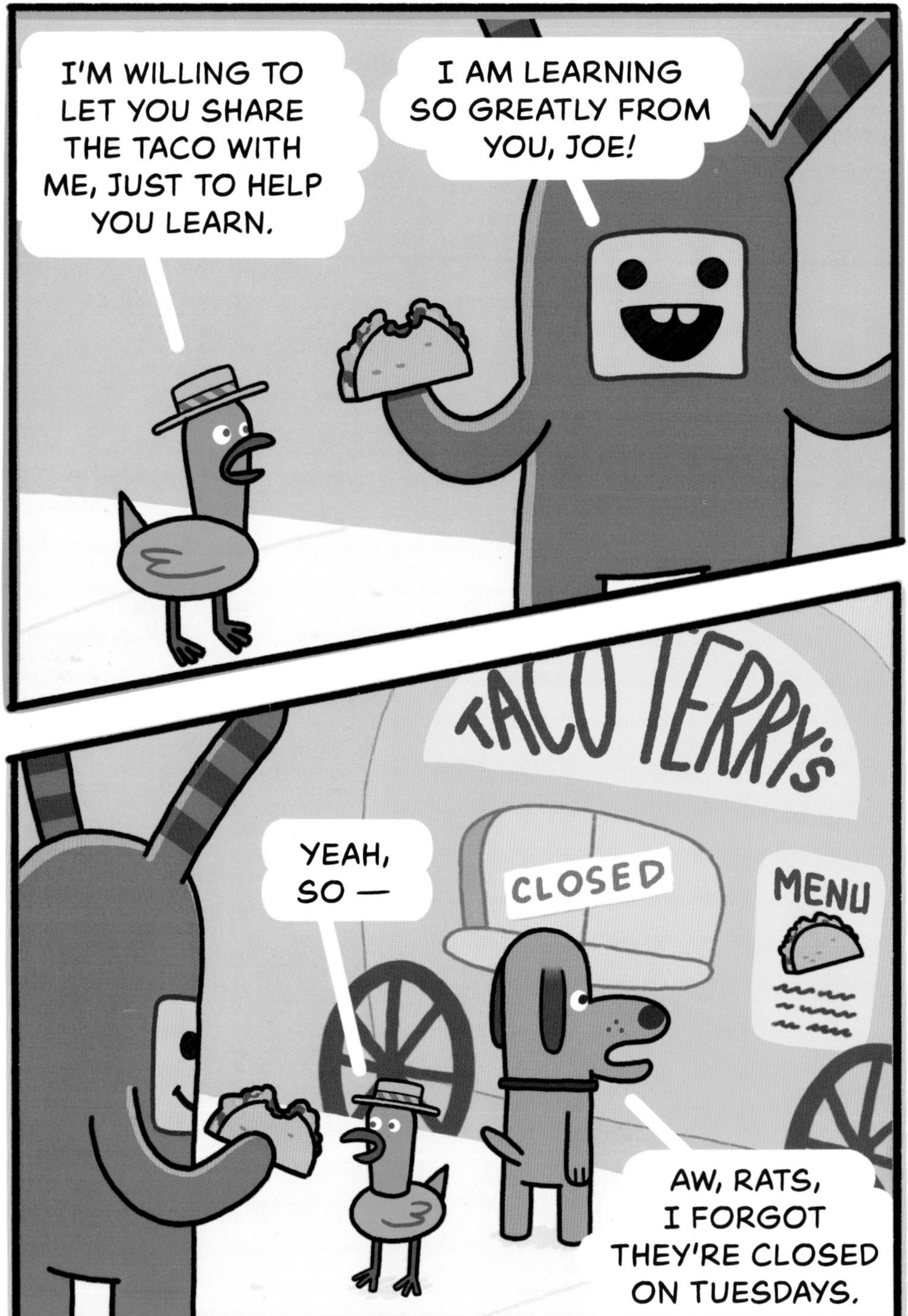

I'M WILLING TO LET YOU SHARE THE TACO WITH ME, JUST TO HELP YOU LEARN.
I AM LEARNING SO GREATLY FROM YOU, JOE!
TACO TERRY'S
CLOSED
MENU
YEAH, SO —
AW, RATS, I FORGOT THEY'RE CLOSED ON TUESDAYS.

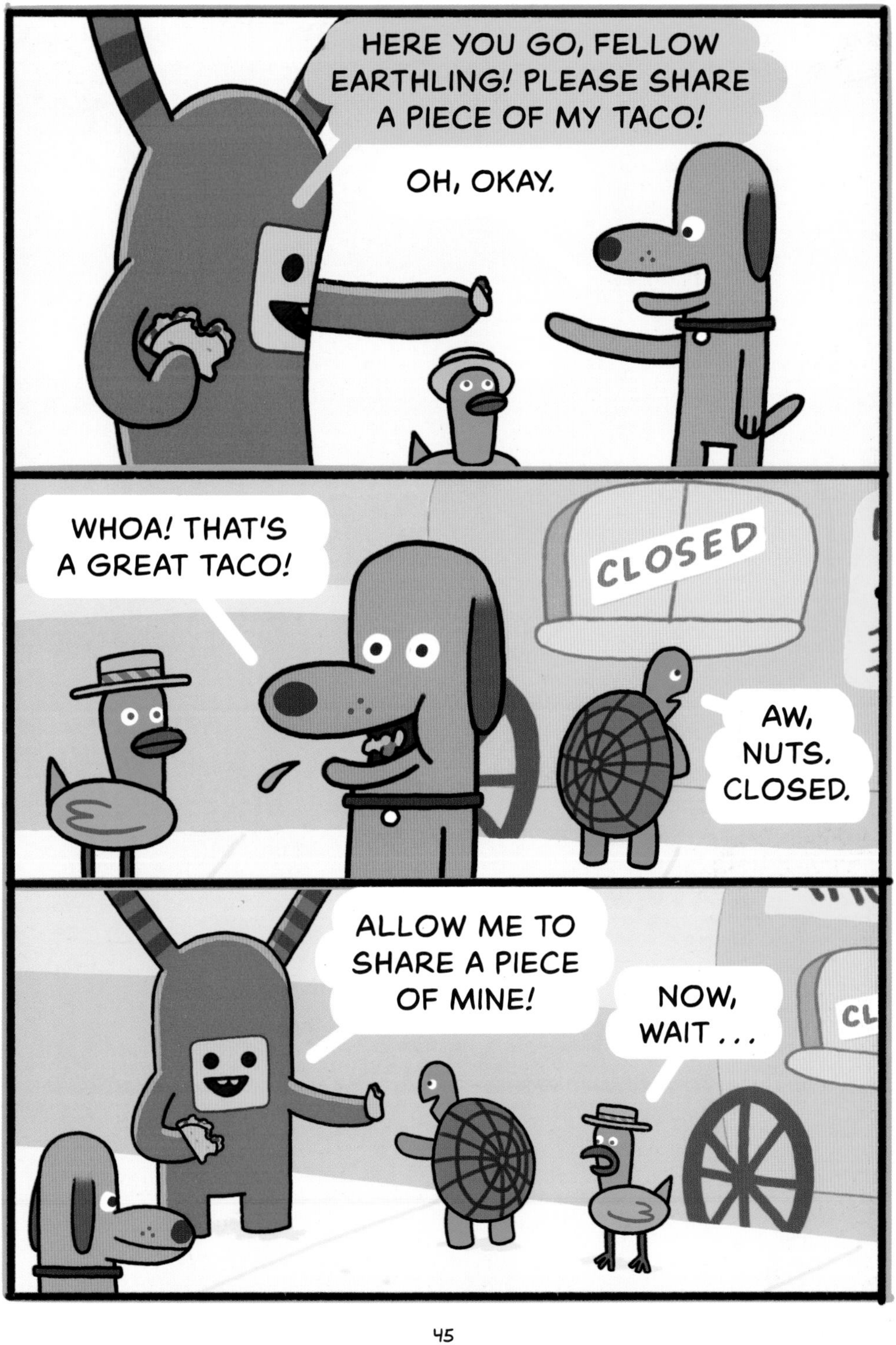
HERE YOU GO, FELLOW EARTHLING! PLEASE SHARE A PIECE OF MY TACO!
OH, OKAY.
WHOA! THAT'S A GREAT TACO!
CLOSED
AW, NUTS. CLOSED.
ALLOW ME TO SHARE A PIECE OF MINE!
NOW, WAIT . . .

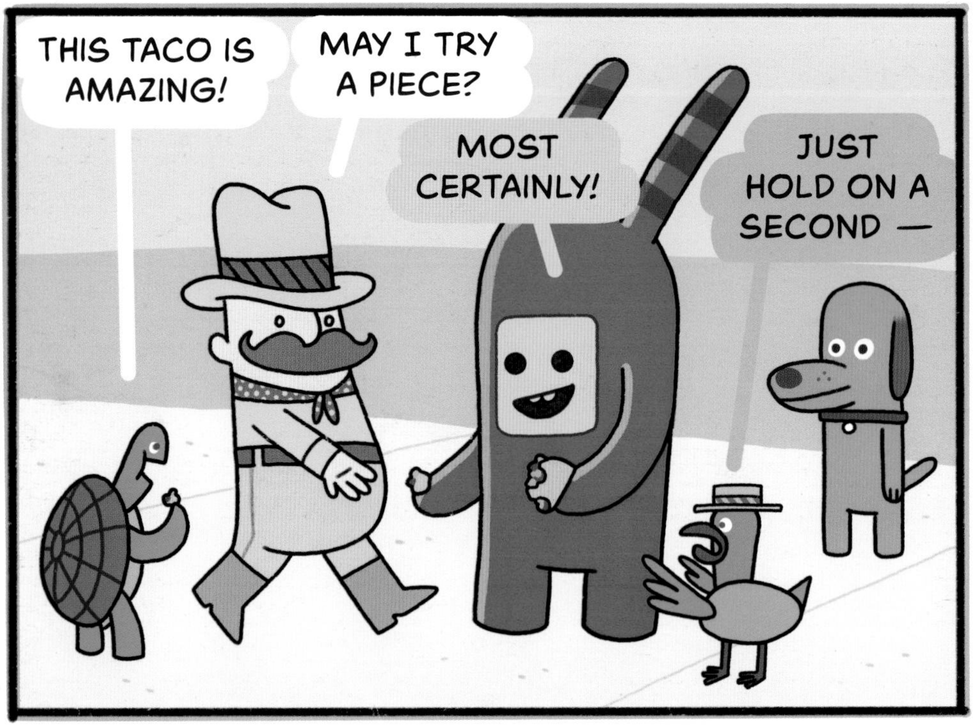
THIS TACO IS AMAZING!
MAY I TRY A PIECE?
MOST CERTAINLY!
JUST HOLD ON A SECOND —

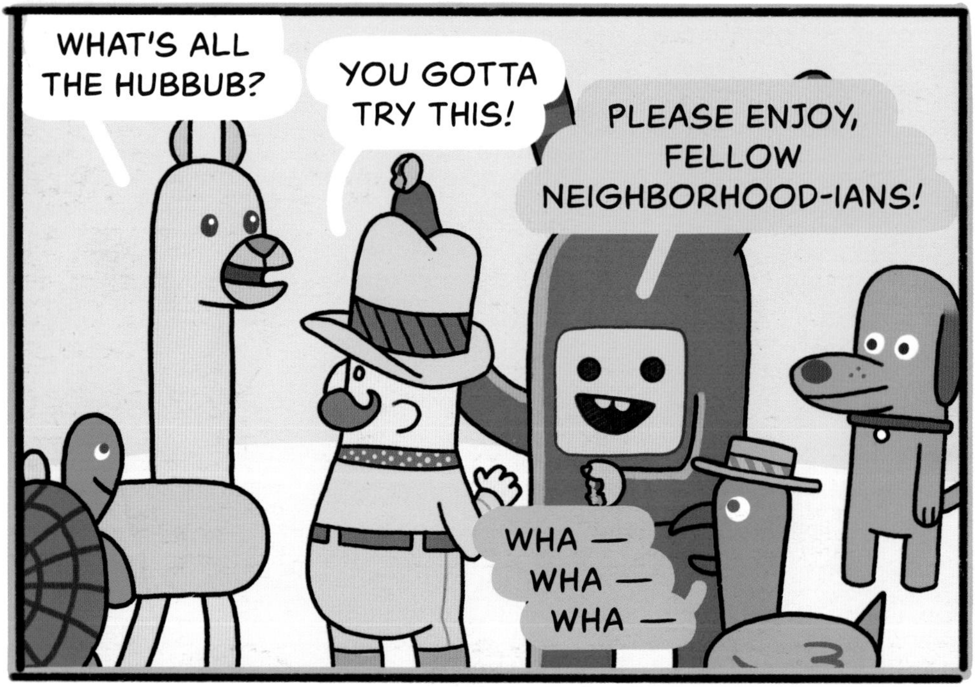
WHAT'S ALL THE HUBBUB?
YOU GOTTA TRY THIS!
PLEASE ENJOY, FELLOW NEIGHBORHOOD-IANS!
WHA —
WHA —
WHA —

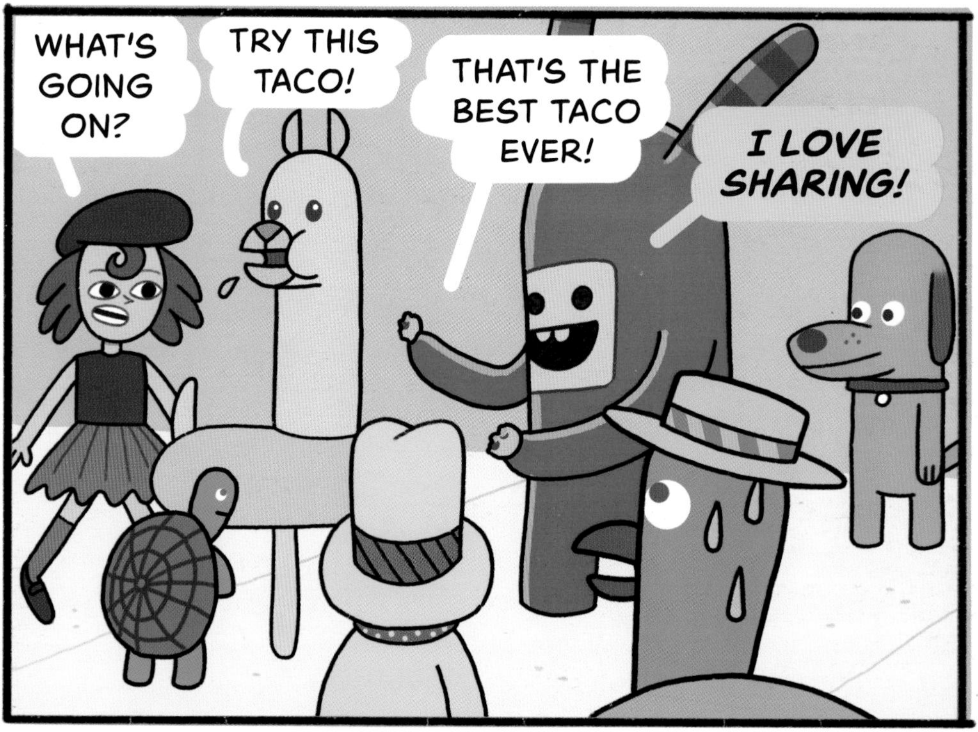
WHAT'S GOING ON?
TRY THIS TACO!
THAT'S THE BEST TACO EVER!
I LOVE SHARING!

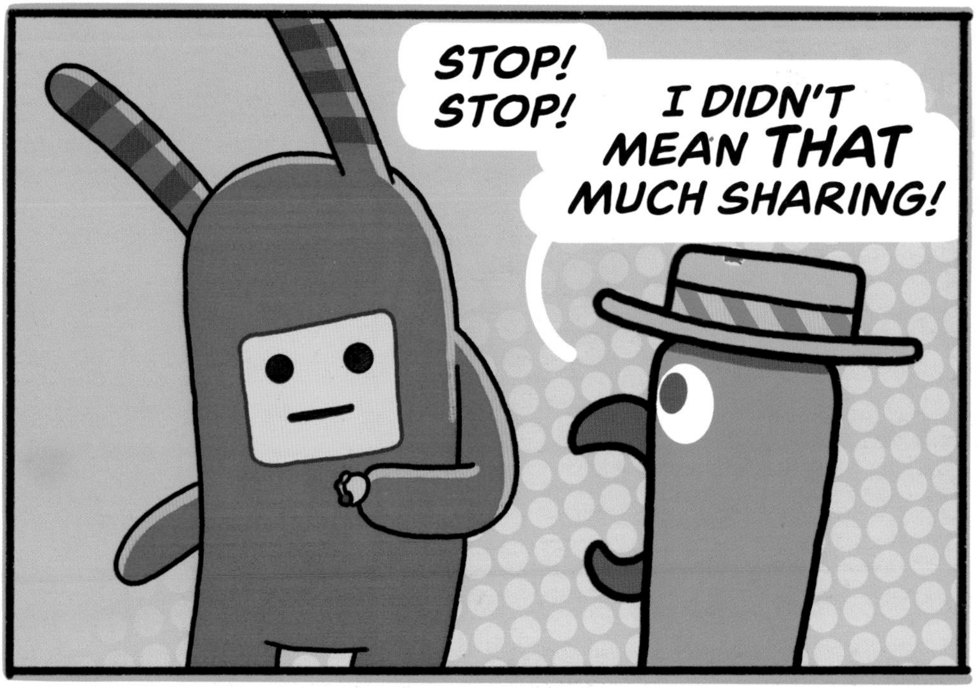
STOP! STOP!
I DIDN'T MEAN THAT MUCH SHARING!

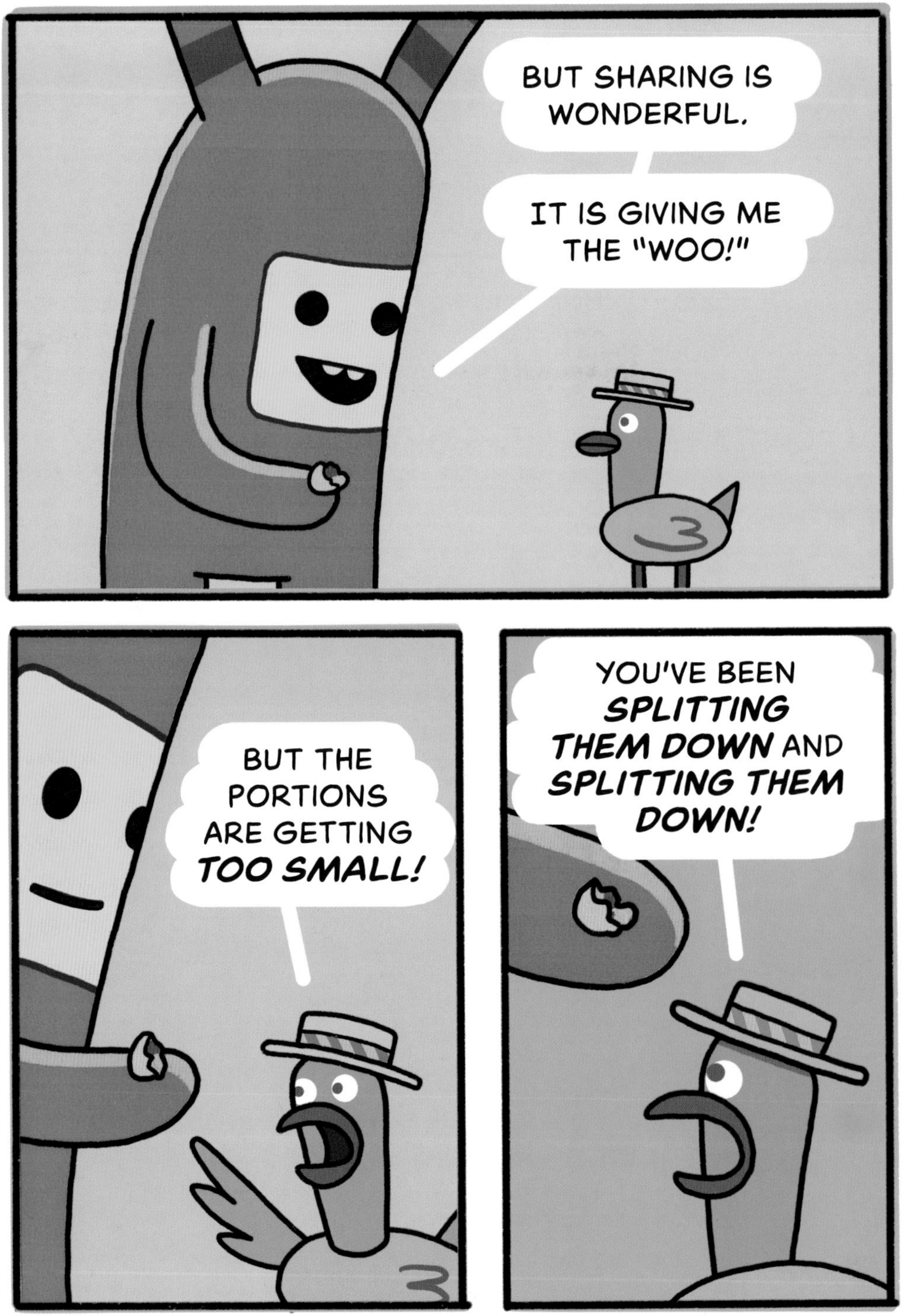
BUT SHARING IS WONDERFUL.
IT IS GIVING ME THE "WOO!"
BUT THE PORTIONS ARE GETTING *TOO SMALL!*
YOU'VE BEEN *SPLITTING THEM DOWN* AND *SPLITTING THEM DOWN!*

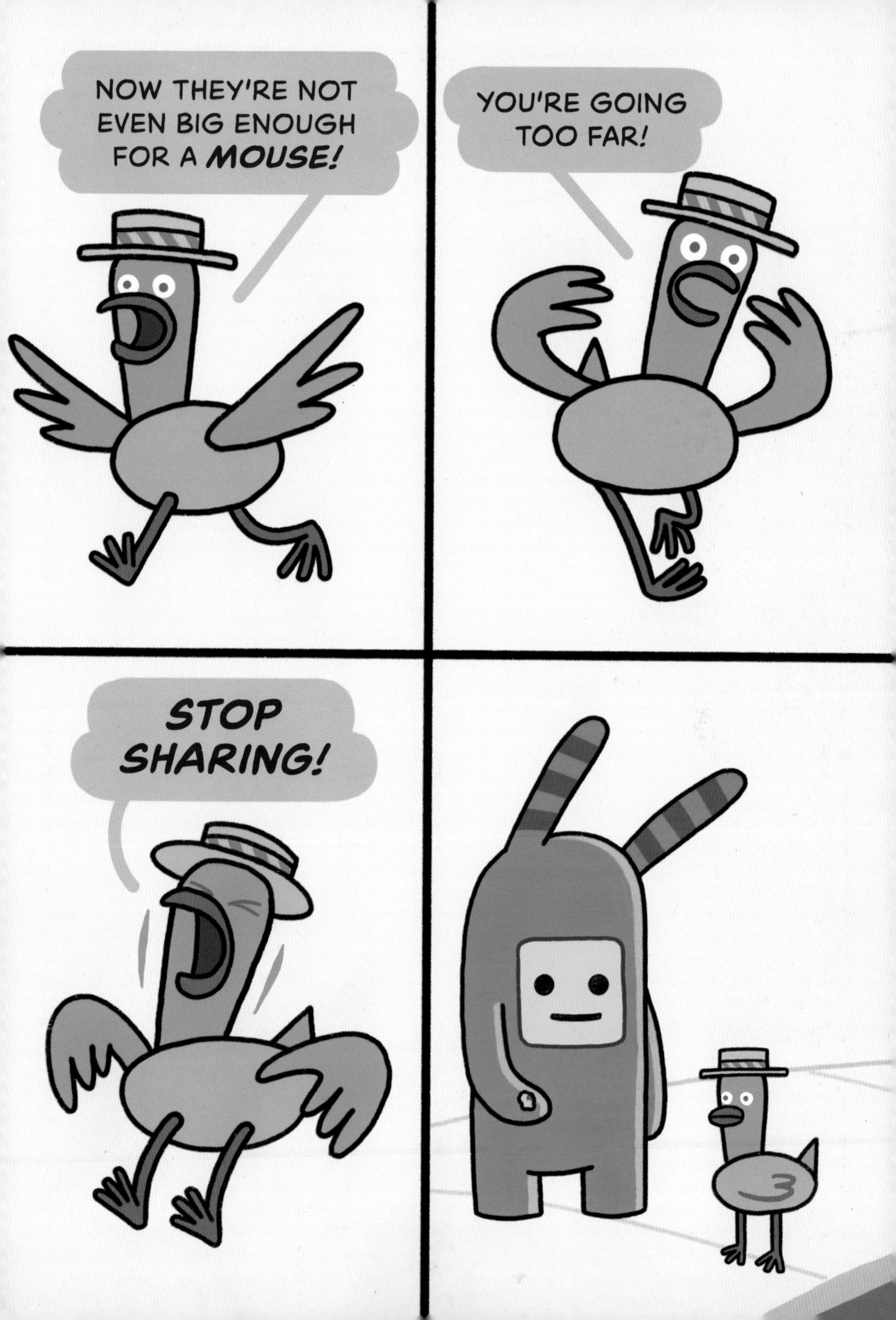
NOW THEY'RE NOT EVEN BIG ENOUGH FOR A *MOUSE!*
YOU'RE GOING TOO FAR!
STOP SHARING!

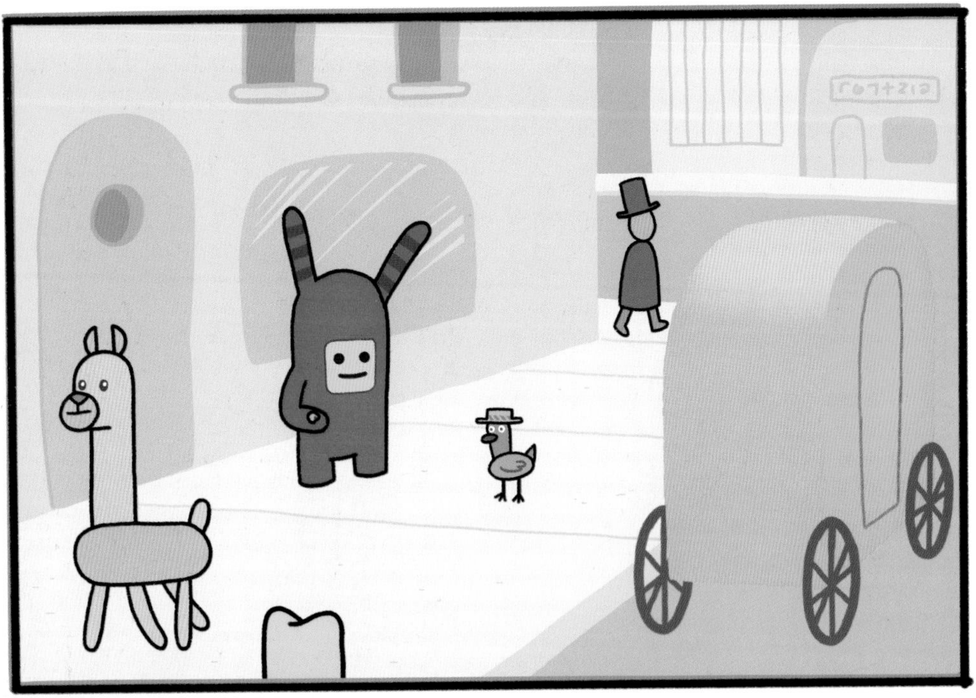

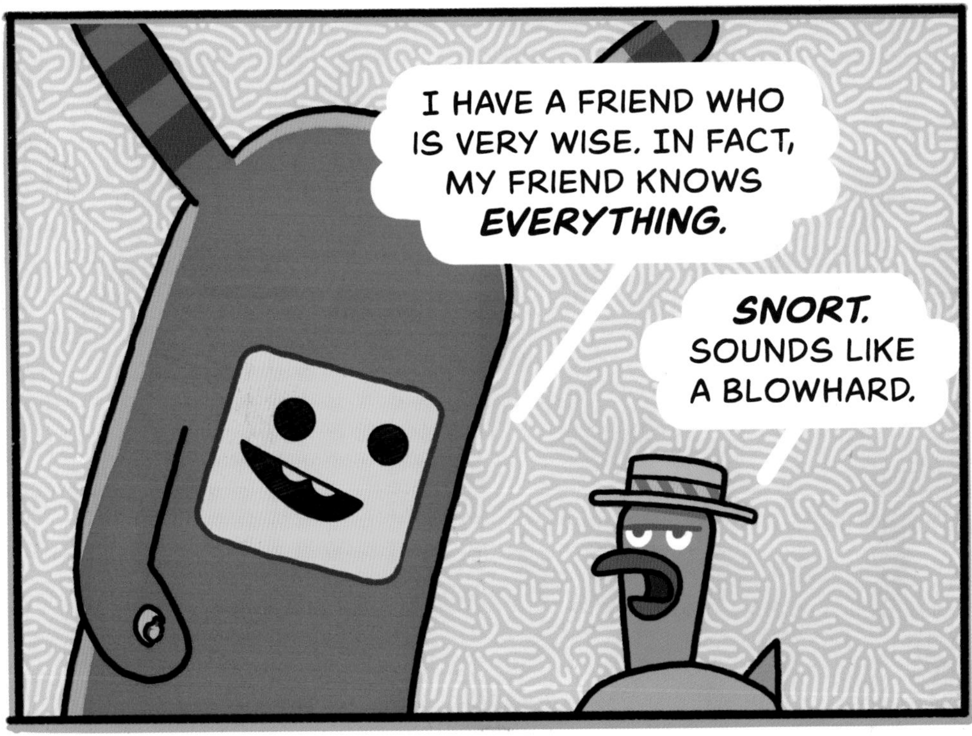
I HAVE A FRIEND WHO IS VERY WISE. IN FACT, MY FRIEND KNOWS **EVERYTHING.**
SNORT. SOUNDS LIKE A BLOWHARD.

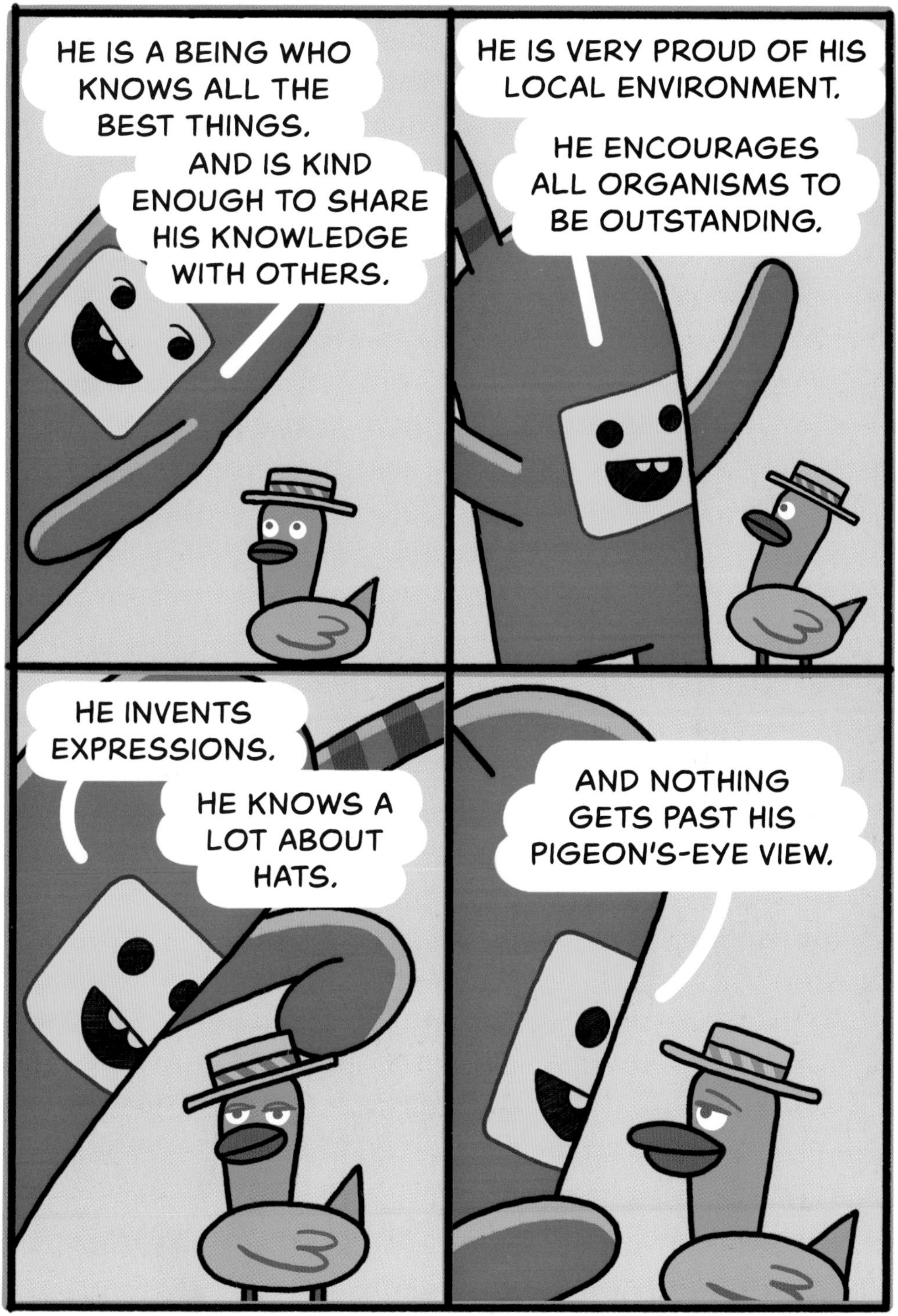
HE IS A BEING WHO KNOWS ALL THE BEST THINGS.
AND IS KIND ENOUGH TO SHARE HIS KNOWLEDGE WITH OTHERS.
HE IS VERY PROUD OF HIS LOCAL ENVIRONMENT.
HE ENCOURAGES ALL ORGANISMS TO BE OUTSTANDING.
HE INVENTS EXPRESSIONS.
HE KNOWS A LOT ABOUT HATS.
AND NOTHING GETS PAST HIS PIGEON'S-EYE VIEW.

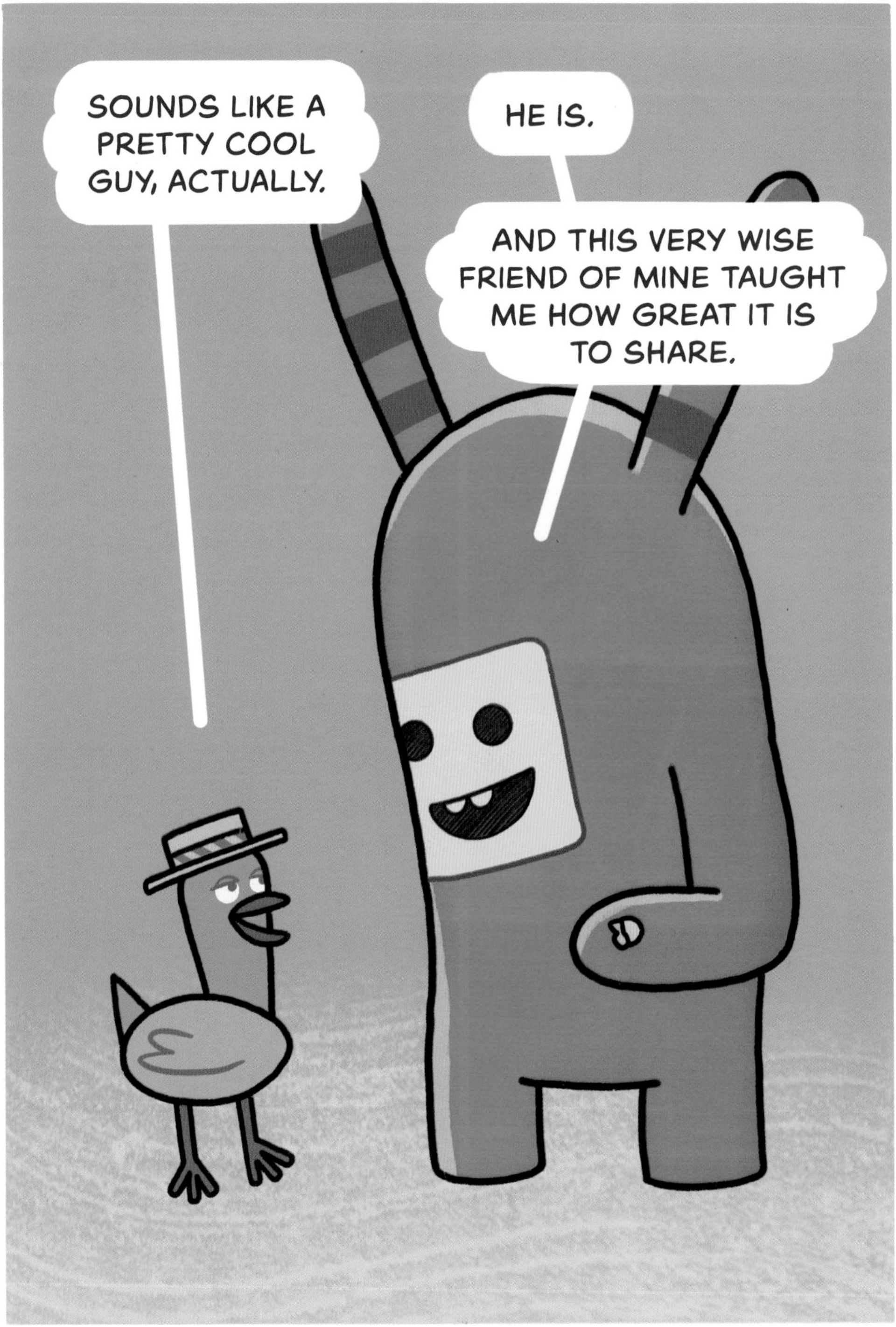
SOUNDS LIKE A PRETTY COOL GUY, ACTUALLY.
HE IS.
AND THIS VERY WISE FRIEND OF MINE TAUGHT ME HOW GREAT IT IS TO SHARE.

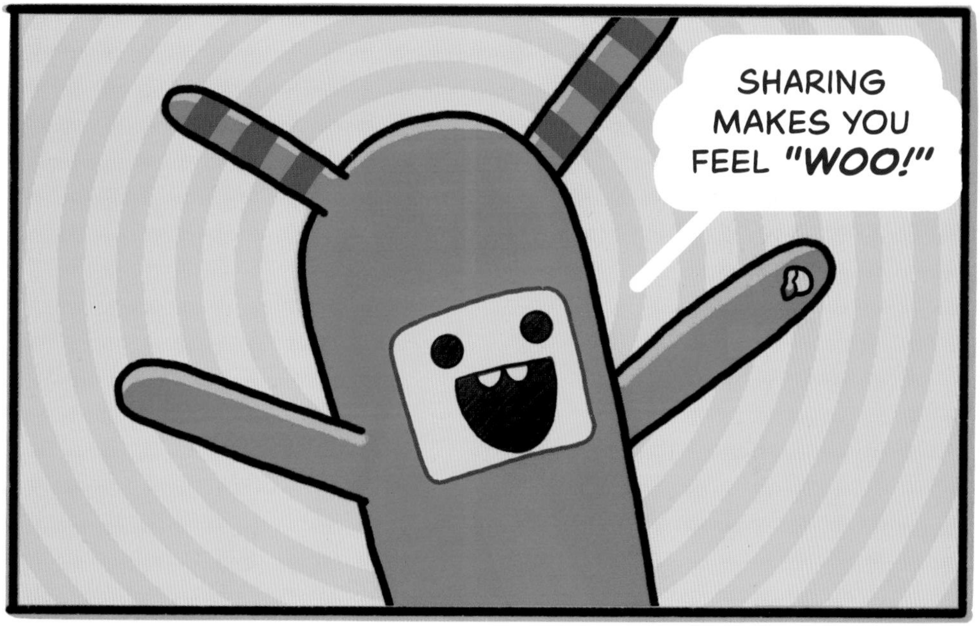
SHARING MAKES YOU FEEL "WOO!"

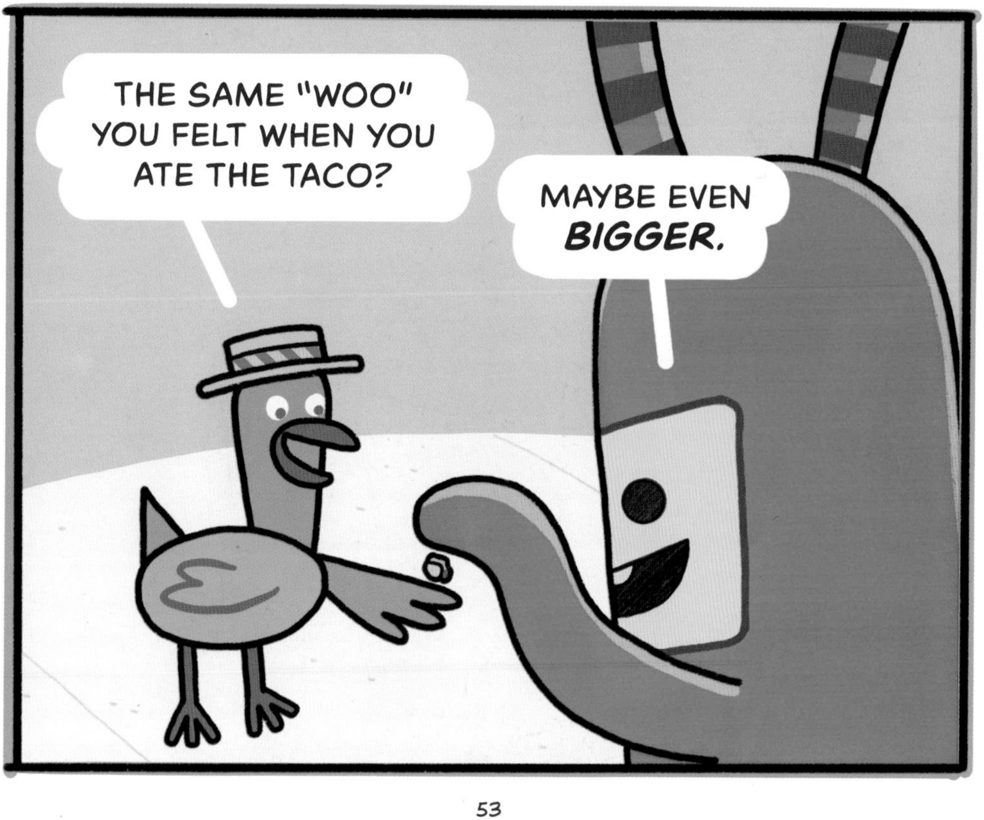
THE SAME "WOO" YOU FELT WHEN YOU ATE THE TACO?
MAYBE EVEN BIGGER.

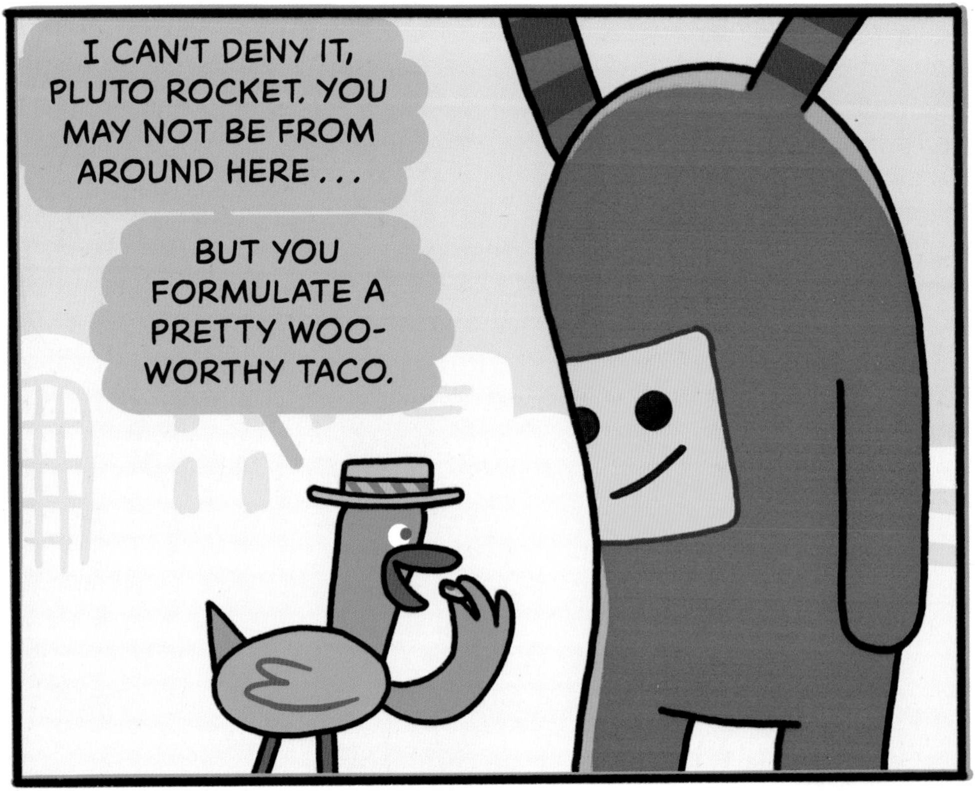
I CAN'T DENY IT, PLUTO ROCKET. YOU MAY NOT BE FROM AROUND HERE . . .
BUT YOU FORMULATE A PRETTY WOO-WORTHY TACO.

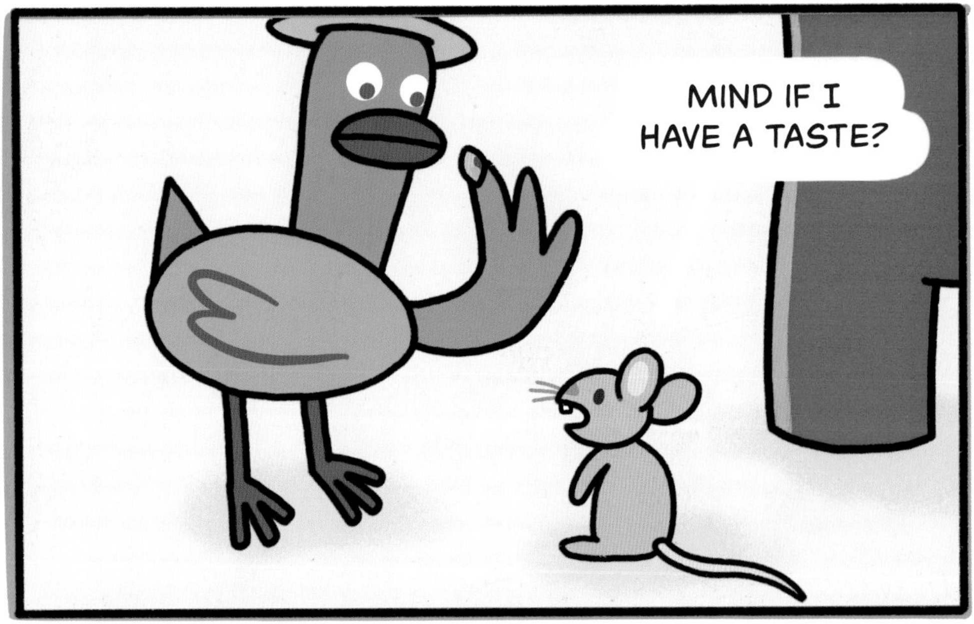
MIND IF I HAVE A TASTE?

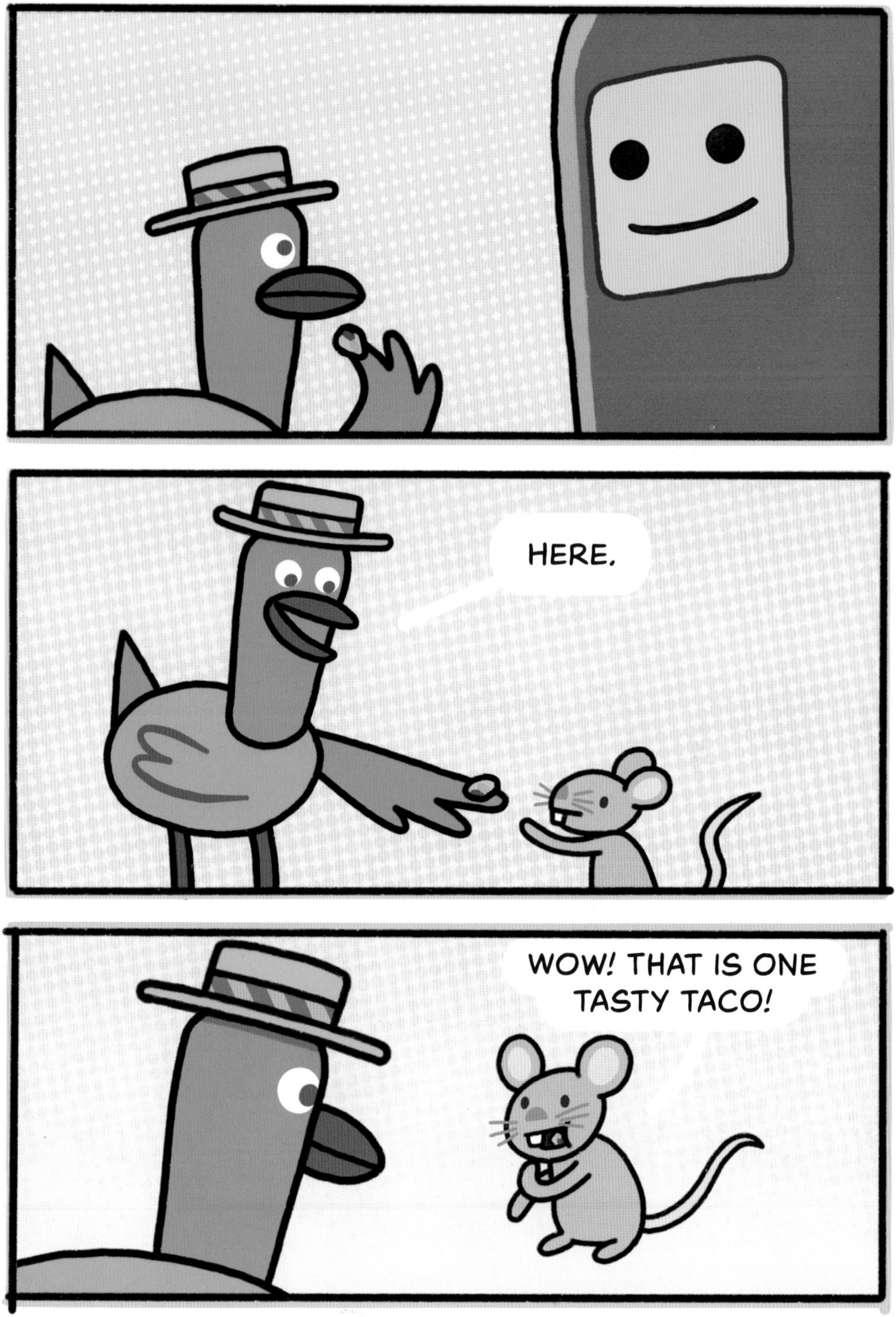
HERE.
WOW! THAT IS ONE TASTY TACO!

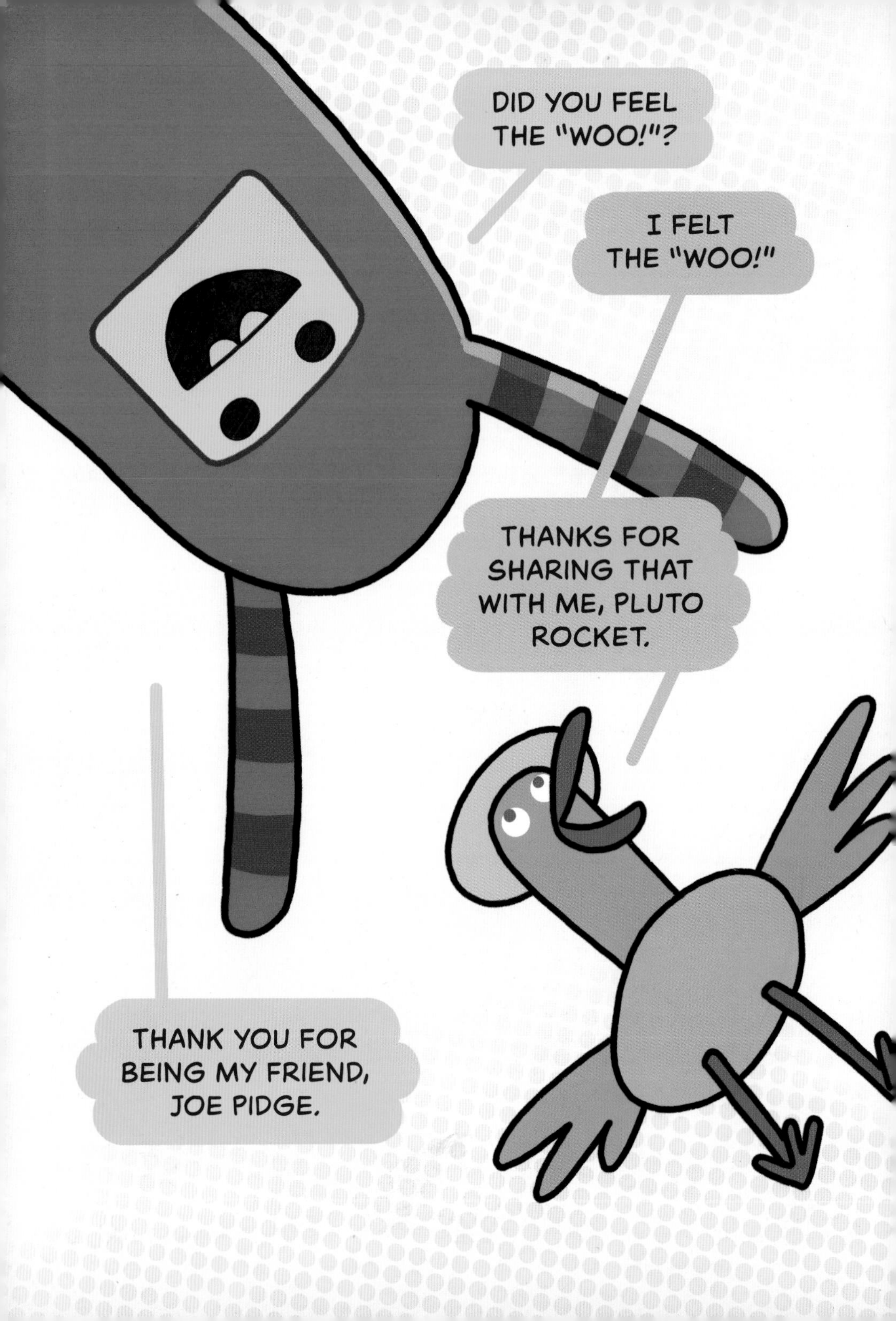
DID YOU FEEL THE "WOO!"?
I FELT THE "WOO!"
THANKS FOR SHARING THAT WITH ME, PLUTO ROCKET.
THANK YOU FOR BEING MY FRIEND, JOE PIDGE.

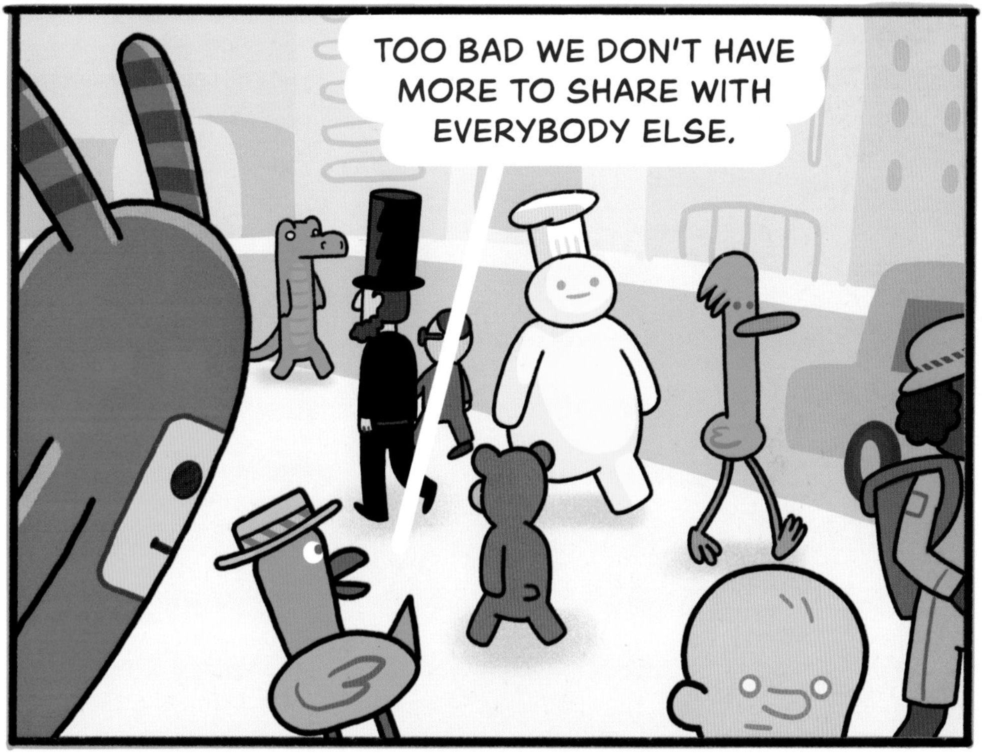
TOO BAD WE DON'T HAVE MORE TO SHARE WITH EVERYBODY ELSE.

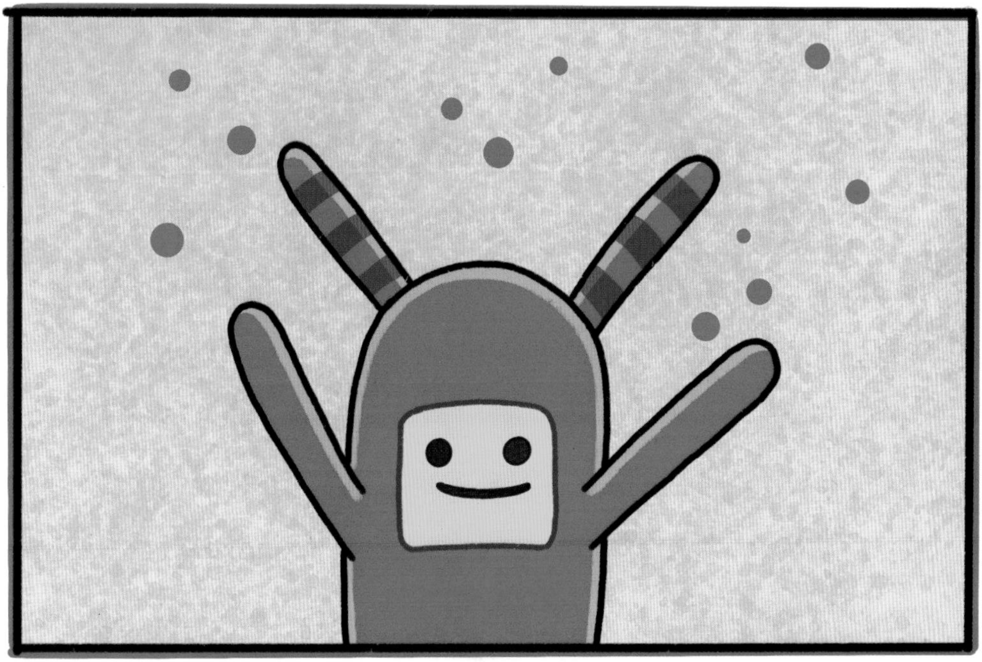

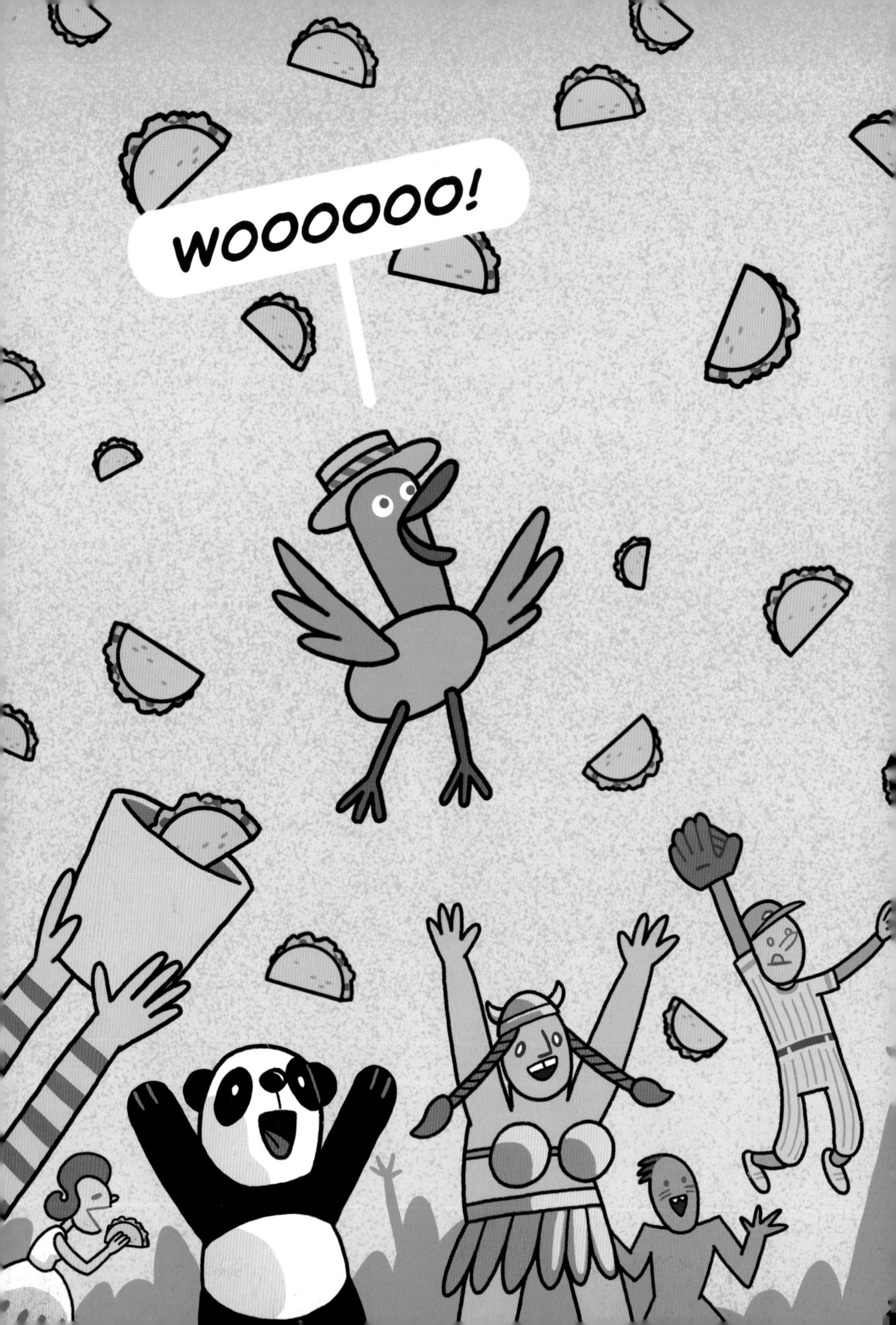
WOOOOOO!

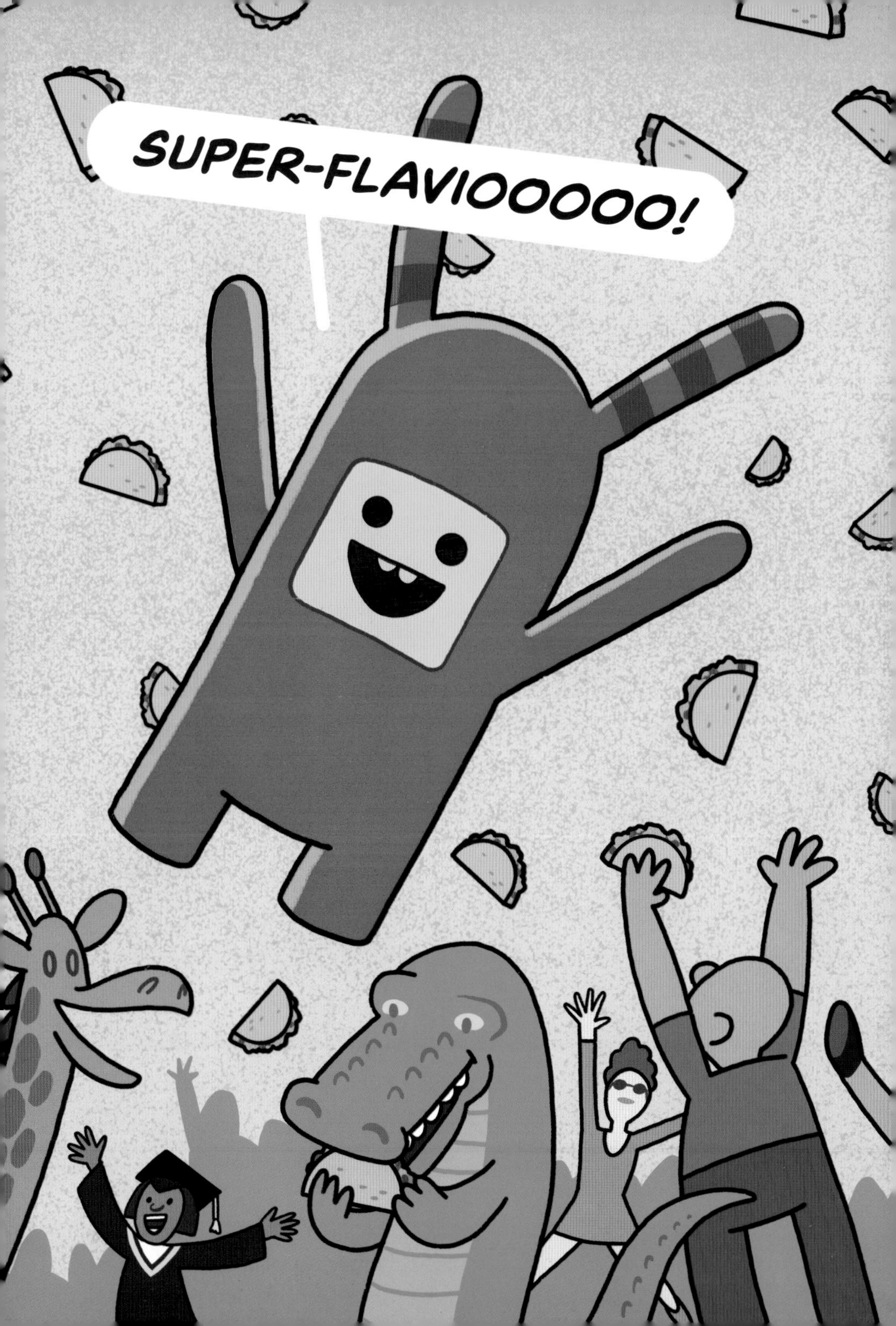
SUPER-FLAVIOOOOOO!

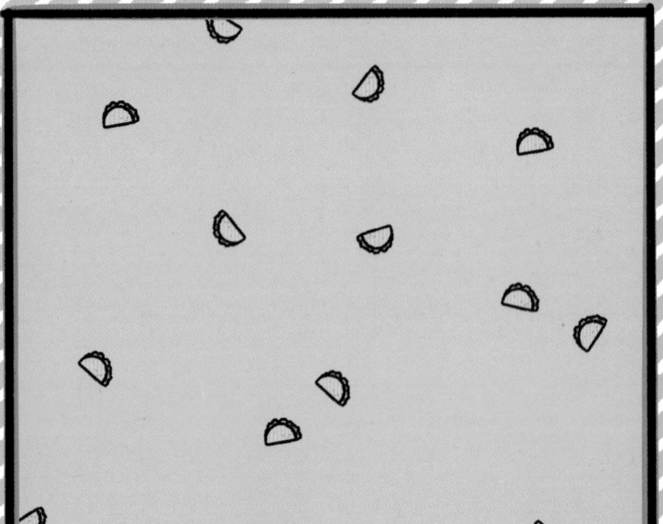
WHAT THE —?
TACO TERRY

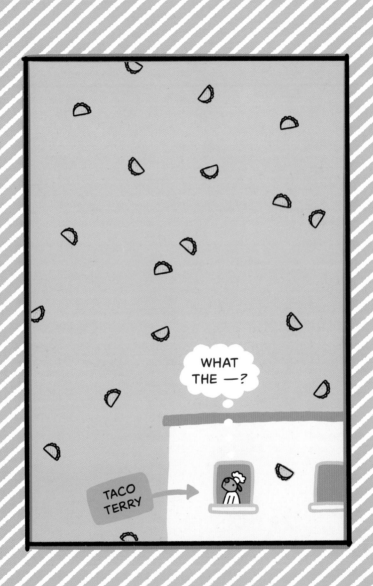

CHAPTER THREE:
SECRET MISSION!

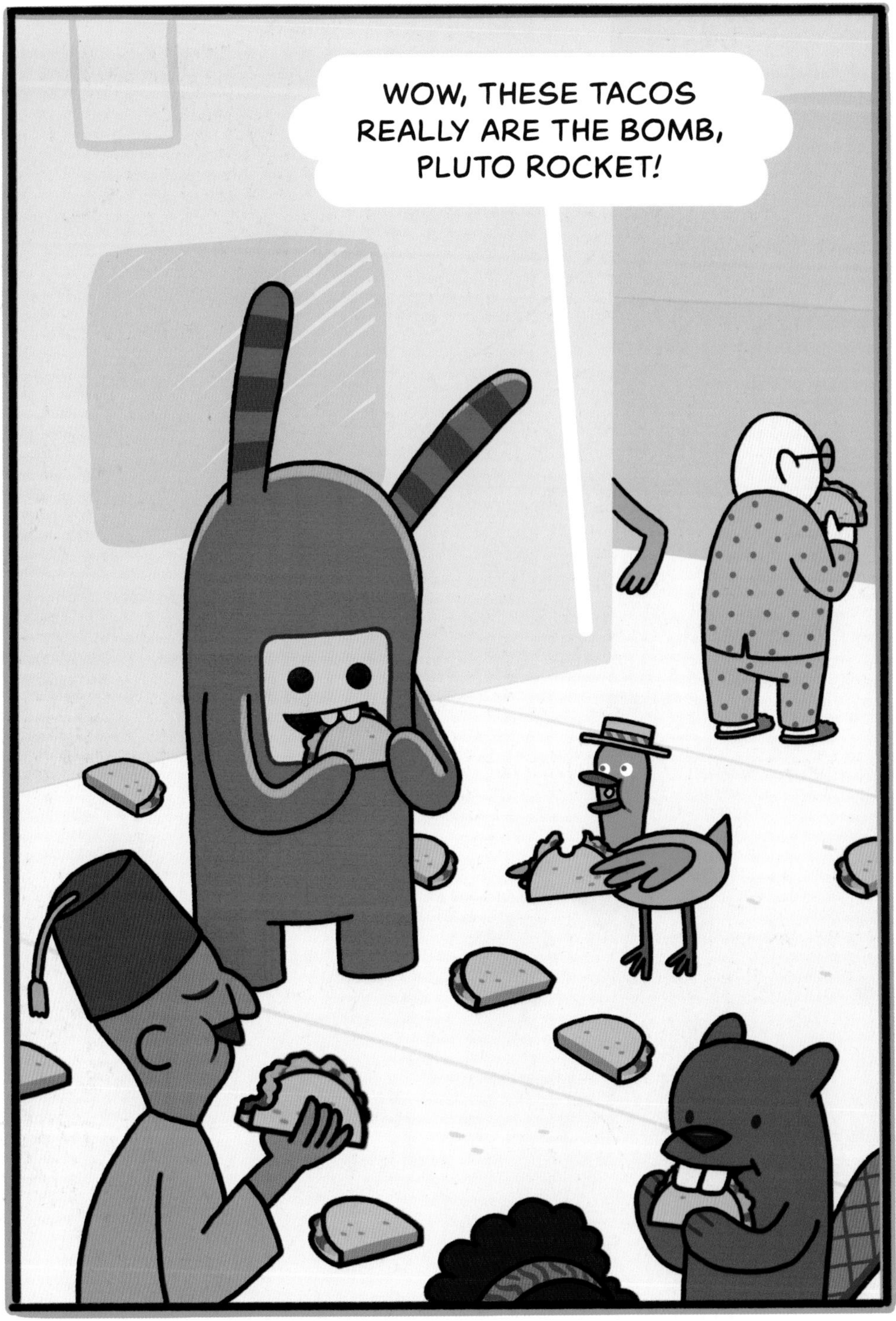
WOW, THESE TACOS REALLY ARE THE BOMB, PLUTO ROCKET!

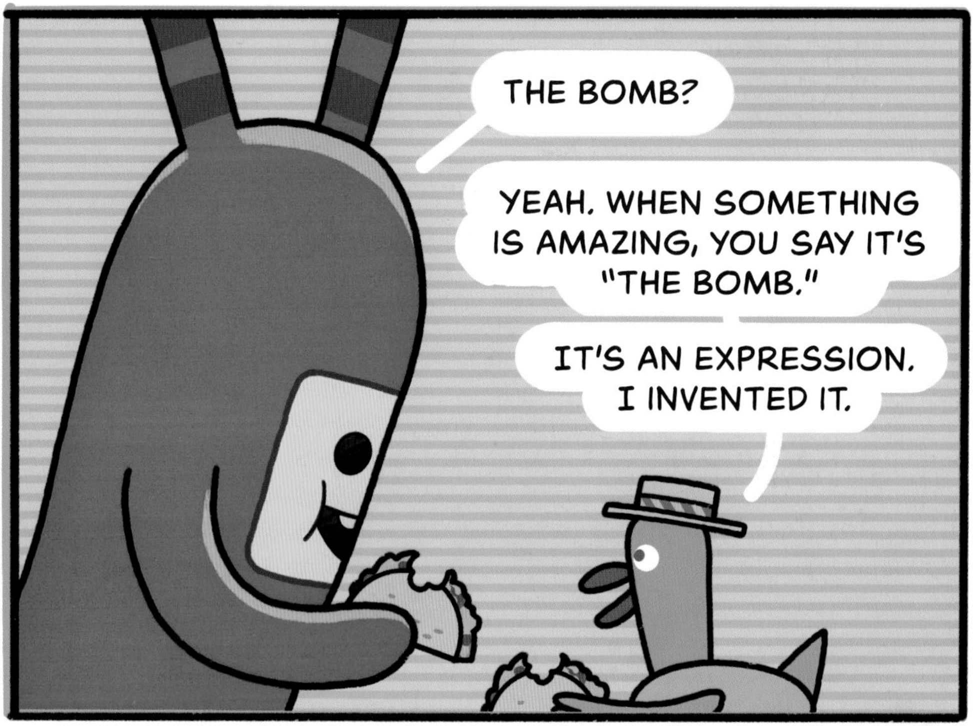
THE BOMB?
YEAH. WHEN SOMETHING IS AMAZING, YOU SAY IT'S "THE BOMB."
IT'S AN EXPRESSION. I INVENTED IT.

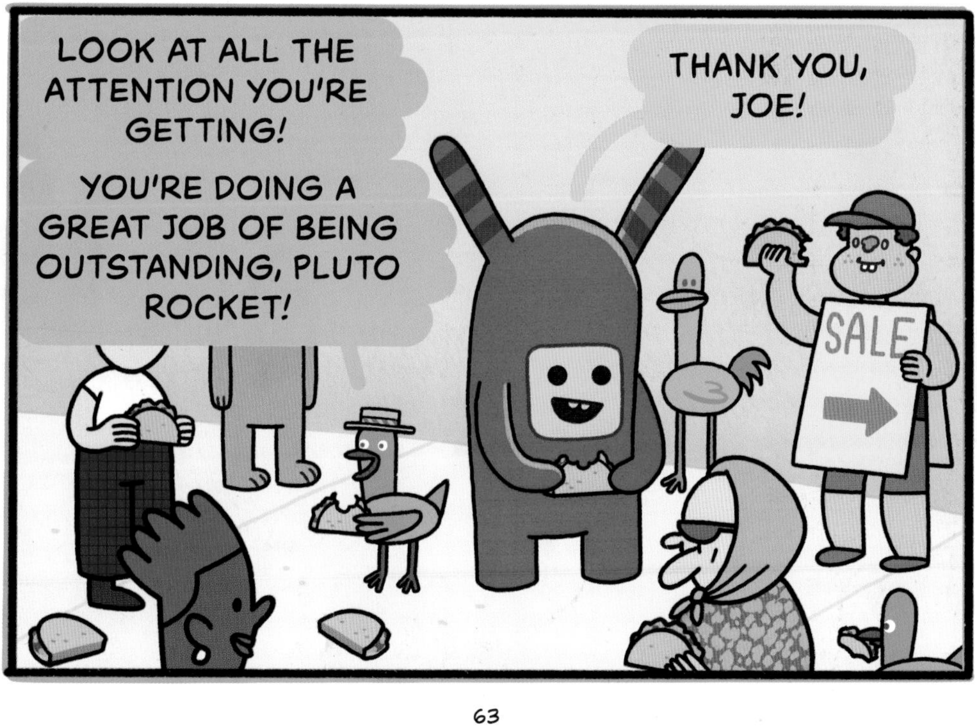
LOOK AT ALL THE ATTENTION YOU'RE GETTING!
YOU'RE DOING A GREAT JOB OF BEING OUTSTANDING, PLUTO ROCKET!
THANK YOU, JOE!
SALE

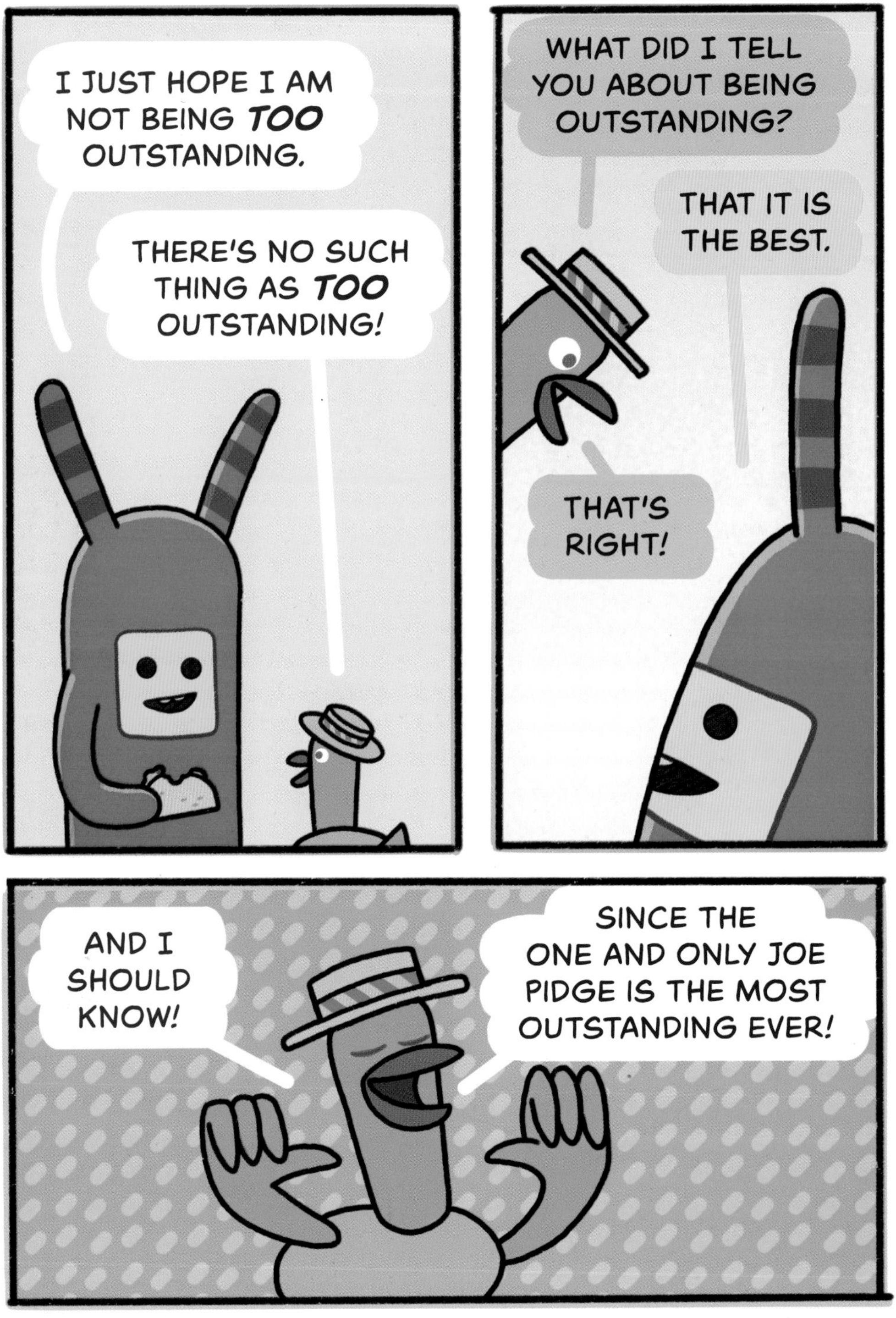
I JUST HOPE I AM NOT BEING TOO OUTSTANDING.
THERE'S NO SUCH THING AS TOO OUTSTANDING!
WHAT DID I TELL YOU ABOUT BEING OUTSTANDING?
THAT IT IS THE BEST.
THAT'S RIGHT!
AND I SHOULD KNOW!
SINCE THE ONE AND ONLY JOE PIDGE IS THE MOST OUTSTANDING EVER!

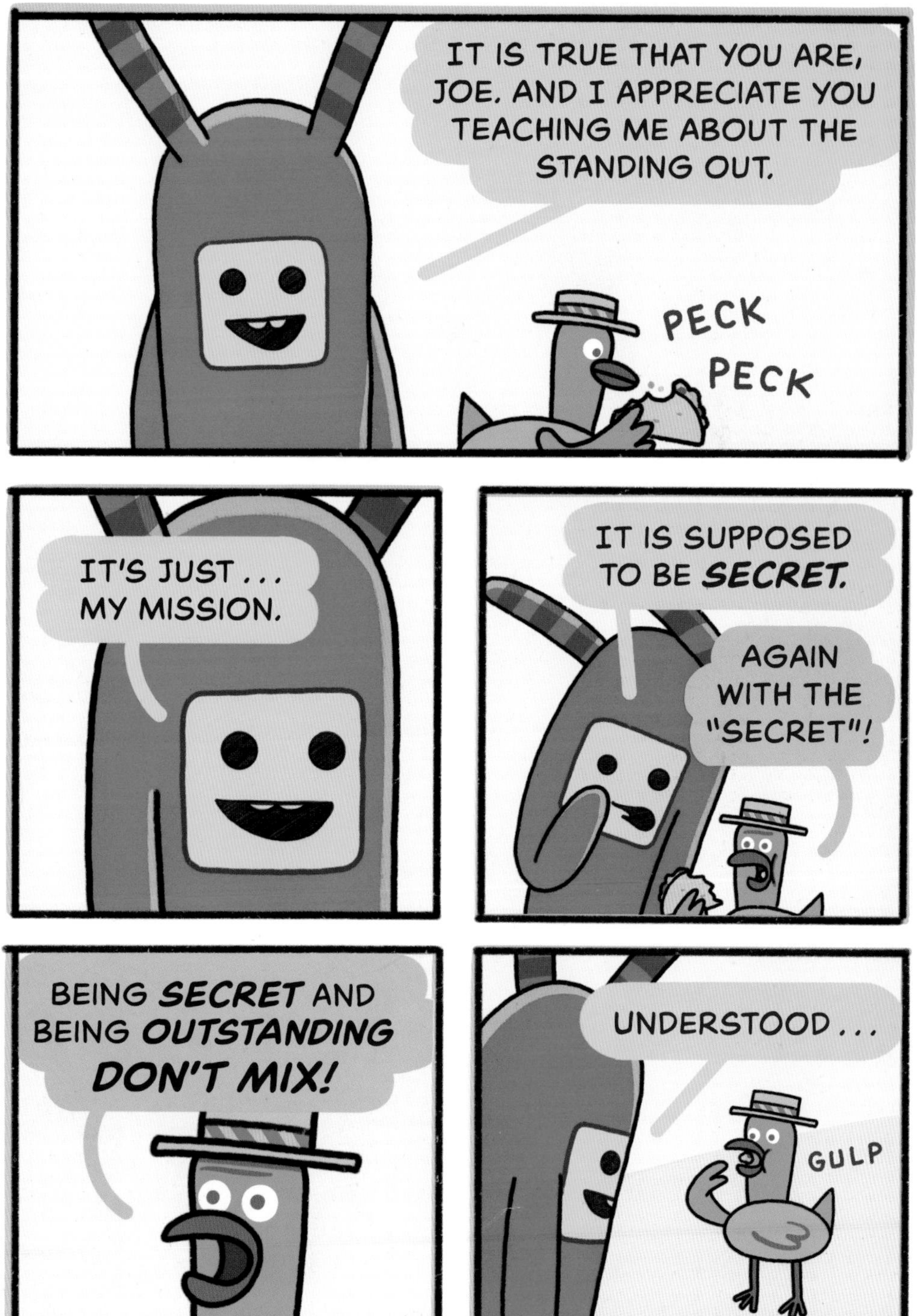
IT IS TRUE THAT YOU ARE, JOE. AND I APPRECIATE YOU TEACHING ME ABOUT THE STANDING OUT.
PECK
PECK
IT'S JUST . . . MY MISSION.
IT IS SUPPOSED TO BE *SECRET.*
AGAIN WITH THE "SECRET"!
BEING *SECRET* AND BEING *OUTSTANDING* *DON'T MIX!*
UNDERSTOOD . . .
GULP

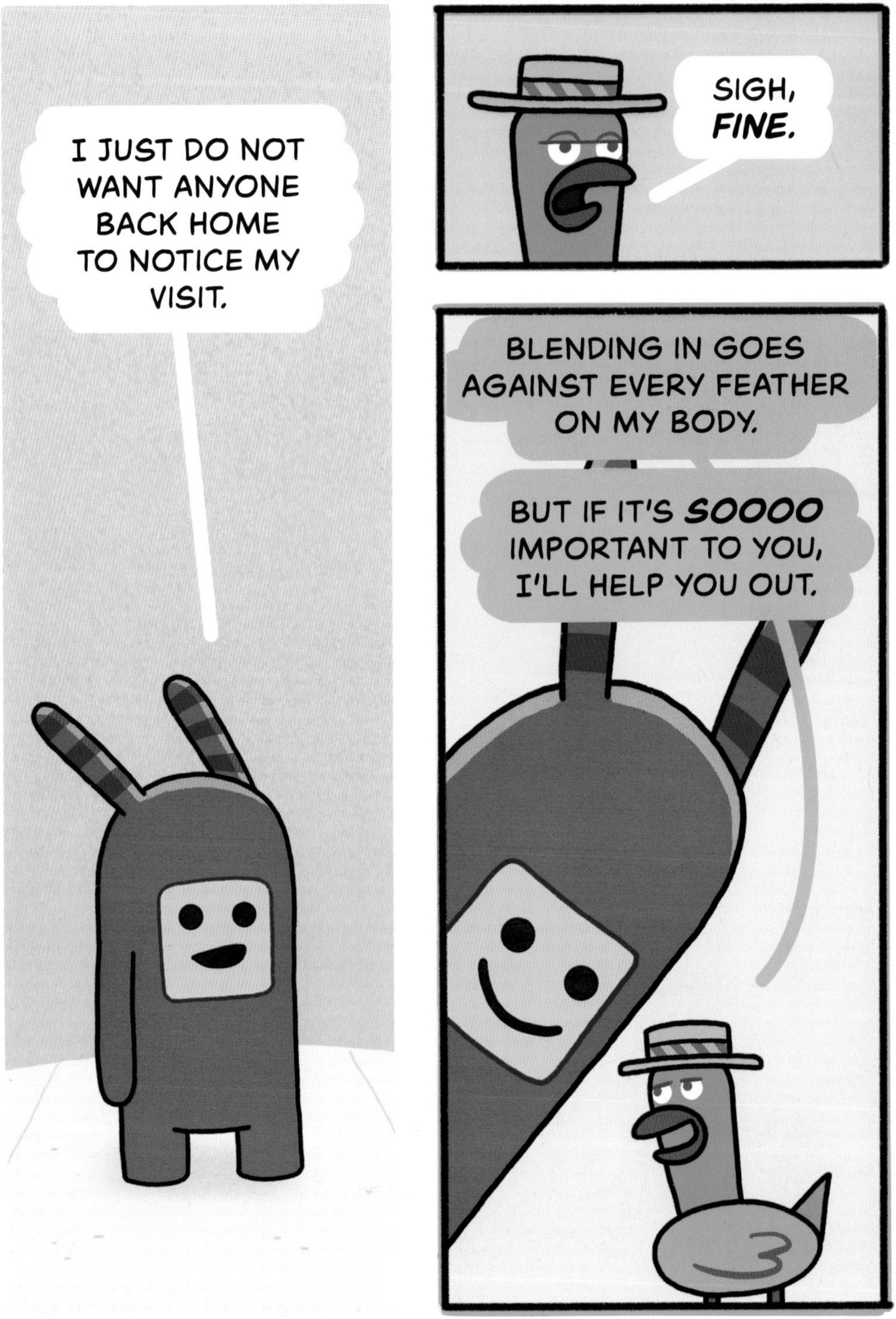
I JUST DO NOT WANT ANYONE BACK HOME TO NOTICE MY VISIT.
SIGH, *FINE.*
BLENDING IN GOES AGAINST EVERY FEATHER ON MY BODY.
BUT IF IT'S *SOOOO* IMPORTANT TO YOU, I'LL HELP YOU OUT.

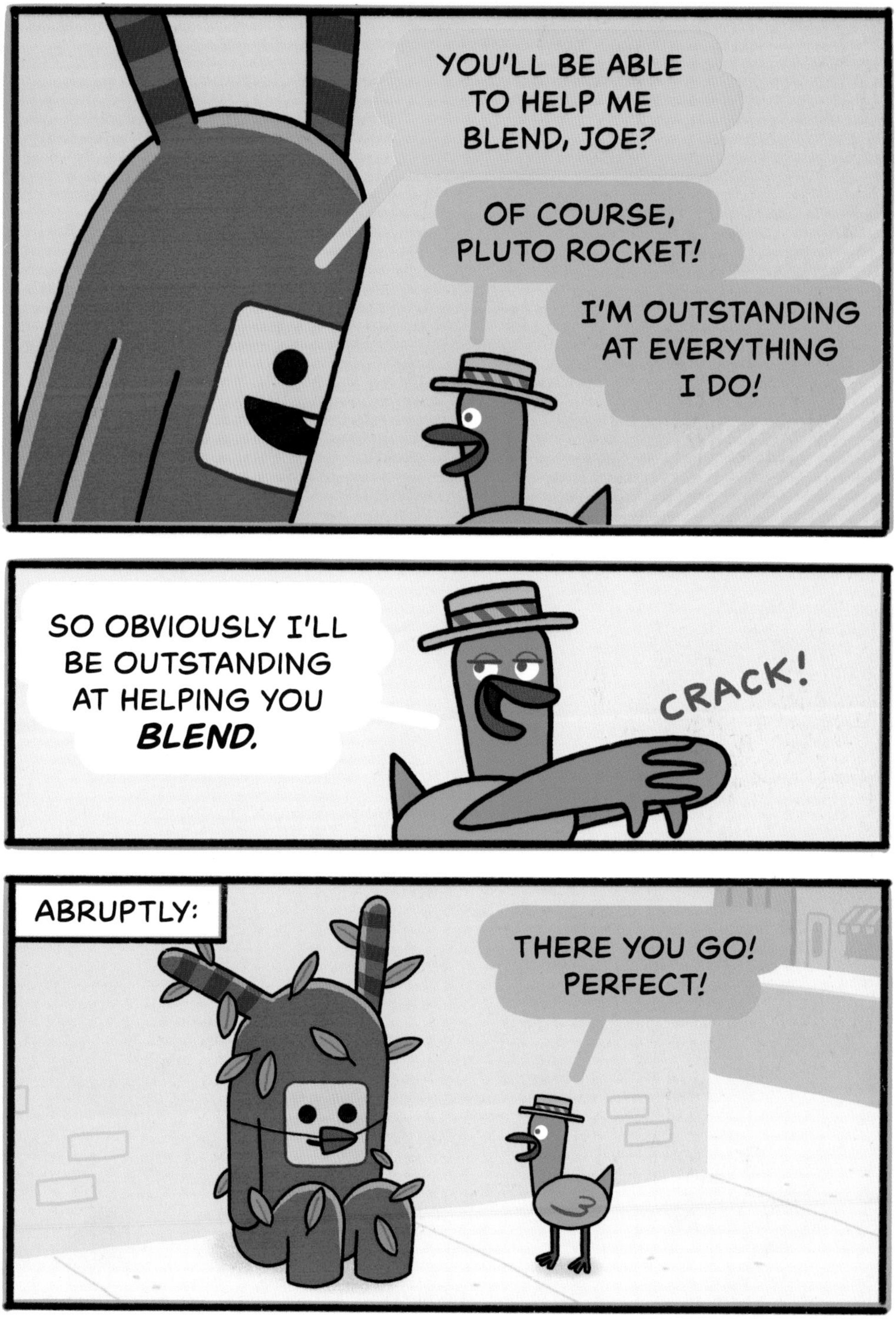
YOU'LL BE ABLE TO HELP ME BLEND, JOE?
OF COURSE, PLUTO ROCKET!
I'M OUTSTANDING AT EVERYTHING I DO!
SO OBVIOUSLY I'LL BE OUTSTANDING AT HELPING YOU BLEND.
CRACK!
ABRUPTLY:
THERE YOU GO! PERFECT!

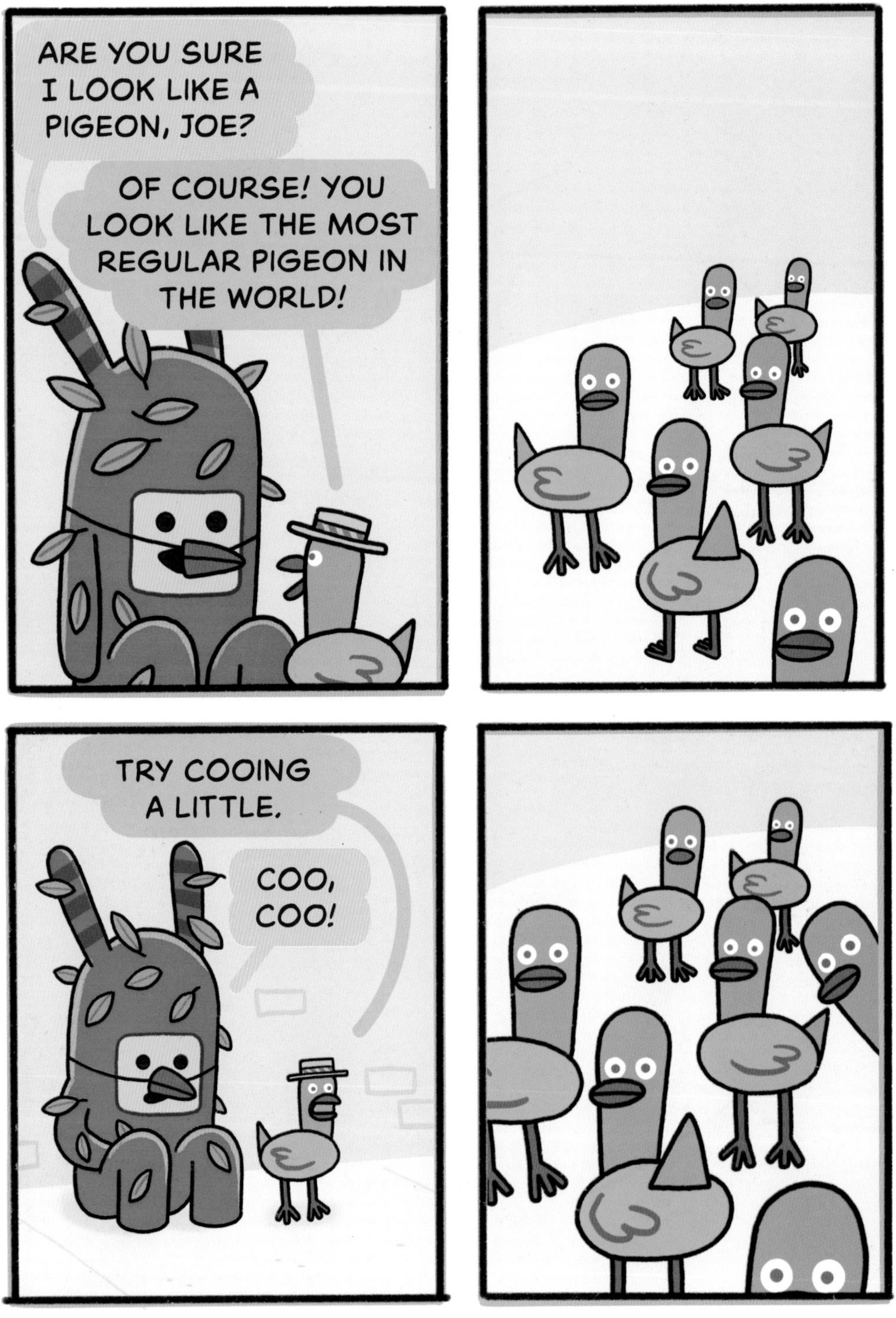
ARE YOU SURE I LOOK LIKE A PIGEON, JOE?
OF COURSE! YOU LOOK LIKE THE MOST REGULAR PIGEON IN THE WORLD!
TRY COOING A LITTLE.
COO, COO!

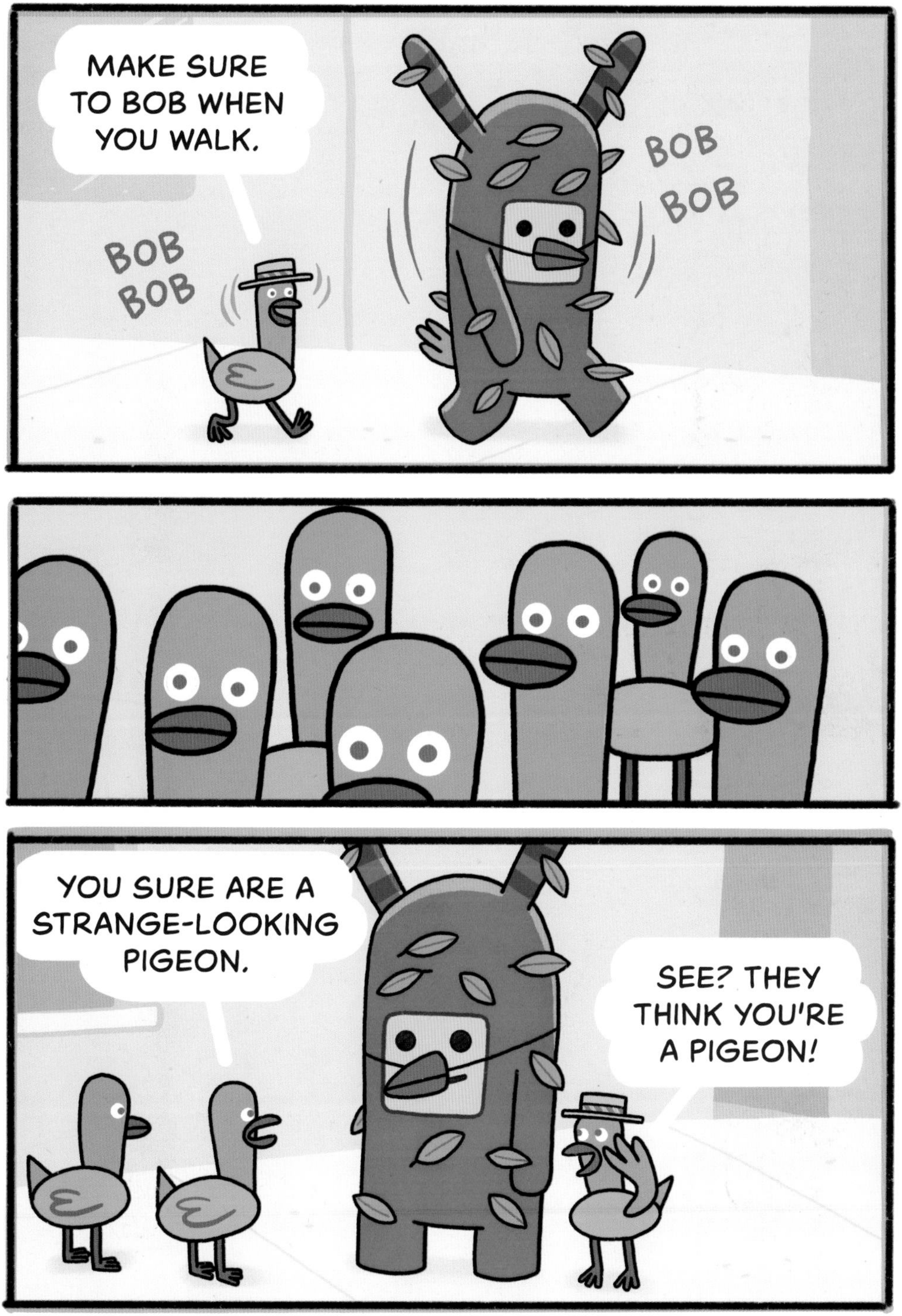
MAKE SURE TO BOB WHEN YOU WALK.
BOB BOB
BOB BOB
YOU SURE ARE A STRANGE-LOOKING PIGEON.
SEE? THEY THINK YOU'RE A PIGEON!

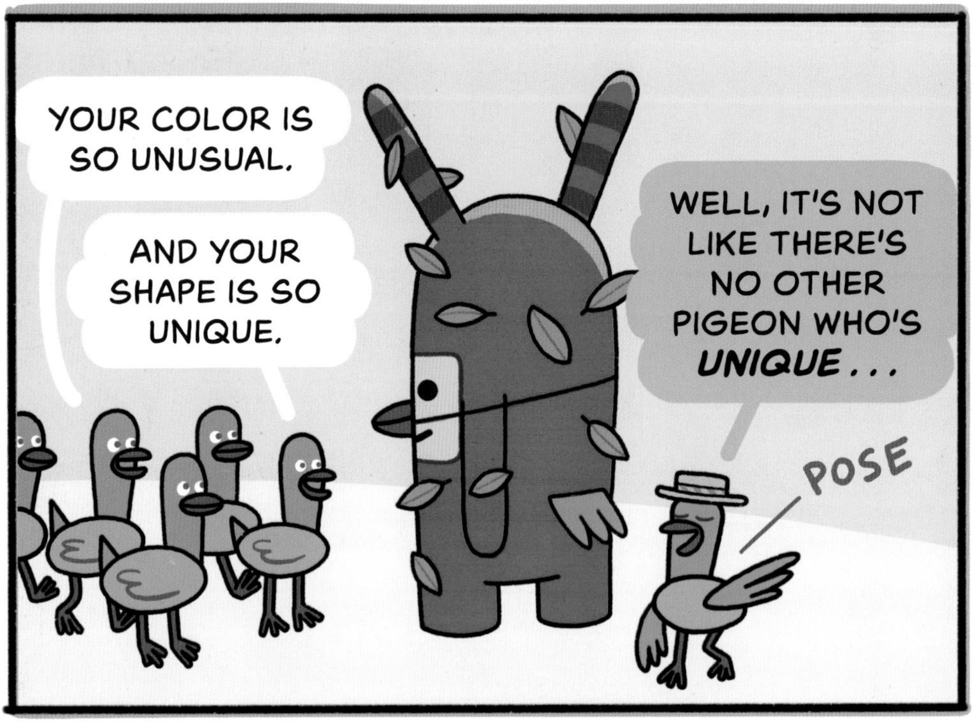
YOUR COLOR IS SO UNUSUAL.
AND YOUR SHAPE IS SO UNIQUE.
WELL, IT'S NOT LIKE THERE'S NO OTHER PIGEON WHO'S ***UNIQUE . . .***
POSE

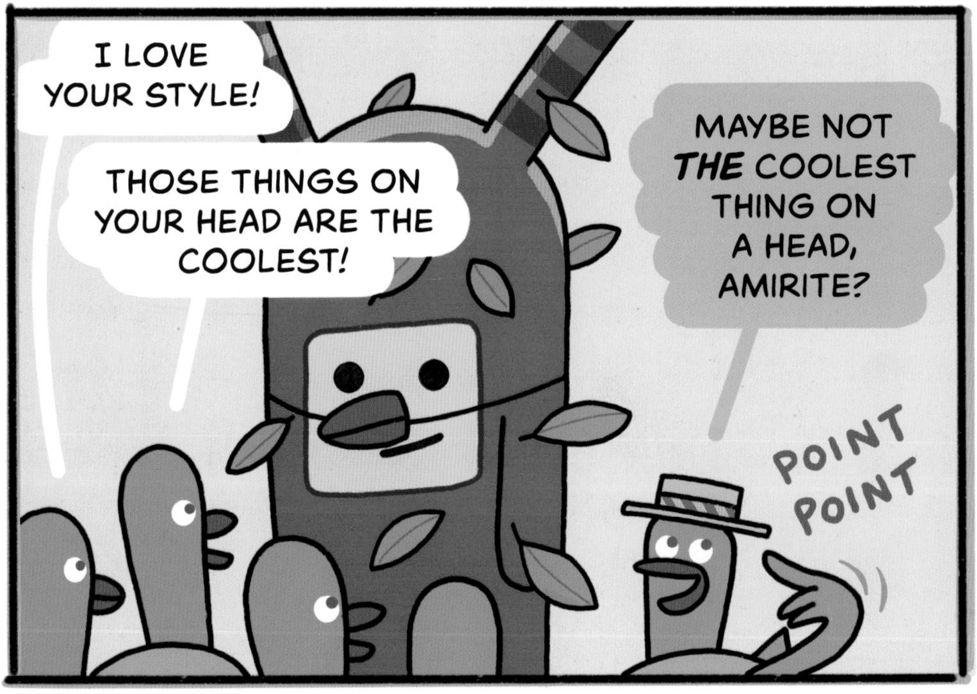
I LOVE YOUR STYLE!
THOSE THINGS ON YOUR HEAD ARE THE COOLEST!
MAYBE NOT ***THE*** COOLEST THING ON A HEAD, AMIRITE?
POINT POINT

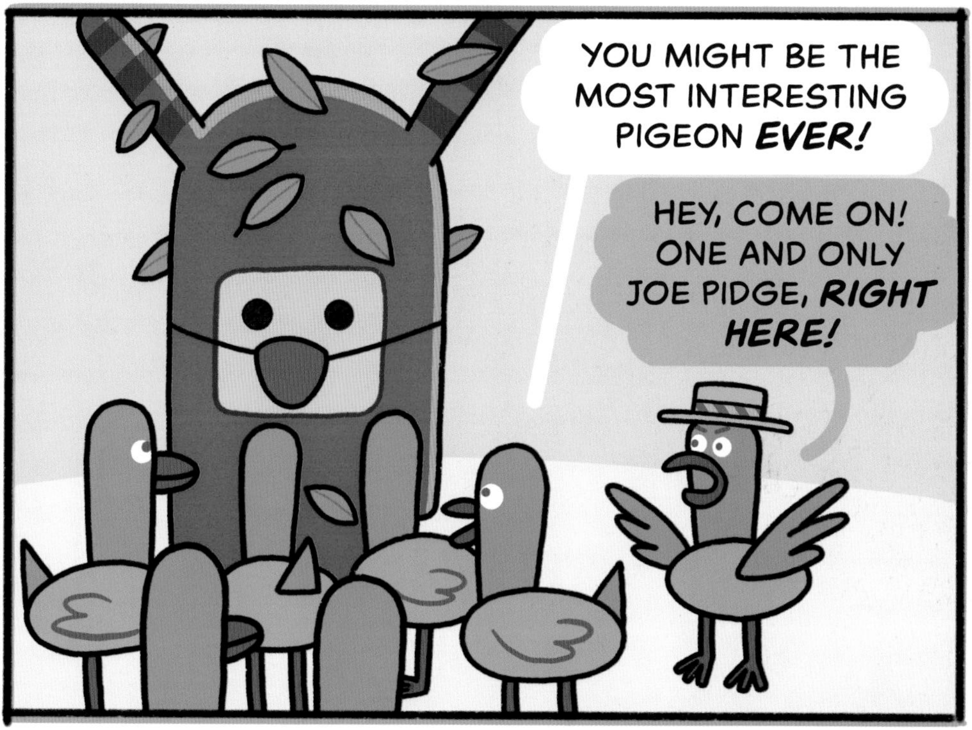
YOU MIGHT BE THE MOST INTERESTING PIGEON ***EVER!***
HEY, COME ON! ONE AND ONLY JOE PIDGE, ***RIGHT HERE!***

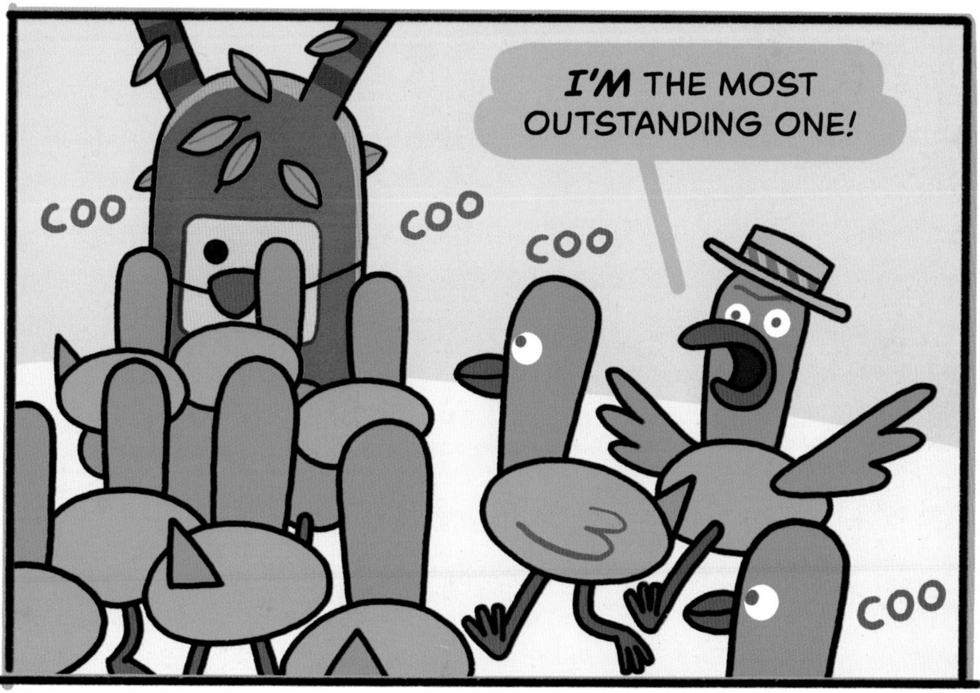
I'M THE MOST OUTSTANDING ONE!
COO
COO
COO
COO

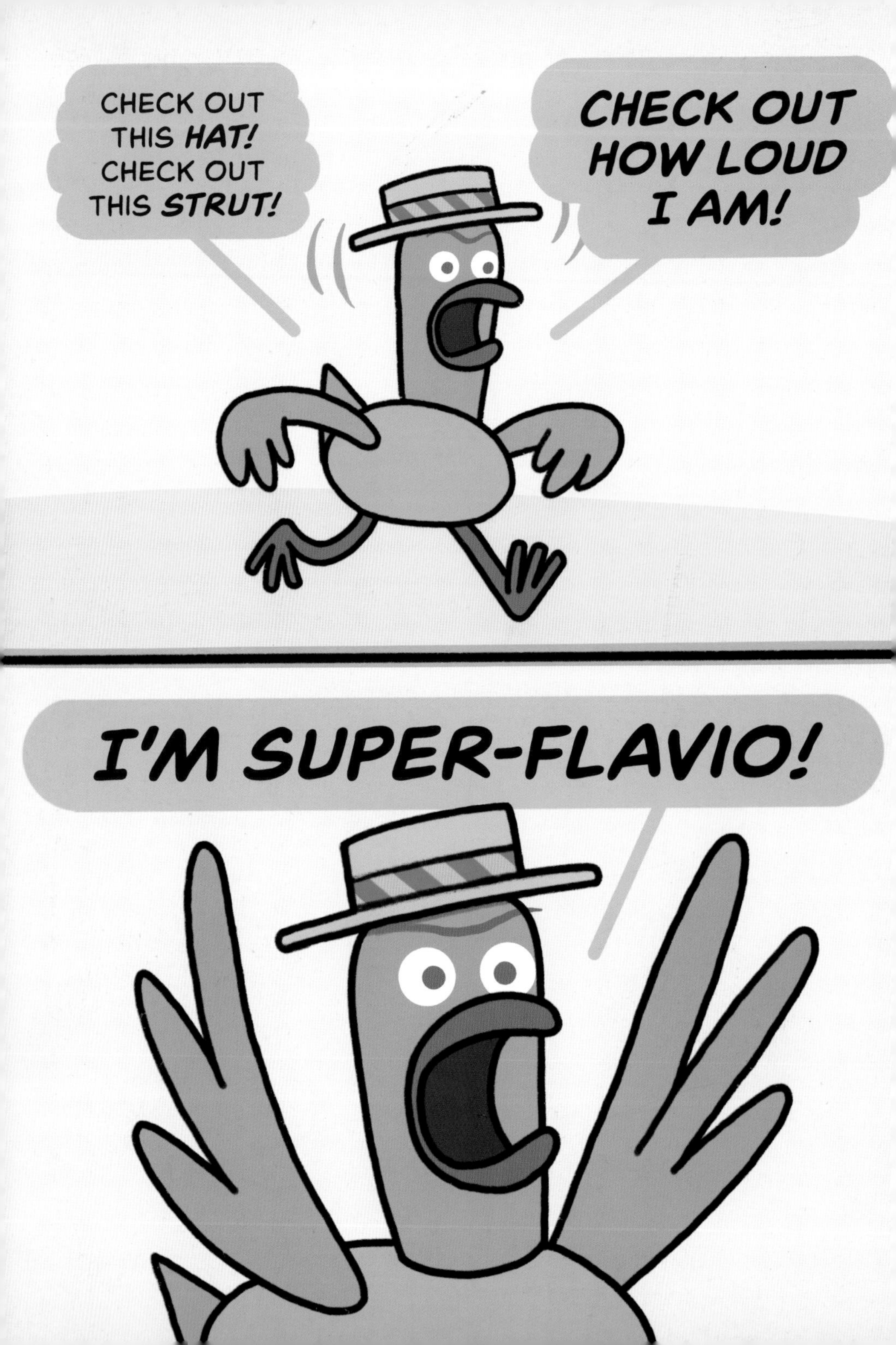
CHECK OUT THIS HAT! CHECK OUT THIS STRUT!
CHECK OUT HOW LOUD I AM!
I'M SUPER-FLAVIO!

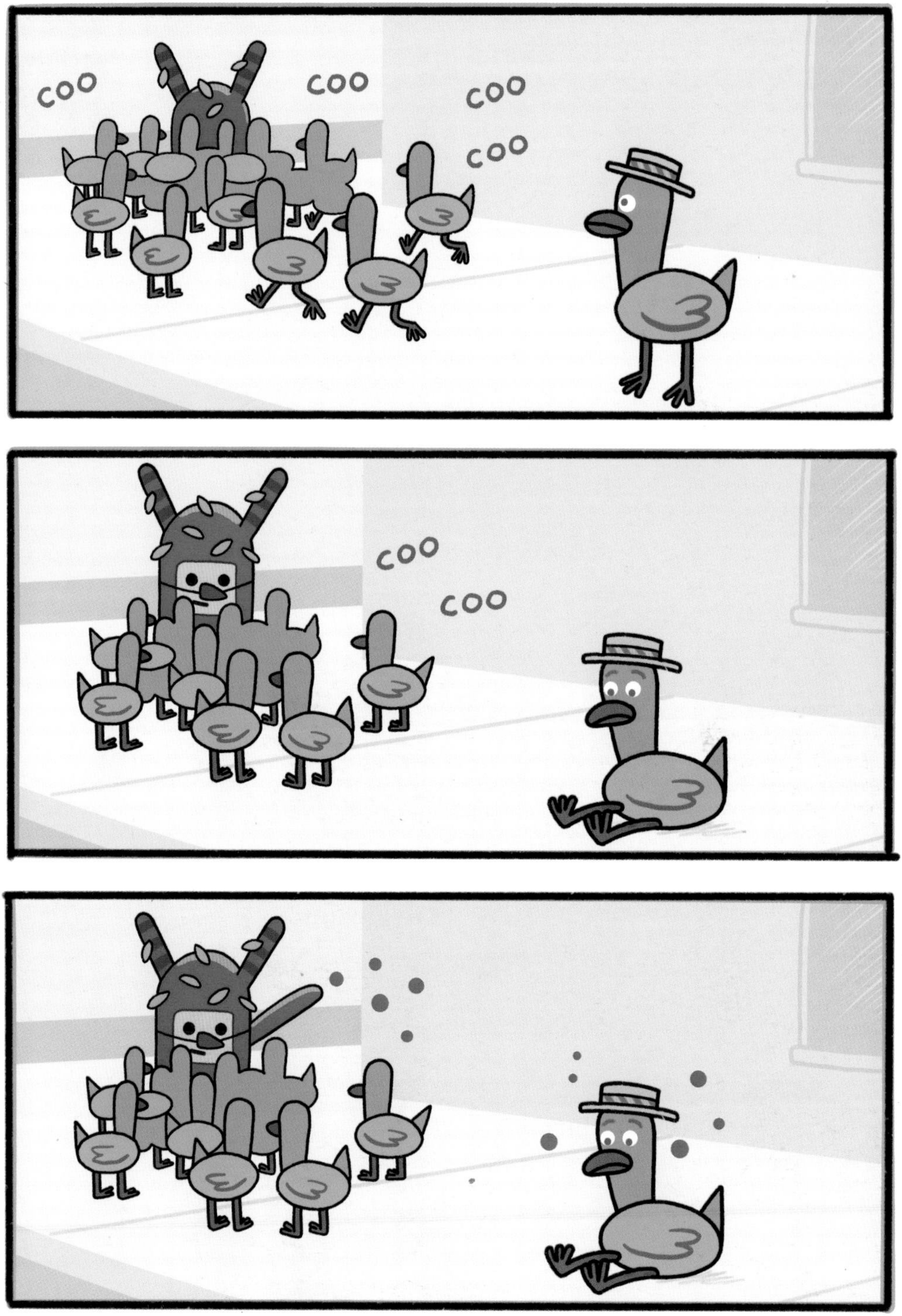
COO
COO
COO
COO
COO
COO

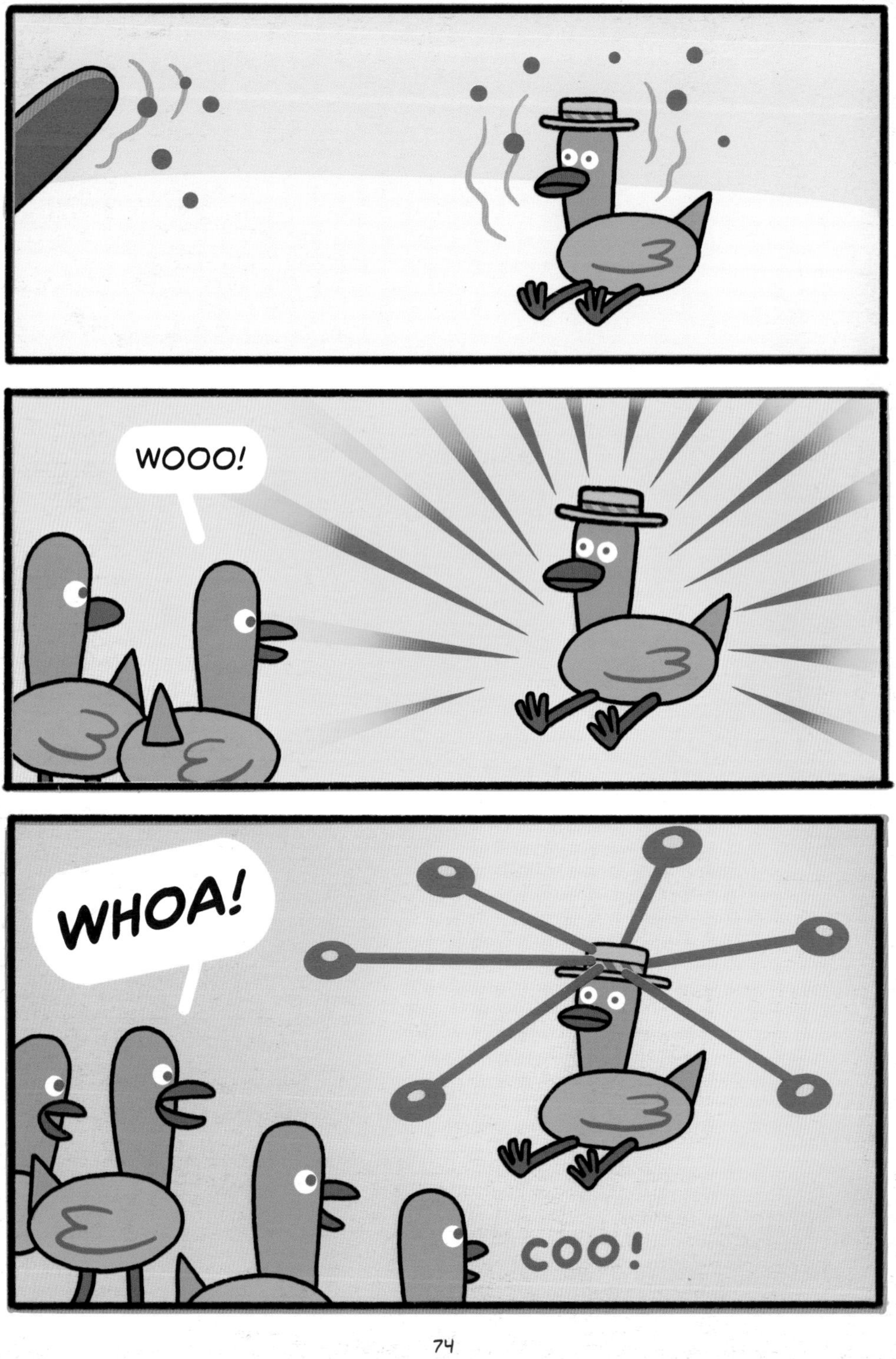
WOOO!
WHOA!
COO!

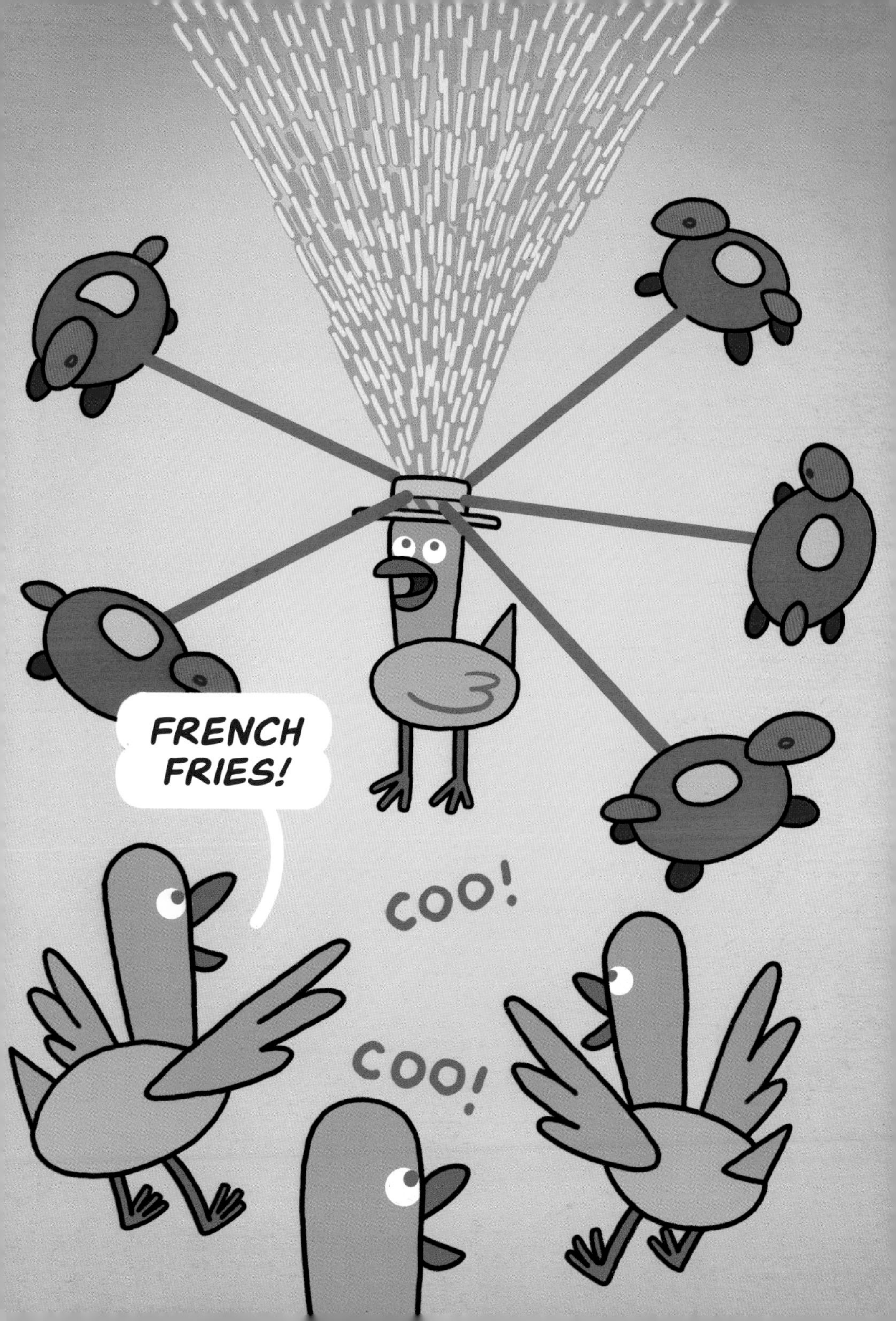
FRENCH FRIES!
COO!
COO!

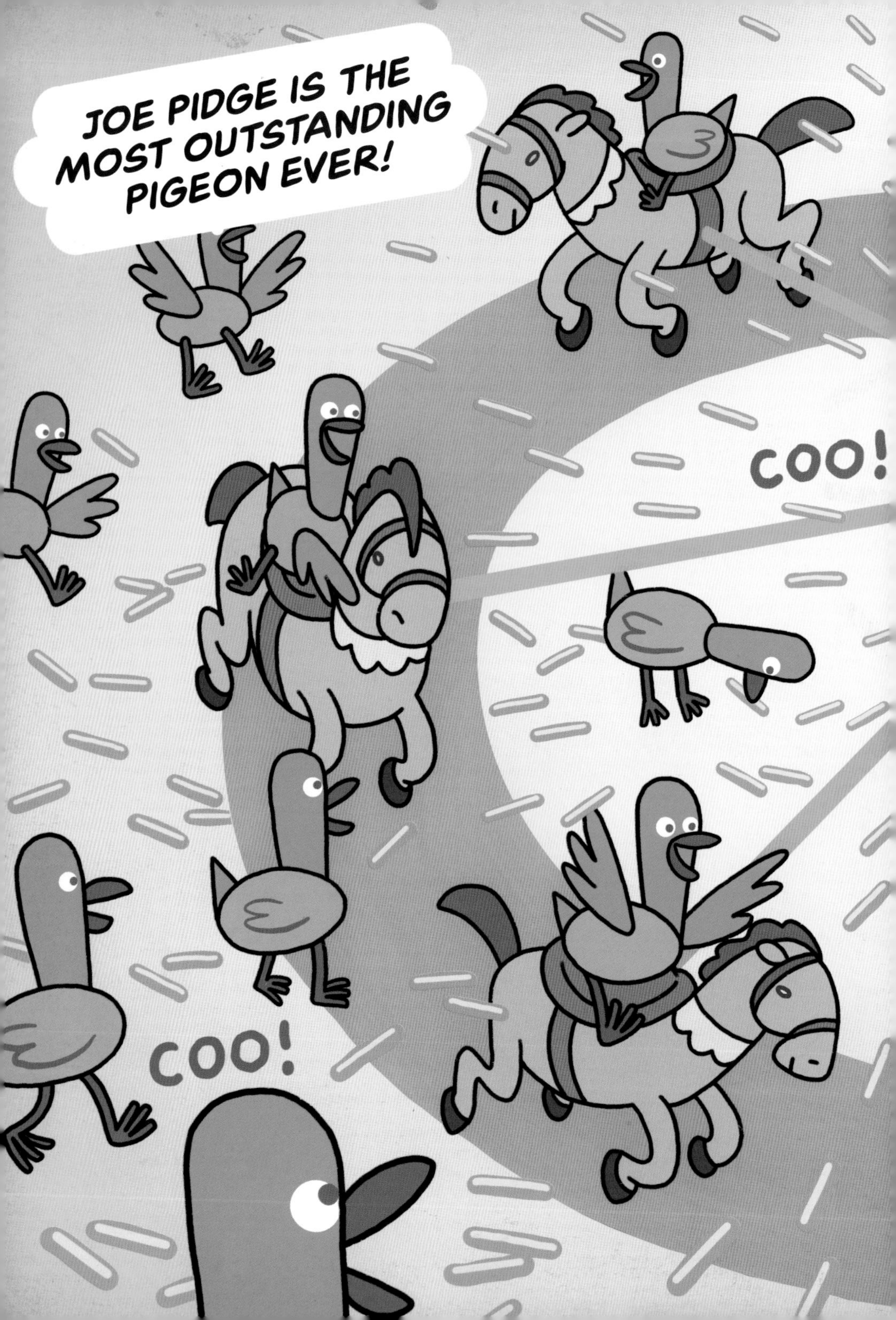
JOE PIDGE IS THE MOST OUTSTANDING PIGEON EVER!
COO!
COO!

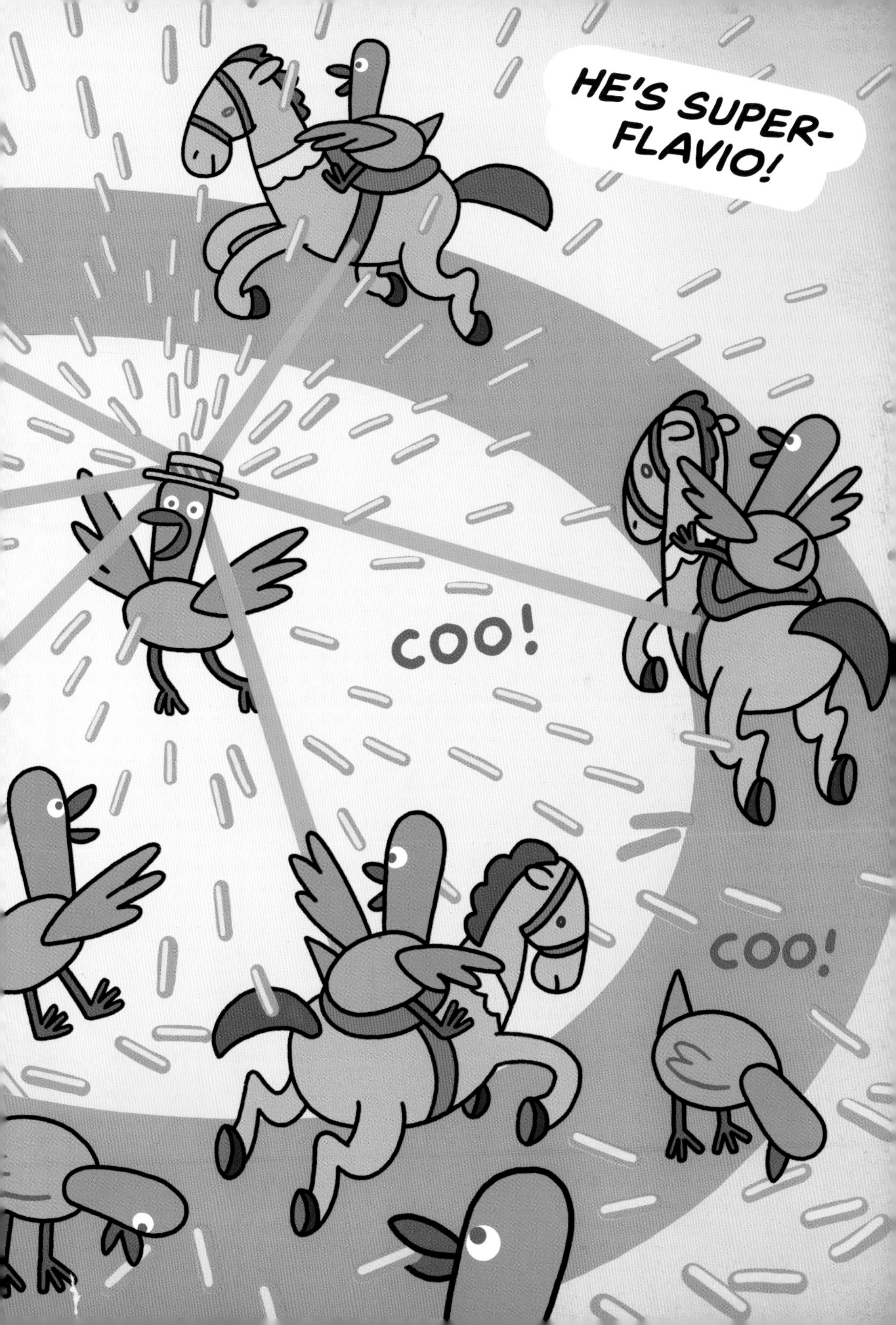
HE'S SUPER-FLAVIO!
COO!
COO!

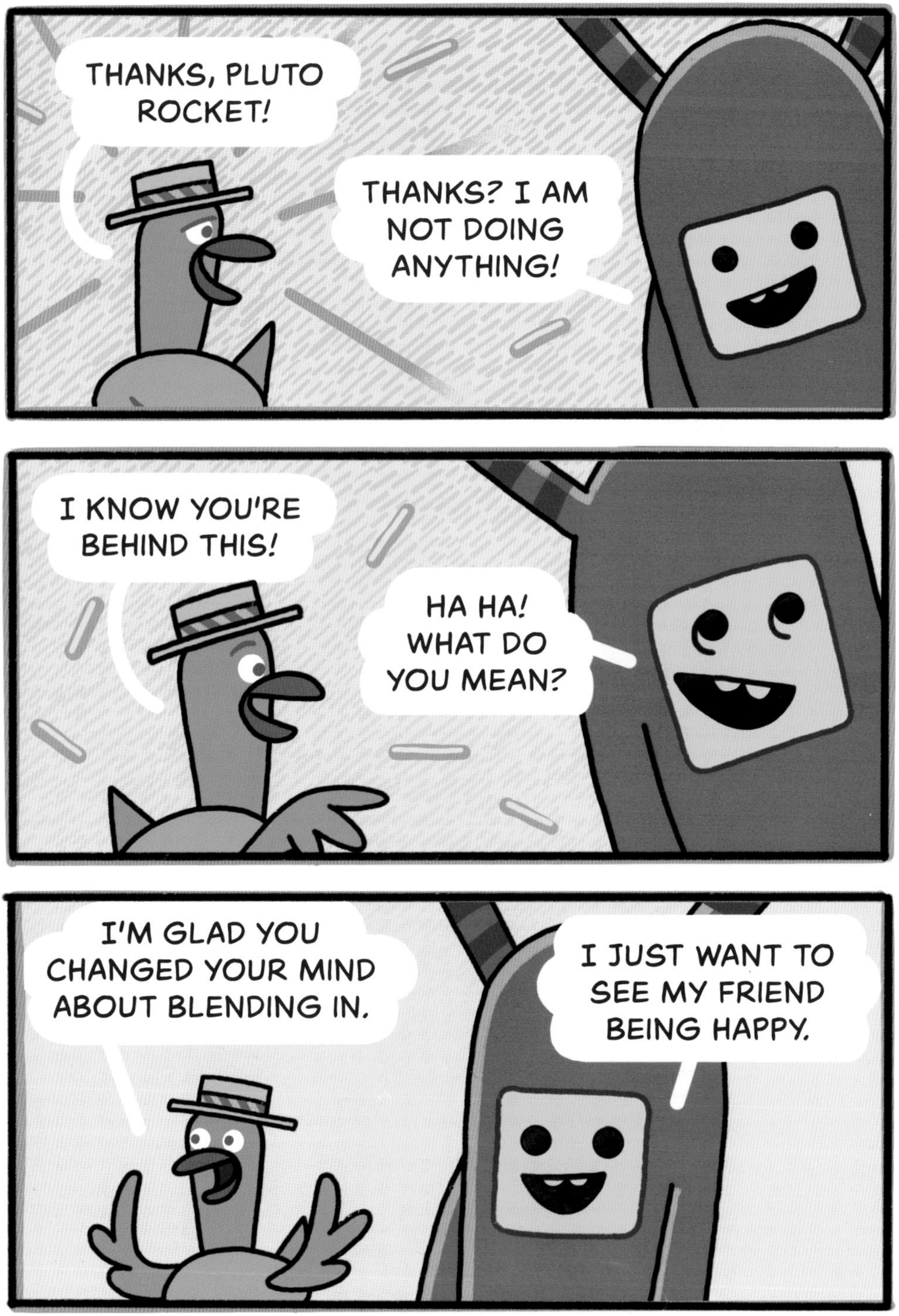
THANKS, PLUTO ROCKET!
THANKS? I AM NOT DOING ANYTHING!
I KNOW YOU'RE BEHIND THIS!
HA HA! WHAT DO YOU MEAN?
I'M GLAD YOU CHANGED YOUR MIND ABOUT BLENDING IN.
I JUST WANT TO SEE MY FRIEND BEING HAPPY.

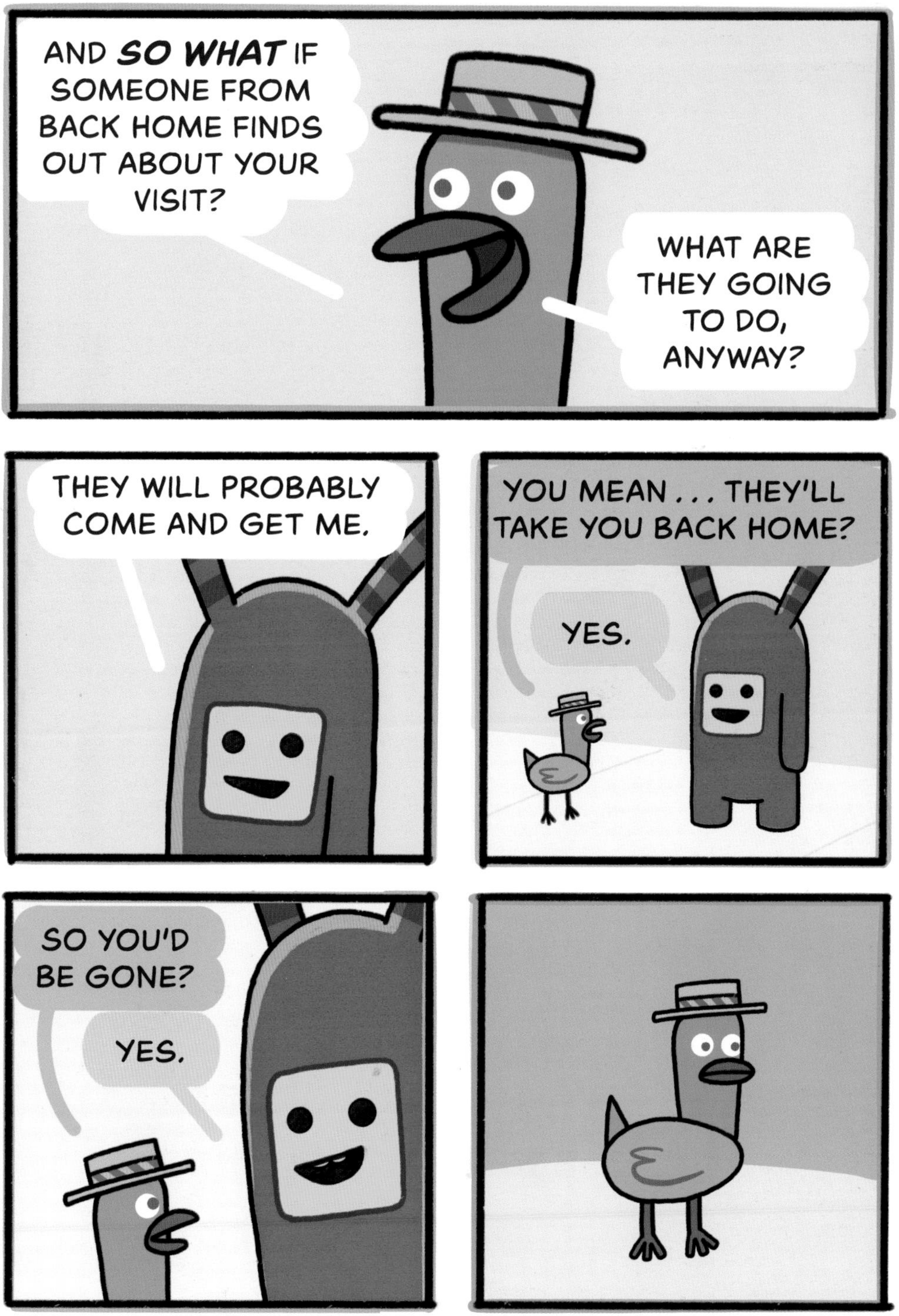
AND **SO WHAT** IF SOMEONE FROM BACK HOME FINDS OUT ABOUT YOUR VISIT?
WHAT ARE THEY GOING TO DO, ANYWAY?
THEY WILL PROBABLY COME AND GET ME.
YOU MEAN . . . THEY'LL TAKE YOU BACK HOME?
YES.
SO YOU'D BE GONE?
YES.

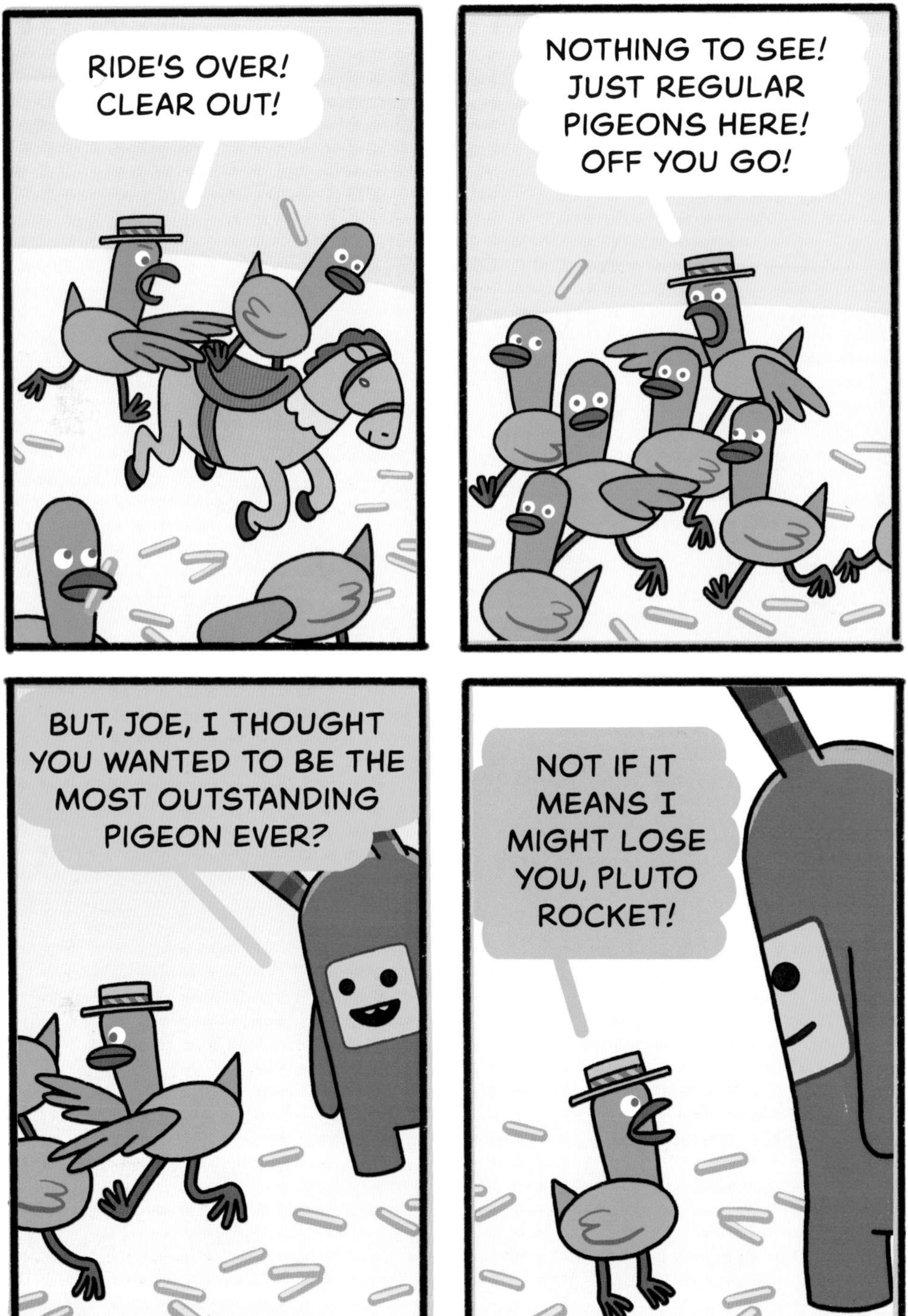
RIDE'S OVER! CLEAR OUT!
NOTHING TO SEE! JUST REGULAR PIGEONS HERE! OFF YOU GO!
BUT, JOE, I THOUGHT YOU WANTED TO BE THE MOST OUTSTANDING PIGEON EVER?
NOT IF IT MEANS I MIGHT LOSE YOU, PLUTO ROCKET!

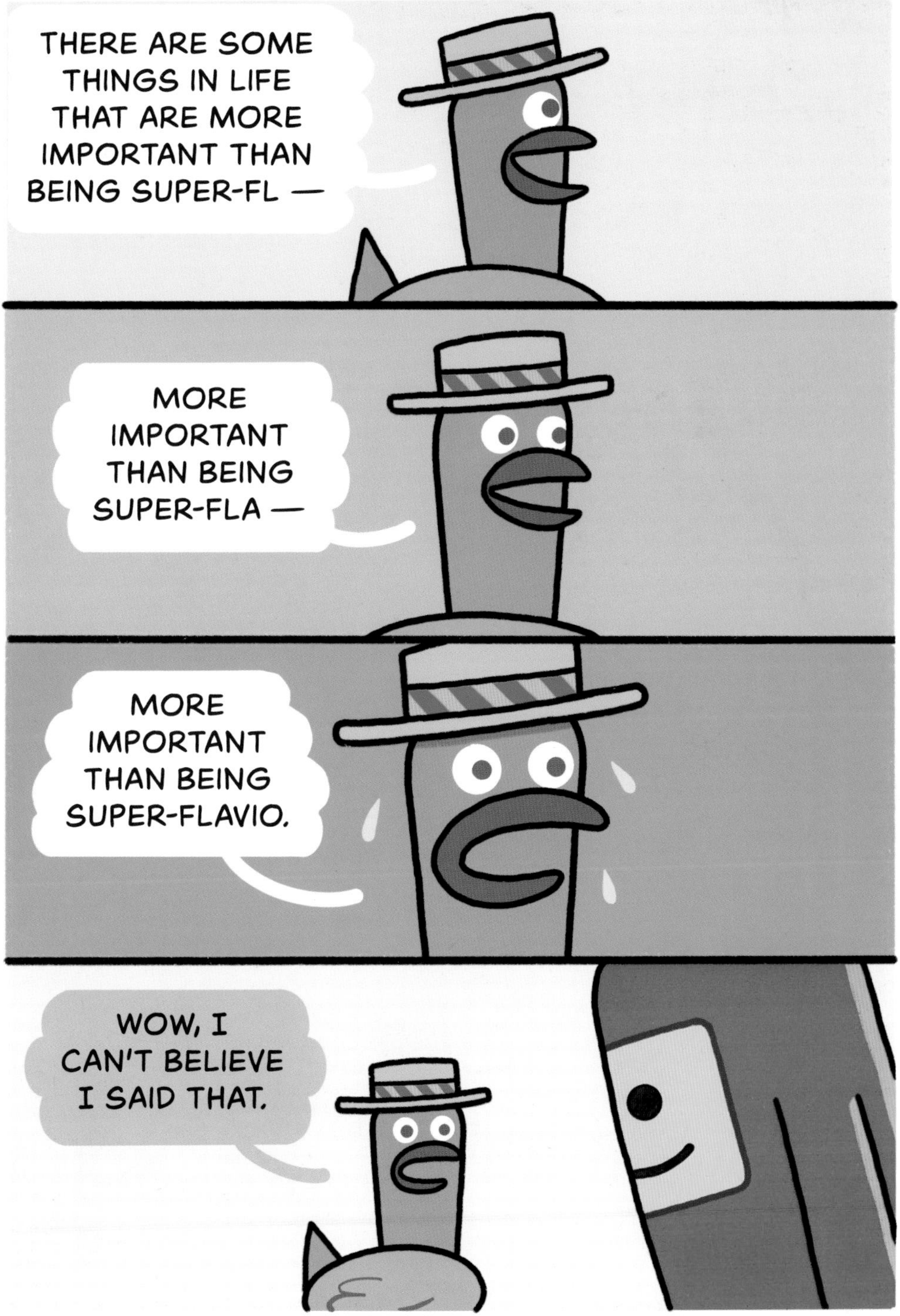
THERE ARE SOME THINGS IN LIFE THAT ARE MORE IMPORTANT THAN BEING SUPER-FL —
MORE IMPORTANT THAN BEING SUPER-FLA —
MORE IMPORTANT THAN BEING SUPER-FLAVIO.
WOW, I CAN'T BELIEVE I SAID THAT.

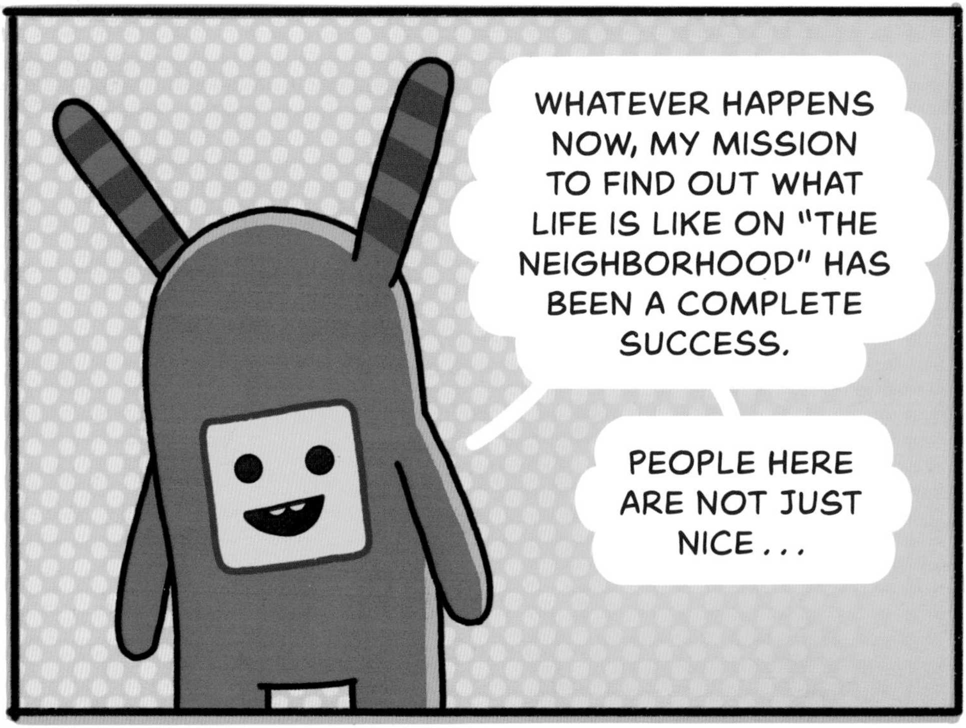
WHATEVER HAPPENS NOW, MY MISSION TO FIND OUT WHAT LIFE IS LIKE ON "THE NEIGHBORHOOD" HAS BEEN A COMPLETE SUCCESS.
PEOPLE HERE ARE NOT JUST NICE . . .

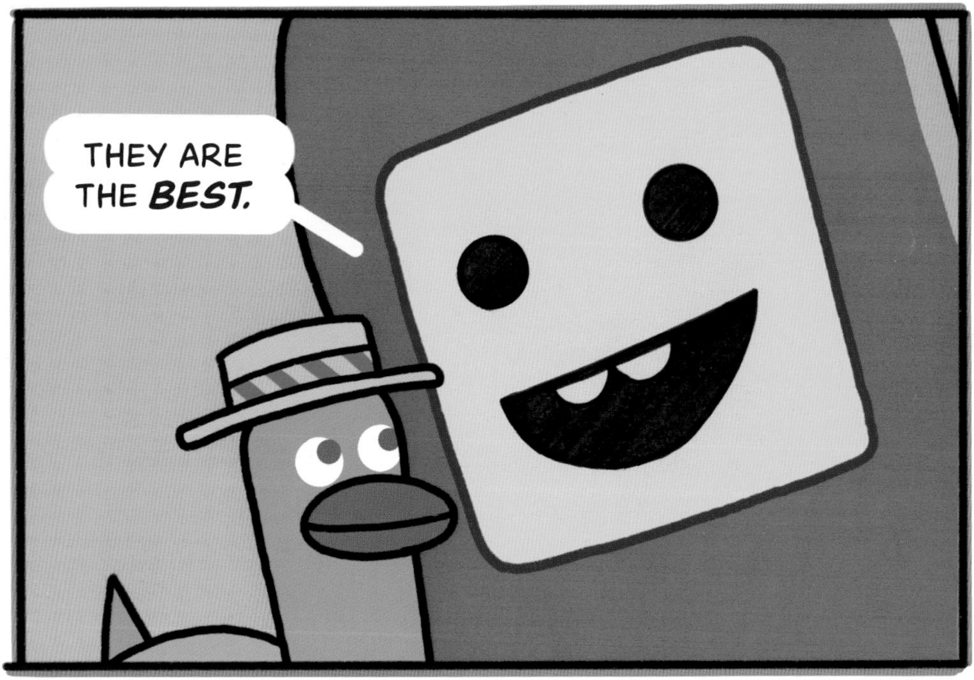
THEY ARE THE ***BEST.***

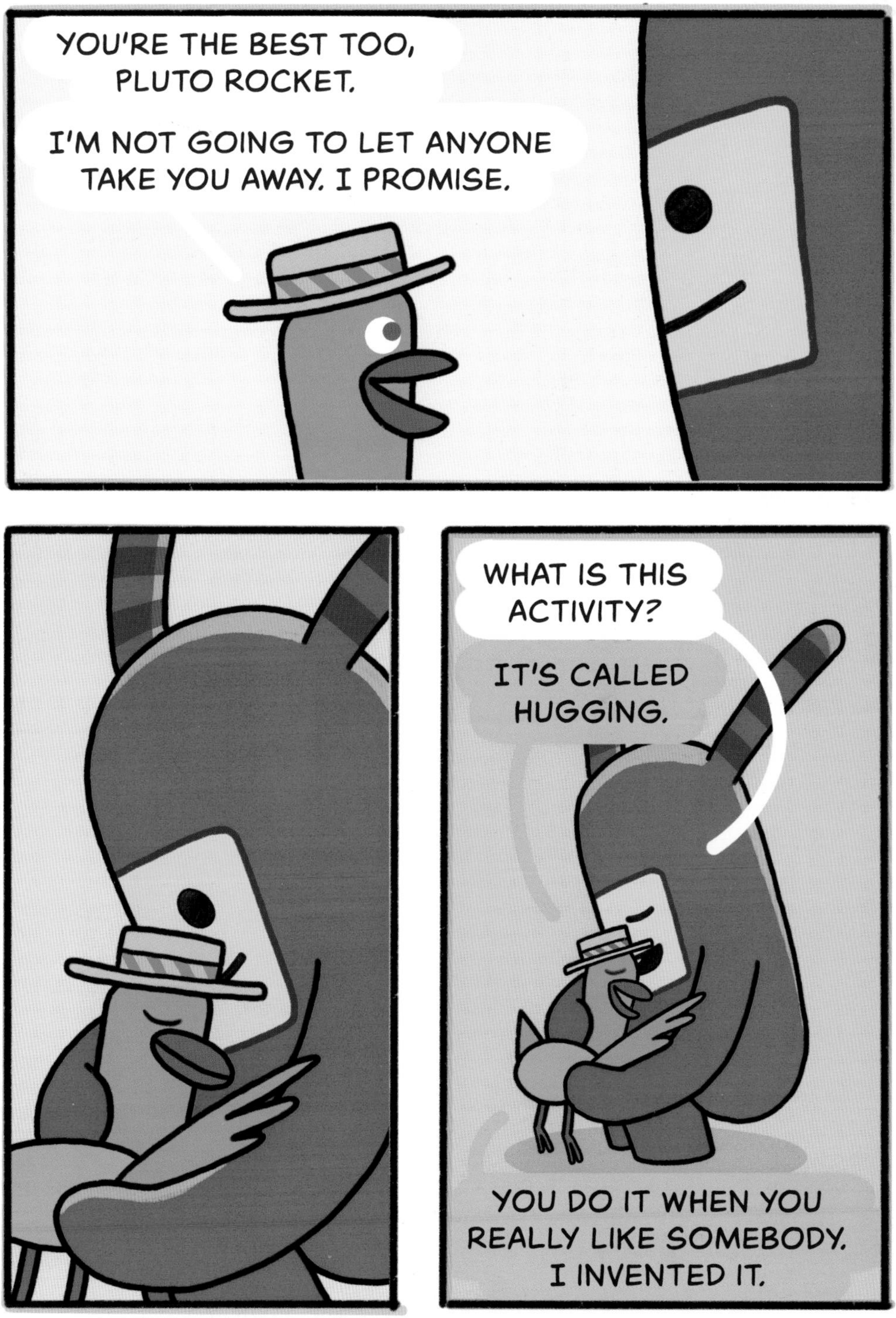
YOU'RE THE BEST TOO, PLUTO ROCKET.
I'M NOT GOING TO LET ANYONE TAKE YOU AWAY. I PROMISE.
WHAT IS THIS ACTIVITY?
IT'S CALLED HUGGING.
YOU DO IT WHEN YOU REALLY LIKE SOMEBODY. I INVENTED IT.

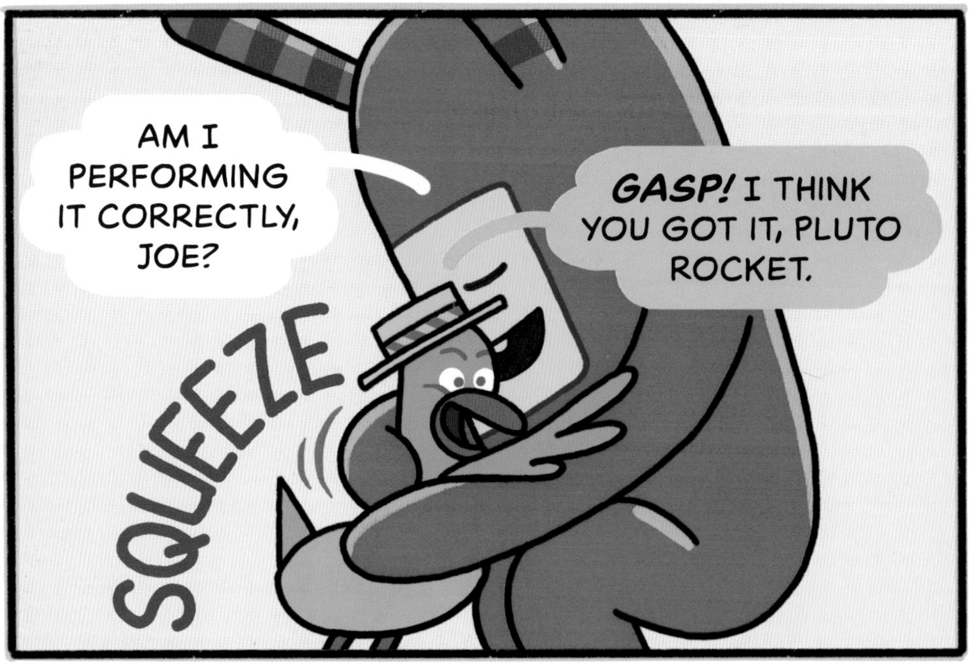
AM I PERFORMING IT CORRECTLY, JOE?
GASP! I THINK YOU GOT IT, PLUTO ROCKET.
SQUEEZE

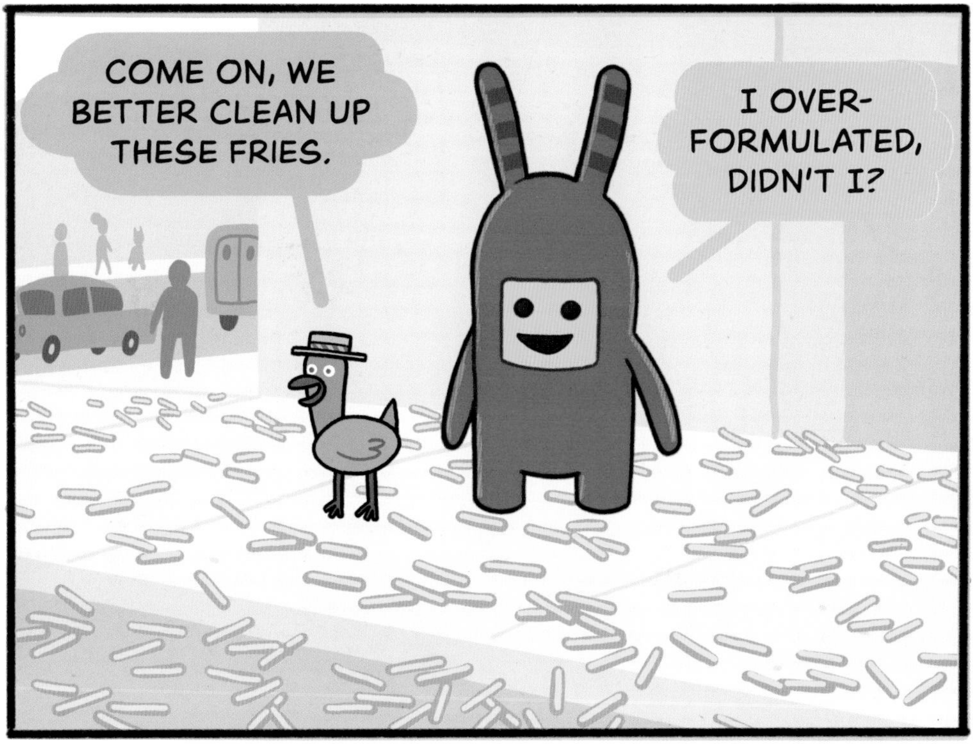
COME ON, WE BETTER CLEAN UP THESE FRIES.
I OVER-FORMULATED, DIDN'T I?

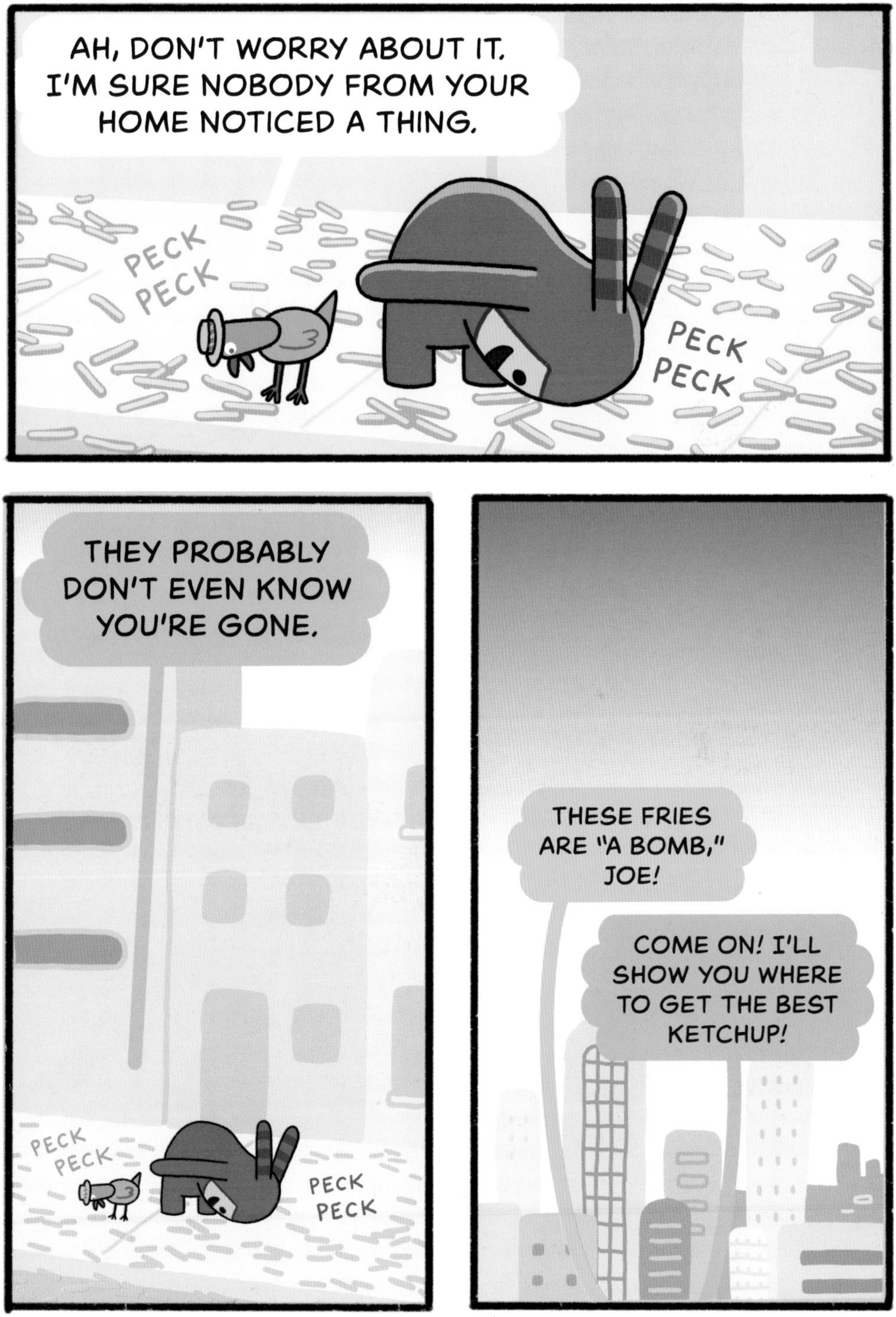
AH, DON'T WORRY ABOUT IT. I'M SURE NOBODY FROM YOUR HOME NOTICED A THING.
PECK PECK
PECK PECK
THEY PROBABLY DON'T EVEN KNOW YOU'RE GONE.
PECK PECK
PECK PECK
THESE FRIES ARE "A BOMB," JOE!
COME ON! I'LL SHOW YOU WHERE TO GET THE BEST KETCHUP!

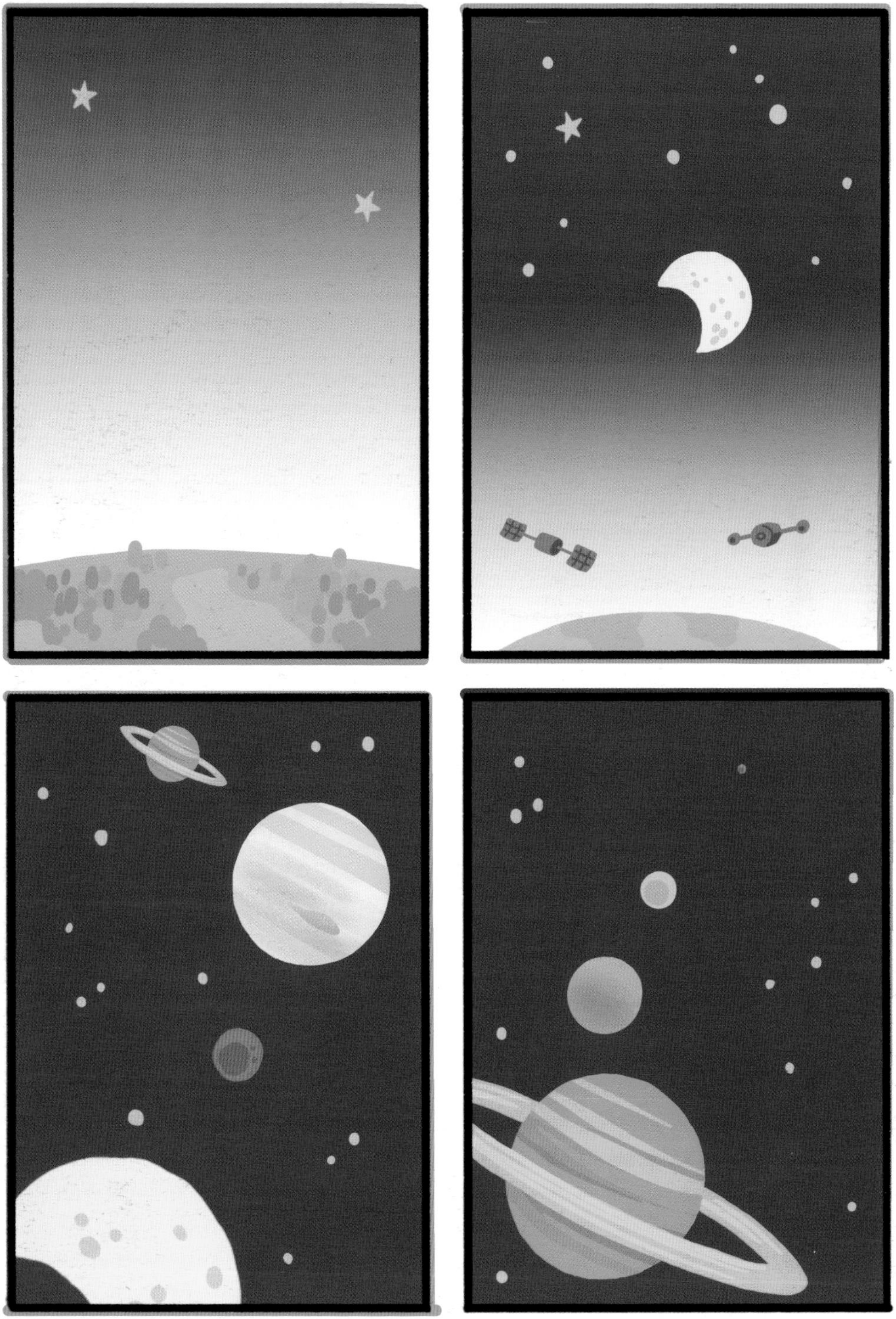

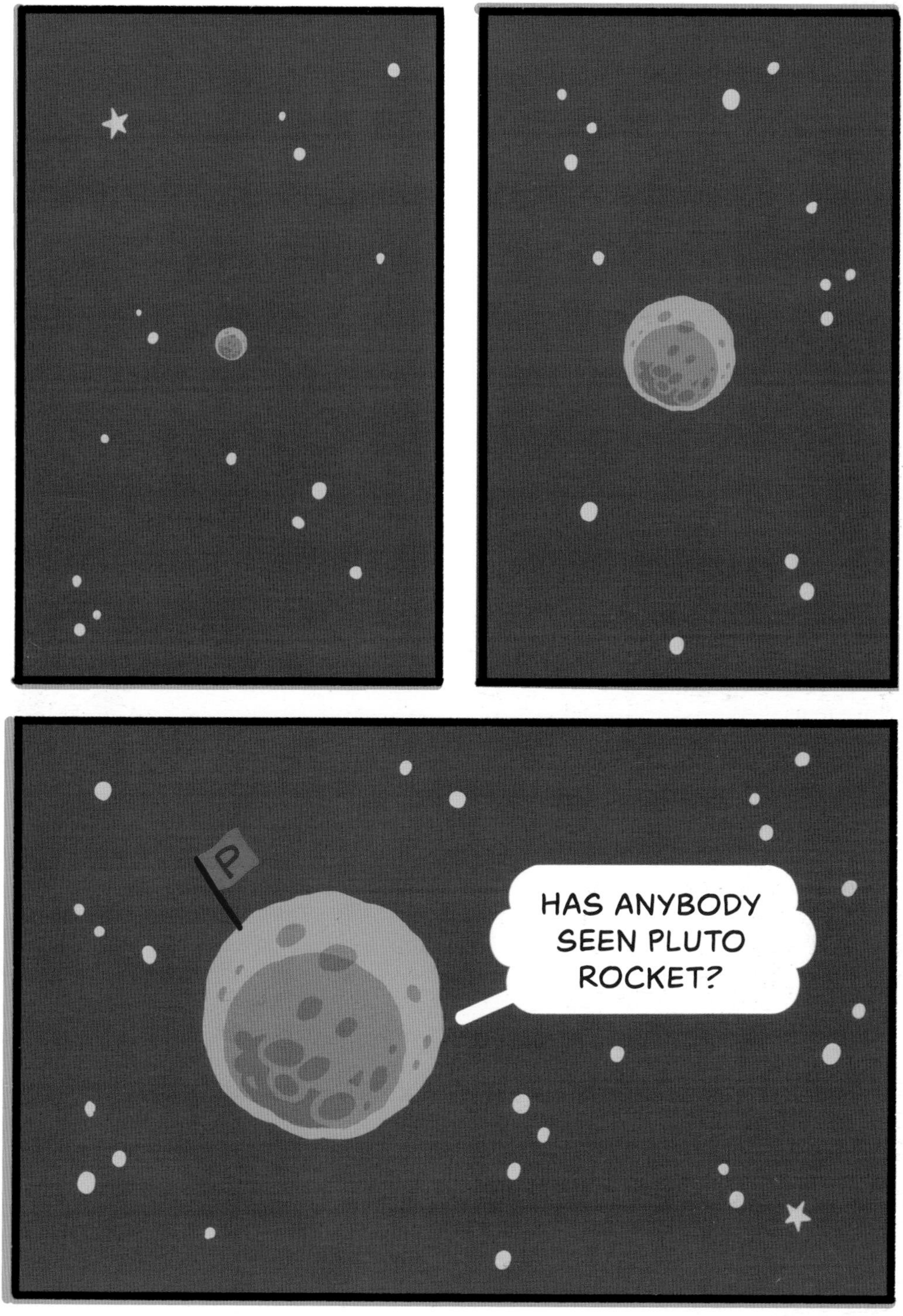
HAS ANYBODY SEEN PLUTO ROCKET?

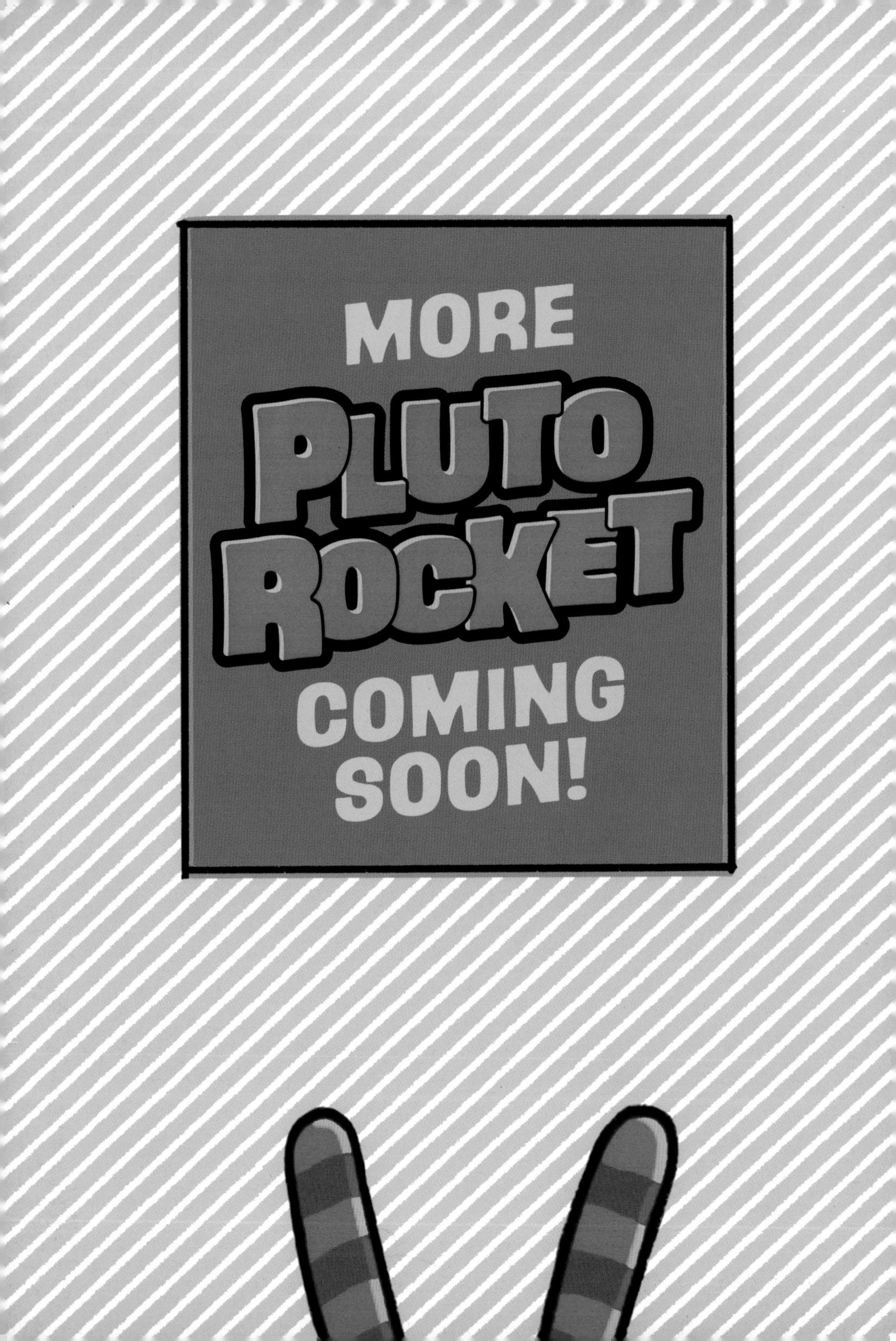
MORE
PLUTO ROCKET
COMING SOON!

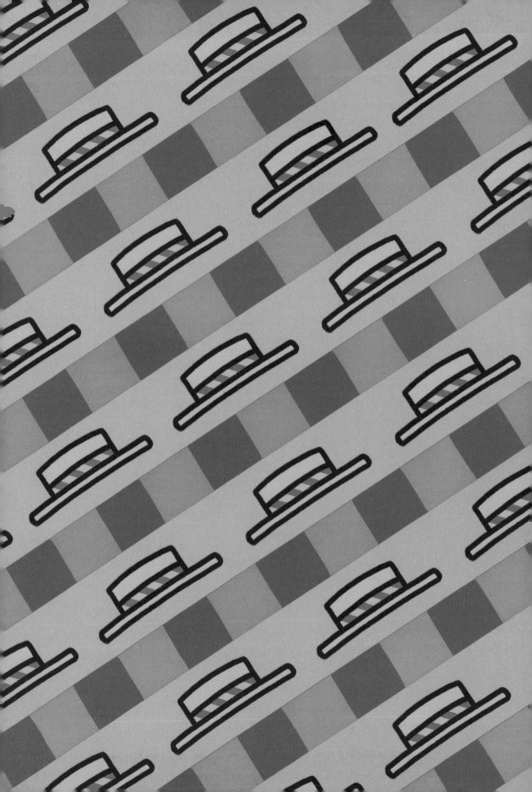